Aphra Behn

The Plays, Histories, and Novels

With Life and Memoirs. Vol. V

Aphra Behn

The Plays, Histories, and Novels
With Life and Memoirs. Vol. V

ISBN/EAN: 9783744749510

Printed in Europe, USA, Canada, Australia, Japan

Cover: Foto ©Andreas Hilbeck / pixelio.de

More available books at **www.hansebooks.com**

Mrs. Behn
B. Cole sculp

THE

PLAYS, HISTORIES,

AND NOVELS

OF THE INGENIOUS

MRS. APHRA BEHN.

WITH

LIFE AND MEMOIRS.

Complete in Six Volumes.

VOL. V.

LONDON:

JOHN PEARSON, 15, YORK ST., COVENT GARDEN.

1871.

ALL THE
HISTORIES
AND
NOVELS

Written by the Late

Ingenious Mrs. *BEHN*,

Intire in Two Volumes.

Publiſhed by Mr. Charles Gildon.

The Eighth Edition, Corrected,
and Illuſtrated with Cuts.

Vol. I. Containing,

I. *The Life and Memoirs of Mrs.* Behn.
II. *The Hiſtory of* Oroonoko: *Or, The* Royal Slave.

III. *The* Fair Jilt: *Or, The Amours of Prince* Tarquin *and* Miranda.
IV. *The* Nun : *Or, The* Perjured Beauty.

LONDON:

Printed for W. Feales, at *Rowe's Head*, againſt St. *Clement's* Church in the *Strand*; R. Wellington, at the *Dolphin* and *Crown*, without *Temple-Bar*; J. Brindley, at the *King's Arms* in *New Bond-ſtreet*; C. Corbett, at *Addiſon's Head*, againſt St. *Dunſtan's Church* in *Fleet-ſtreet*; A. Bettesworth, and F. Clay, in Truſt for B. Wellington.

M.DCC.XXXV.

THE

Epiſtle Dedicatory,

TO

SIMON SCROOP, Eſq;

Of *Danby* in *Yorkſhire*.

Honoured Sir,

I AM extremely pleas'd with this Opportunity of renewing that Ac-quaintance, which I had the Ho-nour and Happineſs to begin with you at the College (where you laid the Foundation of that fine Gentleman you ſince have proved, and where you gave ſuch early and certain Promiſes of your future Merit)

A 3

*Merit) and at the ſame Time of doing Juſ-
tice both to the Reſpect and Honour I have
for you, Sir, and to the Value and Eſteem
I ever had for the Perſon and Memory of
Mrs.* Behn, *by making you a Preſent, that
has more than once already met with a publick and general Applauſe; and by ſecuring
theſe admirable and diverting Hiſtories from
being proſtituted to a Perſon unworthy of the
Honour. And were ſhe alive, ſhe would be
infinitely fond of my* Choice; *in whom ſhe
would have found all the admirable Qualifi-
cations that make up the Character of a noble
Patron, and a generous Friend; an Hereditary Honour, and a Perſonal Virtue: In
whom ſhe would have found an ancient De-
ſcent, dignified with your own particular Honour, Juſtice, Sweetneſs of Temper, Affability, Generoſity and Senſe: In whom ſhe
would have found ſuch a Felicity of Addreſs,
as makes your Diſcourſe at once convince and
charm; a ſprightly Wit and ſound Judgment, which are eminent both in your Converſation and Conduct, in the Choice and
Exerciſe of your Virtues: In whom ſhe would
have found Generoſity without Profuſeneſs;
a native Propenſity to do good to others,
without injuring your Poſterity; a juſt Con-
ſideration of the Object of your Bounty,
before you beſtow a Benefit; and then the
Favour doubled by preventing the Expectation,*
and

*and ſaving the Perſon obliged, the Confuſion
of asking:* In whom ſhe would have found
Prudence *without* Cunning, *the deliberate
Effect of a true Judgment, not the haſty
and mean Reſult of mere Intereſt and Deſign:* In whom therefore ſhe would have made
no Doubt of finding the noble Souls and Principles of Mecænas, Proculeius, Cotta, Fa-
bius, Lentulus, Gallus, *or* Meſſala; *a
Soul exalted with a generous Ambition of
no vulgar Praiſe: for to be a Protector and
Encourager of the Muſes, is an uncommon
Glory; the Prerogative of but a few,* Quos
æquus amavit Jupiter: *and more Ages have
gone to the producing a* Good Patron, *than a*
Good Poet.

*Not but that Poetry, in every Age and
Nation, has pleas'd, and found among the
Rich and Powerful, ſuch as* Juvenal *deſcribes
in his Time,*

———— Didicit jam dives avarus

Tantum admirari, tantum laudare diſertos

Ut pueri Junonis avem ————

*Who give an empty Admiration, and a bar-
ren Praiſe, but want Magnificence of Soul
enough to reward, or preſerve the Author
of their Pleaſure. They have nothing to
ſpare from their Profuſeneſs in their* Trifles;
their Follies are too expenſive to allow any

A 4

Thing

Thing to Learning, good Senfe, *and* divine
Poetry ; *which, like Honefty, are only prais'd
and ftarve.*

Non habet infelix Numitor quod mittat amico,

Quintillæ quod donet habet ; nec defuit illi

Unde emeret multa pafcendum carne leonem

Jam domitum ; conftat leviori bellua fumptu

Nimirum, & capiunt plus inteftina Poetæ.

Sophocles *might get the Government of a
Province for writing a good Play ;* Tyrtæus
*the Command of an Army : but that golden
Age of Poetry is gone ; and at this Diftance,
looks almoft like that fabulous one, the* Gre-
cian *Poets defcrib'd. For now (and almoft
ever fince) no Arts are encourag'd, that are
not immediately employ'd in the Service, Or-
nament, or Pleafure of the* Body; *and thofe
that adorn the* Mind *thrown afide as fuper-
fluous, and as ufelefs as* Ragou's *Shirt;
which would make one think, if (as our fpi-
ritual Writers call it) the Body be but the
Garment or Habit of the* Mind, *that the
Minds of moft Men are mere* Beaux, *wholly
loft in their Drefs, and infenfible to all that
does not either difcompofe or adjuft that.*

Hence

Hence 'tis evident, that whatever Pretence the reſt of the World have to complain of the Times, the Poets only have a juſt Cauſe to do it: For let the Times be ever ſo hard, all other Myſteries and Faculties thrive, and meet with new Supplies. The Sharper *(as numerous as his Tribe is)* ſtill finds freſh Bubbles; *the* Knight of the Poſt *freſh bad Cauſes; Whores and Bawds freſh Cullies;* brawny Fools *freſh City Wives, or diſap-pointed* Quality; Taylors *freſh* Faſhions; Uſurers *freſh* Spendthrifts; Lawyers *freſh* Clients; Courtiers *freſh* Bribes, *freſh* Pro-jects, *and freſh* Places; Soldiers *freſh* Plunder; *and* Divines *freſh* Livings: *But the Poet ſcarce freſh · Straw. And now 'tis as of old,*

———————— Utile multis

Pallere, & toto vinum neſcire Decembri.

I might have made it Anno, *but out of reſpect to the Verſe. Poetry can get no freſh* Star *to ſhine on it, no freſh Patron to en-courage it; that it might be fulfilled, what was long ſince written of it by* Petronius Arbiter———————

Qui pelago credit, magno ſe fœnere tollit;

Qui Pugnas & Caſtra petit, præcingitur Auro;

Vilis adulator picto jacet ebrius oftro,

Et qui follicitat nuptas ac præmia peccat :

Sola pruinofis horret facundia pannis,

Atq ; inopi lingua, defertas invocat artes.

*'Tis Encouragement that advances all Arts,
especially Poetry ; which requires a free,
undisturbed, and easy Life, void of all Cares
and Sollicitudes, which confound the noble
Ideas and Images that should fill a Poet's
Mind. If* Virgil *had mifs'd the Patronage
of the Prince of the* Roman *Empire, he had
never been the Prince of Poets.*

Nam fi Virgilio puer, & tolerabile defit

Hofpitium, caderent omnes a crinibus Hydri, *&c.*

*An enlivening Bottle, a pleafing Converfation,
and an opportune Retreat of fhady Groves,
Hills, Vales, and purling Streams, are Things
that give frefh Vigour to the wearied Pinions
of a foaring Mufe.*

O ! quis me gelidis in montibus Æmi

Siftet, & ingenti Ramorum protegat Umbra ?

*Poetry, the fupreme Pleafure of the Mind,
is begot and born in Pleafure, but opprefs'd
and*

*and kill'd with Pain.   So that this Reflection
ought to raise our Admiration of Mrs. Behn,
whose Genius was of that Force, like Homer's,
to maintain its Gaiety in the midst of Dif-
appointments, which a Woman of her Sense
and Merit ought never to have met with :
But she had a great Strength of Mind, and
Command of Thought, being able to write in
the midst of Company, and yet have her Share
of the Conversation ; which I saw her do in
writing* Oroonoko, *and other Parts of the
following Volume : in every Part of which,
Sir, you'll find an easy Style, and a peculiar
Happiness of thinking.   The Passions, that of
Love especially, she was Mistress of ; and
gave us such nice and tender Touches of them,
that without her Name we might discover the
Author ; as* Protogenes *did* Apelles, *by the
Stroke of his Pencil.*

*In this Edition, Sir, are three Novels not
printed before, and considerable Additions to
her Life ; from all which, I'm persuaded you
will draw a very agreeable Entertainment,
which I always wish you in your Conversation
with the Muses ; for we often seek the Company that pleases us : among which, if I shall
hereafter, by the Indulgence of a better Fortune, be able to place any Thing worthy your
Perusal, I shall enjoy a very sensible Satiffaction ; for,*

A 6

Prin-

Principibus placuiffe viris non ultima laus eft.

And I could find no readier Way to obtain fo agreeable an Event, than thus by putting my felf with fo powerful a Bribe as Mrs. Behn's Hiftories, under your Protection, Sir ; where the Malice of my Enemies, or the Maligni- ty of my Misfortunes, will never be able to give any uneafy, at leaft anxious Thoughts, to,

SIR,

Your moft Humble,

moft Obedient, and

Devoted Servant,

Charles Gildon.

THE

THE

HISTORY

OF THE

LIFE and MEMOIRS

OF

Mrs. *BEHN*.

Written by one of the Fair Sex.

MY intimate Acquaintance with the admirable *Aſtrea*, gave me naturally a very great Eſteem for her; for it both freed me from that Folly of my Sex, of envying or ſlighting Excellencies, I could not obtain,

obtain, and infpired me with a noble Fire to celebrate that Woman, who was an Honour and Glory to our Sex: and this reprinting her incomparable Novels, prefented me with a lucky Occafion of exerting that Defire into Action.

She was a Gentlewoman by Birth, of a good Family in the City of *Canterbury* in *Kent;* her Father's Name was *Johnfon*, whofe Relation to the Lord *Willoughby*, drew him, for the advantageous Poft of Lieutenant-General of many Ifles, befides the Continent of *Surinam*, from his quiet Retreat at *Canterbury*, to run the hazardous Voyage of the *Weft-Indies*. With him he took his chief Riches, his Wife and Children ; and in that Number *Afra*, his promifing Darling, our future *Heroine*, and admired *Aftrea*, who even in the firft Bud of Infancy, difcover'd fuch early Hopes of her riper Years, that fhe was equally her Parents Joy and Fears : for they too often miftruft the Lofs of a Child, whofe Wit and Underftanding outftrip its Years, as too great a Bleffing to be long enjoy'd. Whether that Fear proceeds from Superftition, or Diffidence of our prefent Happinefs, I fhall not determine ; but muft purfue my Difcourfe, with affuring you, none had greater Fears of that Nature, or greater Caufe for 'em : for befides the Vivacity and Wit of her

Con-

Converfation at the firft Ufe almoft of Reafon in Difcourfe, fhe would write the prettieft, foft, engaging Verfes in the World. Thus qualified, fhe accompany'd her Parents in their long Voyage to *Surinam*, leaving behind her the Sighs and Tears of all her Friends, and breaking Hearts of her Lovers, that fighed to poffefs what was fcarce yet arrived to a Capacity of eafing their Pain, if fhe had been willing. But as fhe was Miftrefs of uncommon Charms of Body as well as Mind, fhe gave infinite and raging Defires, before fhe could know the leaft herfelf.

Her Father liv'd not to fee that Land flowing with Milk and Honey, that Paradife which fhe fo admirably defcribes in *Oroonoko*: where you may alfo find what Adventures happen'd to her in that Country. The Misfortunes of that Prince had been unknown to us, if the divine *Aftrea* had not been there, and his Sufferings had wanted that Satisfaction which her Pen has given 'em in the Immortality of his Virtues and Conftancy ; the very Memory of which moves a generous Pity in all, and a Contempt of the brutal Actors in that unfortunate Tragedy. Here I can add nothing to what fhe has given the World already, but a Vindication of her from fome unjuft Afperfions I find are infinuated about this Town in Relation to that Prince.

Prince. I knew her intimately well, and I believe she would not have concealed any Love-Affair from me, being one of her own Sex, whose Friendship and Secrecy she had experienced : which makes me assure the World there was no Affair between that Prince and *Astrea*, but what the whole Plantation were Witnesses of ; a generous Value for his uncommon Virtues, which every one that but hears 'em, finds in himself, and his Presence gave her no more. Besides, his Heart was too violently set on the everlasting Charms of his *Imoinda*, to be shook with those more faint (in his Eye) of a White Beauty ; and *Astrea*'s Relations, there present, had too watchful an Eye over her, to permit the Frailty of her Youth, if that had been powerful enongh. As this is false, so are the Consequences of it too ; for the Lord, her Father's Friend, that was not then arrived, perished in a Hurricane, without having it in his Power to resent it ; Nor had his Resentments been any thing to her, who only waited the Arrival of the next Ships to convey her back to her desired *England;* where she soon after, to her Satisfaction, arrived, and gave King *Charles* II. so pleasant and rational an Account of his Affairs there, and particularly of the Misfortunes of *Oroonoko*, that he desired her to deliver

them

them publickly to the World, and was
satisfy'd of her Abilities in the Management of Business, and the Fidelity of our
Heroine to his Interest. After she was
marry'd to Mr. *Behn*, a Merchant of this
City, tho' of *Dutch* Extraction, he committed to her Secrecy and Conduct, Affairs of the highest Importance in the
Dutch War; which obliging her to stay
at *Antwerp*, presented her with the Adventures of Prince *Tarquin*, and his false
wicked Fair-One *Miranda*. The full Account of which you will find admirably
writ in the following Collection.

But I must not omit entirely some other
Adventures that happened to her during
this Negotiation; tho' I cannot give so just
and large a Representation of them as I
willingly would.

I have told you, that as her Mind, so
her Body was adorned with all the Advantages of our Sex: Wit, Beauty, and
Judgment seldom meet in one, especially in
Woman, (you may allow this from a Woman) but in her they were eminent: and
this made her turn all the Advantages
each gave her, to the Interest she had devoted herself to serve. And whereas the
Beauty of the Face is that which generally
takes with Mankind, so it gives 'em most
commonly an Assurance and Security from
Designs; for they suppose that a beautiful
Woman,

Woman, as she is made for the Pleasure of others, so chiefly minds her own: and in that they are not much mistaken, for they pursue the same Course with the rest of the World, Pleasure; but then 'tis as various as their Tempers, and what they generally imagine may have the least Share in many of them. The Event, I'm sure, shew'd that in *Astrea* (at this Time at least) the Pleasures of Love had not the Predominance, when she diverted the Hopes, which the Vanity of a *Dutch* Merchant of great Interest and Authority in *Holland*, had entertained of a successful Passion, to the Service of her Prince, and his own shameful Disappointment.

They are mistaken who imagine that a *Dutchman* can't love; for tho' they are generally more phlegmatick than other Men, yet it sometimes happens that Love does penetrate their Lump, and dispense an enlivening Fire, that destroys its graver and cooler Considerations; at least it once prov'd so on this Spark, whom we must call by the Name of *Vander Albert* of *Utrecht.*

Antwerp is a City of great Opulence and Compass, and before the Separation of the Seven Provinces from the other Ten, was the *Emporium* of *Flanders*, and is yet a Town of considerable Trade and Resort; 'tis in the *Spanish Netherlands*,

and

and yet near Neighbour to the Domi-
nions of the *States.* For which Reason,
our *Aftrea* chose it for the Place of her
Abode, where she might with the greate
Ease hear from, and meet with *Vander
Albert* ; who, before the War, in her
Husband's Time, had been in love with
her in *England,* and on which she grounded the Success of her Negotiation. *Albert,* as soon as he knew of her Arrival at
Antwerp, and the publick Posts he was in
would give him Leave, made a short
Voyage to meet her, with all the Love his
Nature was capable of (and which by Chance
was much, and more refin'd than most of
his Countrymen, at least according to our
common Notions of 'em) and after a
Repetition of all his former Professions
for her Service, press'd her extremely to
let him, by some signal Means, give un-
deniable Proofs of the Vehemence and
Sincerity of his Passion ; for which he
would ask no Reward, till he had by long
and faithful Services convinc'd her that he
deserv'd it.

This Proposal was so reasonable, and
so extremely suitable to her present Aim
in the Service of her Country, that she
accepted it; and having the Reward in
her own Power, as well as the Judgment
of his Deserts, she put him to that Use,
which made her very serviceable to the
King.

King. I fhall only inftance one Piece of Intelligence, which might have fav'd the Nation a great deal of Money and Difgrace, had Credit been given to it. The latter End of the Year 1666, *Albert* fent her Word by a fpecial Meffenger, that he would be with her at a Day appointed, which nothing could have oblig'd him to but his Engagements to her; but his Affairs requiring his immediate Return into *Holland,* he had fent that Exprefs to get her to be alone, and in the Way, thofe few Minutes he could ftay with her.

The Time comes; *Aftrea* is punctual to the Appointment, and *Albert* informs her, that *Cornelius de Wit,* who, with the reft of that Family, had an implacable Hatred to the *Englifh* Nation, and the Houfe of *Orange,* that was fo nearly related to it, had with *de Ruyter* propos'd to the States, to fail up the River of *Thames,* and deftroy the *Englifh* Ships in their Harbours; fince, by the Propofal of a Peace, the King of *England* had fhewn fo little of the Politician, or was fo ruled by evil Counfellors, that he never thought of treating with Sword in Hand; but to fave the Expence of fitting out a Fleet, had expofed fo confiderable a Part of it to the Refentment of the Enemy. This Propofal of *de Wit,* concurring with the Advice which the *Dutch* Partifans in *Eng-*
land

land had given 'em, was well receiv'd;
and you may depend on it, my charming
Aftrea, that it will be put in Execution
(faid *Albert*) for I can further affure you,
that we have that good Correfpondence
with fome Minifters about the King, that
being enfur'd from all Oppofition, we
look on it as a Thing of neither Danger
nor Difficulty.

. When *Albert* had difcover'd a Secret of
this Importance, and with all thofe Marks
of a fincere Relation of Truth, *Aftrea*
could not doubt but he had fufficient
Grounds for what he had told her, and
fcarce allow'd that little Time that *Albert* ftaid, to the Civilities due for a Service of that mighty Confequence; and
this Interview was no fooner ended, but
fhe got ready her Difpatches for *England.*

But all the particular Circumftances fhe
gave, nor the Confequence of it, if it
fhould be effected, could gain Credit
enough to her Intelligence, to make any
tolerable Preparations againft it: And all
the Encouragement fhe met with, was to
be laugh'd at by the Minifter fhe wrote
to; and her Letter fhew'd, by Way of
Contempt, to fome who ought not to
have been let into the Secret, and fo
bandy'd about, till it came to the Ears
of a particular Friend of her's, who gave
her

her an Account of what Reward she was to expect for her Service, since that was so little valu'd; and desired her therefore to lay aside her politick Negotiation, and divert her Friends with some pleasant Adventures of *Antwerp*, either as to her Lovers, or those of any other Lady of her Acquaintance: that in this she would be more successful than in her Pretences of State, since here she would not fail of pleasing those she wrote to.

Astrea, vex'd at this Letter, and the Treatment she had met with, for a Service the Ancients would have decreed her a Triumph, gave over all sollicitous Thought of Business, and resolv'd to comply with her Friend's Request in what she would take so much Pleasure in the Narration of. But soon after she had the Satisfaction to see her incredulous Correspondents sufficiently punished for neglecting her Advice, and by their Mismanagement, the very particular Thing come to pass she had forewarn'd 'em of; nay, and some powerful Men fall under the Censures of the People for the Misfortunes their Pride, Folly, or private Designs, had brought upon them. But to return from this short Excursion, to her Letter.

LET-

LETTER.

My dear Friend,

YOUR Remarks upon my politick Capacity, tho' they are sharp, touch me not, but recoil on those that have not made Use of the Advantages they might have drawn from thence; and are doubly to blame: First, In sending a Person, in whose Ability, Sense, and Veracity, they could not confide; and next, Not to understand when a Person indifferent tells 'em a probable Story, and which if it come to pass, would sufficiently punish their Incredulity; and which, if follow'd, would have put 'em on their Guard against a vigilant and industrious Foe, who watch'd every Opportunity of returning the several Repulses, and Damages, they had met with of late from them. But I have often observ'd your busy young Statesman, so very opinionated of their own Designs, that they are so far from encouraging those of another, if good, that they cannot forgive their Proposal, and sacrifice a publick Good to their particular Pride.

But I have let these *idle* Reflections (for such must all be that regard our wretched Statef-

Statesmen) divert me from a more agreeable Relation. To comply therefore with your Requeſt, in its full Extent, I ſhall give you an Account of both my own Adventures, and thoſe of a Lady of my Acquaintance; and with her I'll begin, for 'tis but civil to give Place to a Stranger. I ſhall convey her to your Knowledge by the Name of *Lucilla.* She is of a gay, airy Diſpoſition, middle-ſiz'd, fine black Eyes, long flowing dark Hair. Nature has drawn her Eye-brows, which are dark, much finer than Art uſually does thoſe of the affected Beauties of our Acquaintance; her Mouth is ſmall, her Lips plump, ruddy, and freſh, I wont ſay moiſt; her Hand ſmall, Fingers long and taper, and her Shape better than is uſual among the *Flemiſh* Ladies: To this I muſt add, That her Wit is much above the common Rate.

With all theſe Accompliſhments, you may imagine that ſhe was not without her Admirers; among which Number, none came ſo near her Heart, as the eldeſt Son of *Ramirez,* an old ſordid Miſer, that lov'd his Money much above his Sons, or even himſelf; which made the Allowance he gave his two Sons but very ſmall, and not fit to enable them to make any tolerable Figure in the World. For the real Names of theſe two Brothers, I muſt give that of
Miguel

Miguel and *Lopez*, and for the Grace of the Matter, add Don to them.

Don *Miguel*, and Don *Lopez*, I know not how they came by 'em, had Souls as brave and generous, as that of their Father was wretched and bafe ; they with Pain faw the many Advantages of a liberal Education their Father's Covetoufnefs robb'd 'em of ; and by their natural Parts, and winning Behaviour, touch'd their Relations fo nearly, that they long contributed to their Improvement, even till now the Brothers were become two of the moft accomplifh'd and gallant Youths of the City. Their Quality gave them Admittance to the beft Families, and their Accomplifhments to the Hearts of the faireft Ladies ; but few ever paffed farther than the Confines of theirs, and the lighter Touches of an Amoret was all that made them figh, till they faw the incomparable *Lucilla*, and her fair Coufin, of whom, not knowing her, I fhall fay nothing. Don *Miguel*, as gay as he was, and as infenfible as he fancy'd himfelf, no fooner faw *Lucilla*, but he found the Difference betwixt the Force of her Eyes, and thofe of the reft of the Ladies of his Acquaintance ; and as a Proof of it, he was not fooner touch'd with Love than Jealoufy ; for her Coufin fitting by her, he obferv'd his Brother's Eyes often caft that Way, and was very uneafy at it; and that Friendfhip that grew up with their Years, and increas'd as they grew, found now a fudden Check. I will not, like your Romance-Writers, give you an Account of all his private Reflections on this Occafion nor the Conflict and Struggling between his old Gueft, Friendfhip, and this new Intruder, Love. It is enough to tell you, that as foon as Opportunity ferv'd, he took care to put himfelf out of Pain, or at leaft to give himfelf a Certainty, whether his Brother was his Rival, or not; and was not a little pleas'd, that *Lucilla* had only found the Way to his Heart, while his Brother faw nothing fo fair as her Coufin. Don *Miguel*, and Don *Lopez*, as they were in love, fo they were too accomplifh'd to be unfuccefsful; and there remain'd no Obftacle to their Happinefs, but their Father's Avarice, which would never be brought to any Reafon, in allowing them what was fit for Perfons of their Rank. They come in therefore to a Confultation, what Meafures to take to cure their Father of fo ungenerous a Diftemper of the Mind; and by that Means accomplifh what they both longed for more than Glory.

They found their Father's Avarice had not fo engrofs'd his Soul, as to beat off all Sentiments of Religion; on the contrary, he was extremely credulous of all the fuperftitious

ſtitious Parts of Religion, and particularly of all Narrations of Spectres, Witches, Apparitions, &c. they therefore concluded to attack him on that Side that could make the leaſt Defence. He conſtantly ſpent Part of the Morning in telling his Money, and counting his Bags: His Sons therefore having procur'd a Pick-lock to his Cloſet, took care to place in it a Figure that was very dreadful, ſo that the old Gentleman ſhould find him counting his Bags and Money when he came in, which happen'd accordingly. He was not a little frighted, and haſtily retir'd, nor came thither again in three or four Days; but on his next coming, he was extremely ſurpriz'd to find the Number of his Bags increas'd, which for ſome time had been leſſen'd every Morning; ſo that he concluded, it was a Reward of his Abſtinence from a Sight that pleas'd him too much: Yet was ſo well pleas'd with this Increaſe, that he repeated his Viſits for three or four Mornings together, and found his Bags decreaſe on that. He was very much troubled in Mind, and conſulting his Confeſſor on all that had happen'd, he aſſur'd him, it could be none but the Devil he had ſeen; and that he was to fear the Conſequence of taking Poſſeſſion of any of the Money ſo left there by that evil Spirit, and it was much to be doubted whether he had not exchang'd the whole.

So concluding with fome wholefome Advice againſt Avarice, he difmifs'd his Penitent, who again for fome Time forbore his Clofet; and on his next Viſit, finding all he had ever loſt return'd, and abundance more added, a Fit of Avarice coming on him, he refolv'd to try if he cou'd outwit the Devil; and by removing it from that Place, which he fuppos'd taken Poffeffion of by the foul Fiend, fecure both the Money and his own Peace of Mind. Accordingly in the Night he digs a Hole in the Garden, and conveys all the Bags into it, and covers them fafely up. His Sons, the next Day, coming to the Clofet, and finding all removed, were not a little difappointed, and troubled to think how they ſhould at leaſt recover that Money which was lent 'em by their Friends to carry on this Defign. All the Difficulty lay in difcovering where their Father had hid it; and to do that, nothing occur'd that would hold Water, till Don *Lopez* concluded to make once more the Experiment of his Fear of Apparitions, againſt the next Night; therefore they prepared the Chamber for their Defign, and invited fome of their Friends, on purpofe to make the old Gentleman drunk; which having effected, he was carefully carried to Bed, and three or four Statues, out of the Garden, convey'd up into his Room, and plac'd on each
Side

Side and Corner of his Bed, with People
behind 'em to flaſh and make Lightning,
to diſcover to him theſe imaginary Spectres.
All Things being in this Order, a Maſtiff-
Dog, with a great Iron-Chain, was let
into the Room, the rattling of which, in a
little Time, awaken'd the old Gentleman,
who began to pray very heartily; but
Fear ſtill prevailing, as in Deſpair, made
him think to get out of the Room, when
he heard the Noiſe on the other Side of the
Room, the moſt diſtant from the Door.
On his firſt Motion to riſe, the Perſon behind the Image flaſh'd with his Lightning,
and diſcover'd a white pale Ghoſt to the
frighted Miſer: So he ſtarted back into
his Bed again, and thus he was ſerv'd on
each Side, till in Deſpair, and ready to die
with Fear, he could ſcarce utter ſo much
as one Prayer. Then he heard a Voice, with
a thouſand Terrors and Threats, demand
him, he having taken the Price of his Soul
in the Money he had removed. The old
Man replied, with a thouſand Croſſes to
guard himſelf, that the Money was in ſuch
a Place, and that he would ſurrender not
only that, but his own too, to be at eaſe.
When they had thus got the Knowledge of
the Place where the Treaſure was hid;
they eaſily, in the Fear he was in, convey'd
away the Statues, and left all Things in Order, as if nothing had happen'd; and re-

pairing to the Garden, found the Money, but took no more thence but what they had before put there.

The next Day the old Gentleman ſends for them to his Chamber, ill with the Fright, and lets 'em know, that he had thus long been in an Error, in ſetting his Mind on hoarded Bags, which ought to be plac'd in Heaven at his Years; but having had various Warnings againſt it, he now reſolv'd a new Life, and in order to that would immediately ſettle his Affairs. So he divided his Eſtate equally betwixt them; and having found his own Sum of Money left, as he thought, by the Devil, he gave a third Part to charitable Uſes, and divided the other betwixt his Sons, and retired to a Monaſtery, where he ſoon made a very religious End.

The Sons having by theſe Means, gain'd their Point, did not long defer the Happineſs for which they undertook this; and thus was my Friend *Lucilla,* and her Couſin, made the moſt fortunate of our Sex, if Love and Money could make 'em ſo.

But I have been too long in this, to add ſome pleaſant Adventures of my own, which I muſt defer till the next Opportunity; having only Room enough left to ſubſcribe myſelf your Friend and Servant,

ASTREA.

LETTER.

L E T T E R.

Dear Friend,

THO' our Courtiers will not allow me
to do any great Matters with my
Politicks, I am fure you muft grant, that
I have done fo with my Eyes, when I fhall
tell you I have made two *Dutchmen* in
love with me. *Dutchmen!* do you mind
me, that have no Soul for any Thing but
Gain, that have no Pleafure but Intereft or
the Bottle ; but in Affairs of Love, go to
the moft facred Part of it more brutally
than the moft fordid of their Four-footed
Brethren ; nay, they are fo far from the
Warmth of Love, that thro' their phlegmatick Mafs there is not Fire enough to give
'em a vigorous Appetite, fo far are they
from the Finenefs of a vehement Paflion.
Yet I, Sir, this very numerical Perfon, your
Friend and humble Servant, have fet two
of 'em into a Blaze; two of very different
Ages (I was going to fay Degrees too, but
I remember there are no Degrees in *Holland.*) *Vander Albert* is about Thirty-two,
of a hale Conftitution, fomething more
fprightly than the reft of his Countrymen ; and tho' infinitely fond of his Intereft,
B 4

and

and an irreconcilable Enemy to Monar-
chy, has by the Force of Love been obliged to let me into fome Secrets that
might have done our King, and, if not
our Court, our Country no fmall Service.
But I fhall fay no more of this Lover till
I fee you, for fome particular Reafons
which you fhall then likewife know. My
other is about twice his Age, nay, and
Bulk too, tho' *Albert* be not the moft Bar-
bary Shape you have feen ; you muft know
him by the Name of *Van Bruin*, and he
was introduced to me by *Albert* his Kinfman, and obliged by him to furnifh me
in his Abfence with what Money, and
other Things I fhould pleafe to command,
or have Occafion for, as long as he ftaid
at *Antwerp*, where he was like to continue
fome Time about a Law-Suit then depend-
ing. He had not vifited me often, before
I began to be fenfible of the Influence of
my Eyes on this old Piece of Worm-eaten
Touchwood ; but he had not the Confidence (and that's much) to tell me he
loved me, and Modefty you know is no
common Fault of his Countrymen : tho' I
rather impute it to a Love of himfelf,
that he would not run the Hazard of being turn'd into Ridicule in fo difpropor-
tion'd a Declaration. He often infinuated, that he knew a Man of Wealth and
Subftance, tho' ftricken indeed in Years,

and

and on that Account not so agreeable as a younger Man, that was passionately in love with me ; and desired to know whether my Heart was so far engaged, that his Friend should not entertain any Hopes. I reply'd, that I was surprized to hear a Friend of *Albert*'s making an Interest in me for another ; that if Love were a Passion I was any way sensible of, it could never be for an old Man, and much to that Purpose. But all this would not do, in a Day or two I received this eloquent Epistle from him ; for he had heard *Albert* praise my Wit, and he thought, that what he wrote to one so qualify'd, must be in an extraordinary Stile, which I shall give you as near as I can in our Language ; and which I indeed was indebted to an Interpreter myself for, tho' 'twas wrote in *French*, which I have some Knowledge of.

LETTER.

Most Transcendent Charmer,

I Have strove often to tell you the Tempests of my Heart, and with my own Mouth scale the Walls of your Affections ; but terrify'd with the Strength of your

Fortifications, I concluded to make more
regular Approaches, and firſt attack you
at a farther Diſtance, and try firſt what
a Bombardment of Letters would do ;
whether theſe Carcaſſes of Love, thrown
into the Sconces of your Eyes, would
break into the midſt of your Breaſt, beat
down the Court of Guard of your Aver-
ſion, and blow up the Magazine of your
Cruelty, that you might be brought to a
Capitulation, and yield upon reaſonable
Terms. Believe me, I love thee more
than Money ; for indeed thou art more
beautiful than the Ore of *Guinea*, and I
had rather diſcover thy *Terra Incognita*,
than all the Southern *Incognita* of *America*.
O ! thou art beautiful in every Part, as
a goodly Ship under Sail from the *Indies ;*
thy Hair is like her flowing Pennants as
ſhe enters the Harbour, and thy Forehead
bold and fair as her Prow ; thy Eyes bright
and terrible as her Guns ; thy Noſe like
her Rudder, that ſteers my Deſires ; thy
Mouth the well wrought Mortar, whence
the Granadoes of thy Tongue are ſhot
into the Gun-room of my Heart, and ſhat-
ter it to Pieces ; thy Teeth are the grap-
pling Irons that faſten me to my Ruin,
and of which I would get clear in vain ;
thy Neck is curious and ſmall like the very
Topmaſt-head, beneath which thy lovely
Boſom ſpreads itſelf like the Main-ſail

before

before the Wind ; thy Middle is taper as the Bolt-fprit, and thy Shape as flender and upright as the Main-maft ; thy Back-parts like the gilded carv'd Stern, that jets over the Waters ; and thy Belly, with the Perquifites thereunto belonging, the Hold of the Veffel, where all the rich Cargo lies under Hatches ; thy Thighs, Legs, and Feet the fteady Keel that is ever under Water. O that I cou'd once fee thy Keel above Water ! And is it not pity that fo fpruce a Ship fhould be un-mann'd, fhould lie in the Harbour for want of her Crew ? Ah ! let me be the Pilot to fteer her by the *Cape of Good Hope*, for the *Indies* of Love. But Oh ! fair *Englifh* Woman ! thou art rather a Firefhip gilded, and fumptuous without, and driven before the Wind to fet me on Fire ; for thy Eyes indeed are like that, deftruc-tive, tho', like Brandy, bewitching : alas ! they have grappled my Heart, my Fore-caftle's on Fire, my Sails and Tackling are caught, my upper Decks are confum'd, and nothing but the Water of Defpair keeps the very Hulk from the Combuftion ; fo you have left it only in my Choice, to drown or burn. Oh ! for Pity's fake, take fome Pity, for thy Compaffion is more defirable than a ftrong Gale, when we are got to the Windward of a *Salleeman* : your Eyes, I fay again and again, like a

B 6

Chain-

Chain-fhot, have brought the Main-maft of my Refolution by the board, cut all the Rigging of my Difcretion and Inte- reft, blown up the Powder-room of my Affections, and fhatter'd all the Hulk of my Bofom; fo that without the Planks of your Pity, I muft inevitably fink to the Bottom. This is the deplorable Con- dition, tranfcendent Beauty! of your un- done Vaffal,

VAN BRUIN.

To this I returned this following ridi- culous Anfwer, which I infert to give you a better Picture of my Lover's Intellects.

L E T T E R.

Extraordinary Sir,

I Received your extraordinary Epiftle, which has had extraordinary Effects, I affure you, and was not read without an extraordinary Pleafure. I never doubt- ed the Zeal of your Countrymen in ma- king new Difcoveries, in fixing new Trades, in fupplanting their Neighbours, and in ingroffing the Wealth and Traf- fick of both the *Indies;* but, I confefs, I never expected fo wife a Nation fhould

at

at laft fet out for the *Ifland of Love:* I thought that had been a *Terra del Fuego* in all their Charts, and avoided like Rocks and Quick-fands: nay, I fhould as foon have fufpected them guilty of becoming Apoftles to the *Samæoids*, and of preaching the Gofpel to the *Laplanders*, where there is nothing to be got, and for which Reafon the very Jefuits deny them Baptifm; as of fetting out for fo unprofitable a Voyage as *Love.* Hark ye, good Sir, have you thoroughly confider'd what you have done? Have you reflected on the fad Confequences of declaring yourfelf a Lover; nay, and an old Lover to a young Woman? to a Woman that would expect all the Duties of Gallantry, even from a young Servant; but great and terrible Works of Supererogation from an antiquated Admirer? Have you enough examined what Degrees of Generofity *Love* neceffarily infpires, that Foe to Intereft, that Hereditary Enemy of your Country? Nay, have you thought whether by holding this Correfpondence with Love, you may not be declared a Rebel, an Enemy to your Country, and be brought into Sufpicion of greater Intelligence with the *French*, by entertaining their Gallantry and Love, than *de Witt,* by all his Intrigues with that *Monarch?* I confefs I tremble for you. Alas! alas! how deplorable a

Spectacle

Spectacle would it be to thefe Eyes, to fee that agreeable Bulk difmember'd by the enraged Rabble, and Scollops of your Flefh fold by Fifh-wives for Guilders and Duckatoons! Have you maturely confider'd the evil Example you fet your Neighbours, who may be influenced by a Perfon of your Port and Figure? And fhould the Evil by this Means fpread, *Holland* were undone; for then there were fome Danger of Honefty's fpreading, and then good-night the beft Card in all your Hands, for the winning the Game and Money of *Europe.* Lord, Sir, think what a dreadful Thing it is to be the Ruin of one's Country! But if publick Evils don't affect you, have you fet before the Eyes of your Underftanding the Charge of fitting out fuch a Veffel (as you have made me) for the *Indies* of Love? and I fear the Profits will never anfwer the Expence of the Voyage.

There are Ribbons and Hoods for my Pennants; Diamond Rings, Lockets, and Pearl Necklaces for my Guns of Offence and Defence; Silks, Holland, Lawn, Cambrick, *&c.* for Rigging; Gold and Silver Laces, Imbroideries and Fringes fore and aft, for my Stern and for my Prow; rich Perfumes, Paint and Powder for my Ammunition; Treats, rich Wines, expenfive Collations, Gaming-Money, Pin-
Money,

Money, with a long *Et cætera* for my Cargo ; and Balls, Mafquerades, Plays, Walks, airing in the Country, and a Coach and Six, for my fair Wind.

You may fee by my Concern for your Intereft and Perfon, that the Approaches you have made, have not been a little fuccefsful ; and if you are but as furious a Warrior when you come to ftorm, as you are at a Bombardment, the Lord have Mercy upon me.

But to deal ingenuoufly with you, I doubt your Prowefs in two or three particular Retrenchments, which I fear you'll hardly be able to gain. There is firft your Age, a formidable Baftion you'll fcarce carry ; then your mighty Bulk will with the laft Difficulties be brought to treat with my Love : but what is yet more dreadful, your Treachery to *Vander Albert* is a Fort that muft prove impregnable, if any Thing can be fo to fuch a Pen and fuch a Head. But if you carry the Town by Dint of Valour, I hope you'll allow me Quarter, and be as merciful to me as you are ftout ; and then I fhall not fail of being, extraordinary Sir,

Your humble Servant,

ASTREA.

LET.

L E T T E R.

Magnanimous Heroine,

I Have received your Packet in anſwer
to my Epiſtolary Advice Boat, which
did lately and honeſtly remonſtrate my
preſent State. You give me Hopes, that
out of your Imperial Bounty, you will
have me tugg'd home to the Harbour of
your Good-will, place me in the Dock
of your Friendſhip, refit me for the Ocean
of your Love, and ſend me out a cruiſing
for the Service of your Pleaſure ; which
Thought exalts my Heart more than
Punch, and makes me deſpiſe all Dangers
of interloping, ſpite of the Joint-ſtock of
Vander Albert : for the Scars I ſhall receive
in your Warfare, will be more valued by
me, than thoſe I have got in my robuſt
Youth, in the Heroick Combats of *Snick-
or-ſnee ;* when with a furious and triumphant Rage, I have chopped off the Fore-
flap of my Antagoniſt's Shirt, and laid
him Noſeleſs flat on his Back. You ſeem
tho' to make ſome Bones of two or three
Scruples about my Perſon and Age: you
ſay I am too bulky to be your Lover;

let

let not Errors mifguide you, Child ——
Portlinefs is comely and graceful; and fince
Bulk is valu'd in all Things elfe, why not
in Man then? You value a great Houfe
more than a little one, an Elephant more
than an Ox, a firft-rate Ship more than
a Frigate, a Caftle more than a Fort, and
the Ocean more than a Fifh-pond; then
why not *Van Bruin* more than *Vander Albert?* Oh! but you fay I am too old
too ——, but that's more than you know,
you little Wag you: and thereby hangs
a Tale. I am not green Wood indeed,
and fixty, or fixty five, has the Advantage of fo many Years feafoning. In all
Things elfe too we value Age; old Wine,
old Seamen, old Soldiers, and old Medals,
old Families, and why not then old *Van
Bruin?* But then you object my betraying my Friend, —— but that fhews that
you are not fo witty as you would be
thought —— for is any Man fo much
my Friend, as I am to myfelf; I that
never part from myfelf as long as I
live, as I may from *Vander Albert;* and
fhould I not then prefer a Friend that
will certainly always ftick to me, to one
that may defert me the next Moment?
and here I fhould be falfe to that dear
Friend, to be true to *Vander Albert.* But
what do you talk of Friendfhip? I'd
fooner deny my Faith for you, than for a
new

new rich *Japan* Traffick.   But Words are
superfluous ; when you parley, 'tis a Sign
you will hearken to a Capitulation, and
deliver up the Fort if you like the Terms ;
and to shew you that what you proposed
has not terrify'd me, I send you *Cart-
Blank* to fill up yourself —— For adod !
adod ! you must be mine, and you shall
be mine :   I'll win thee and wear thee,
with my old tough Vigour, you pretty
little turly-murly Rogue you, and I come
this Evening to sign Articles, and put in a
new Garrison ; but ever remain,

Your Deputy, and Happy

VAN BRUIN.

Tho' I had no Need of sending an Answer to this, where he threatens me with
a speedy Visit, yet the more to divert
myself and my Company, I sent him the
following Billet.

L E T T E R.

Most Magnificent Hero,
YOU have made me extremely proud
of myself, to find I can come into
a Competition with the only Cause and

Effect

Effect of your National Valour, *Punch,*
and *Snick-or-snee :* Nor am I lefs pleas'd,
too find you fo notable a Logician ; for I
love Reafoning with an infinite Paffion,
efpecially in a Lover : and it muft be al-
lowed, that you have gain'd your Point
in the Defence of your Bulk, and might for
a further Vindication have added, That
Elephants have danc'd on the Ropes,
which fhews their Bulk deftroy'd not
their Activity, and by Confequence ——
but a Word to the Wife ——— When
the Sons of God went in to the Daughters
of Men, they begat a Race of Giants——
Well, I don't know, if our Planets fhould
happen to be in Conjunction, what ftrange
Things might come to pafs, and what a
wonderful Race we fhould produce ; but
I'm fatisfy'd, that betwixt the Gaiety of
the Mother, and the robuft portly Activity of the Father, it could not be lefs than
dancing Elephants. You have indeed
furprizingly vanquifh'd my Objection of
your Age, and I fhall take Care to ufe you
like venerable Medals, valuable for their
Antiquity and Ruft ; tho' an old Lover
look'd lately more like an old Gown, than
old Gold, or an old Family, and fitter
for my Maid than myfelf ; or at leaft
fome decay'd Beauty, that had not a Stock
of Charms enough to purchafe a young
one : But you have convinc'd me of that
Error

Error too. Alas ! I fear that deluding
Tongue of your's will quite remove my
Objection too of your Treachery to *Vander Albert;* since you go on a National
Principle, and even bribe my Judgment
with the Compliment of sacrificing your
Faith or Religion (which if it be your Interest, is very considerable in a *Dutchman*) to the Love of me. So that I defer Proposals of Articles, till our *Plenipo's*
meet, and proceed regularly on these Pre-
liminaries, at the Place of Conference;
which is agreed on all Hands, to be the
Abode of

Your most happy

ASTREA.

You may imagine, this Letter brought
my *Hogen-Mogen* Lover, with no little
Haste, to my Apartment, whither we'll
now adjourn; for 'twou'd be impertinent
to trouble you with any more of these
foolish Letters ; one or two may divert,
as a Minute or two of a Coxcomb's Company, which on a longer Visit grows nau-
seous : But to give you all, would make
you pay too dear for so trifling a Pleasure.
The other Part of this Courtship consist-
ing in odd Grimaces, ridiculous Postures,
and antick Motions, cannot be so well de-
scrib'd to you, as to give you a true Image
of

of 'em ; so far at least, as to render 'em as diverting to you as they were for a while to me. But imagine to yourself an old, over-grown, unwieldly *Dutchman,* playing aukwardly over all that he suppos'd would make him look more agreeable in my Eyes. Age he found I did not admire, he therefore endeavour'd to conceal it by Dress, Peruke, and clumsey Gaiety : Respect he was inform'd I expected from a Lover, which he would express with such comical Cringes, such odd sort of Ogling, and fantastick Address, that I could never force a serious Face on whatever he said ; for let the Subject be ever so grave, his Person and Delivery turn'd it into a Farce. There was no Piece of Gallantry he observ'd perform'd by the young Gentlemen of the City, but he attempted in Imitation of them, even to Poetry ; but that indeed was in his own Language, and so might be extraordinary for aught I know.

Thus I diverted myself with him in *Albert's* Absence, till he began to assume and grow troublesome, on my bare Permission of his Address ; for a very little Incouragement serves that Nation, full of their own dear selves : so that to rid myself of him, I found no more ready Way, than to let *Albert* know all his Treachery to him, and the many consi-

derable

derable Proffers he had made to win me to his Defires. But *Albert*, with an unufual Refentment of thefe Affairs, threaten'd his Death, which was going farther than I defir'd ; for tho' I had no Kindnefs for either of them, yet I had fo much for myfelf, as not to be the Occafion of any Murder, or become the Talk of the City on fo ridiculous an Occafion: fo I pacified *Albert*, and made him fee how foolifh fuch an Attempt on an old Man would look, and perfuaded him only, the next Vifit he made, to upbraid him with his Treachery, and forbid him the Houfe ; and if Need were, to threaten him a little. But this produced a very ridiculous Scene, and worthy of more Spectators : For my *Neftorean* Lover would not give ground to *Albert*, but was as high as he, challeng'd him to *Snick-or-fnee*, for me, and a thoufand Things as comical; in fhort, nothing but my pofitive Command could fatisfy him, and on that as he promis'd no more to trouble me ; fure as he thought of me, he was Thunder-ftruck when he heard me not only forbid him the Houfe, but ridicule all his Addreffes to his Rival *Albert :* and with a Countenance full of Defpair, went away, not only from my Lodgings, but the next Day from *Antwerp*, leaving his Law-fuit to the Care of his

Friends,

Friends, unable to ſtay in the Place where he had met with ſo dreadful a Defeat.

Thus you ſee the Prowefs of my Perſon ; how unſuccefsful ſoever my Mind has been in our Stateſmens Opinions, you will in a little Time find who is in the right of it. I'm ſorry I can't at this Time furniſh you with any more refin'd Intrigues. Thofe of a Prince that have happen'd here, are too long ; and I have met with none that have touch'd me ſo far as to concern my Heart, which is not the moſt infenſible of all my Sex, I aſſure you : and I am ſo far from finding one fit to make a Lover of, that I can't meet with one that raiſes me to the Warmth of a Friend. But here my Letter puts me in Mind, that I have exercis'd your Patience enough for once, and I ſhall therefore conclude myſelf

Your faithful Friend,

ASTREA.

B U T now 'tis Time to proceed to her Affairs with *Vander Albert*, her other *Dutch* Lover, which was pleaſant enough, and in which ſhe contriv'd to preſerve her Honour, without injuring her Gratitude ; for ſhe could not deny but he had done Services that did juſtly challenge a
Return

Return for fo much Love as produc'd
'em.

There was a Woman of fome Remains of Beauty in *Antwerp*, that had
often given *Aftrea* Warning of the Infidelity of *Albert*, affuring her he was of
fo fickle a Nature, that he never lov'd
paft Enjoyment, and fometimes made
his Change before he had even that Pretence ; of which Number herfelf was,
for whom he had profefs'd fo much Love
as to marry her, and yet deferted her that
very Night in the height of her Expectation. This Woman came now into *Aftrea*'s Mind, at the fame Time to gratify
her Admirer with a Belief of his Happinefs, and do Juftice to an injur'd Woman. She gives her Notice of her Defign, and orders the Appointment fo,
that *Albert* met *Catalina* (for that was
her Name) for *Aftrea*, and poffefs'd her
with all the Satisfaction of a longing
Lover. But *Catalina*, infinitely pleas'd
with the Adventure, appoints the next
Night, and the following ; and finding
his Tranfports ftill frefh and high, began
to confide in her own Charms ; and keeping him longer than ufual, made the Day
difcover a double Difappointment, of her
in her future Pleafures, and him in the
paft ; for he could not forgive her even
the Joys fhe had imparted by the falfe

Bait

Bait of another's Charms, but flung from
her with the higheſt Reſentment and
Indignation, and return'd to *Aſtrea* to
upbraid her with her ungenerous Dealing ; who, for her Plea, urg'd his Duty
to his Wife, and how unreaſonable it was
in him, to deſire the ſacrificing of the
Reputation of the Woman he profeſs'd
to love.

Tho' *Albert* was forc'd to acquieſce in
what ſhe ſaid, he could not loſe his Deſire, now increas'd by the Pleaſure of Revenge, which he promis'd himſelf in the
Enjoyment of her, even againſt her Will,
and almoſt without her Knowledge. Mrs.
Behn had an old Woman of near Three-
ſcore, whom, out of Charity, ſhe kept as
her Companion, having been an old decay'd Gentlewoman ; but ſhe, guilty of
the common Vice of the Age, Avarice,
ſtill covetous of what they cannot enjoy,
was corrupted by *Albert*'s Gold, to put
him dreſs'd in her Night-Cloaths to Bed
in her Place (for ſhe made her her Bed-
fellow) when *Aſtrea* was out at a Merchant's of *Antwerp*, paſſing the Evening
in Play and Mirth, as her Age and Gaiety required : The Son of which Merchant
was a brisk, lively, frolickſome young Fellow, and with his two Siſters, and ſome
Servants, waited on *Aſtrea* home ; and
as a Concluſion of that Night's Mirth,

 propos'd

propos'd to go to Bed to the old Woman and furprize her, whilft they fhould all come in with the Candles, and compleat the merry Scene. As it was agreed, fo they did ; but the young Spark was more furpriz'd, when, in the Encounter, he found himfelf met with an unexpected Ardour, and a Man's Voice, faying, *Have I now caught thee, thou malicious Charmer! Now I'll not let thee go till thou haft done me Juftice for all the Wrongs thou haft offer'd my doating Love.*

By this Time the reft of the Company were come in, all extremely furpriz'd to find *Albert* in *Aftrea*'s Bed, inftead of the old Woman; who being thus difcover'd, and *Albert* appeas'd with her Promife to marry him at her Arrival in *England*, was difcarded, to provide herfelf, according to her Deferts. But *Albert* taking his Leave of her with a heavy Heart, and returning into *Holland* to make all Things ready for his Voyage to *England*, and Matrimony, died at *Amfterdam* of a Fever : Whilft *Aftrea* proceeded in her Journey to *Oftend* and *Dunkirk*, where, with Sir *Bernard Gafcoign*, and others, fhe took Shipping for *England ;* in which fhort Voyage fhe met with a ftrange Appearance, that was vifible to all the Paffengers and Ship's Crew. Sir *Bernard Gafcoign* had brought with him from *Italy*

feveral

feveral admirable Telefcopes and Profpec-
tive-Glaffes ; and looking thro' one of
them, when the Day was very calm
and clear, efpy'd a ftrange Apparition
floating on the Water, which was alfo
feen by all in their Turns that look'd thro'
it : which made 'em conclude that they
were painted Glaffes that were put at the
Ends, on Purpofe to furprize and amufe
thofe that look thro' em ; 'till after having taken 'em out, rubb'd and put 'em
in again, they found the fame Thing floating toward the Ship, and which was now
come fo near as to be within View without the Glafs. I have often heard her
affert, that the whole Company faw it.
The Figure was this : A four-fquare Floor
of various-colour'd Marble, from which
afcended Rows of fluted and twifted Pillars, embofs'd round with climbing Vines
and Flowers, and waving Streamers, that
receiv'd an eafy Motion from the Air ;
upon the Pillars a hundred little *Cupids*
clamber'd with fluttring Wings. This
ftrange Pageant came almoft near enough
for one to ftep out of the Ship into it,
before it vanifh'd ; after which, and a
fhort Calm, followed fo violent a Storm,
that having driven the Ship upon the
Coafts, fhe fplit in Sight of Land : but the
People, by the Help of the Inhabitants,
and Boats from the Shore, were all fav'd ;

C 2

and

and our *Aſtrea* arrived ſafe, tho' tir'd, to *London*, from a Voyage that gain'd her more Reputation than Profit.

The reſt of her Life was entirely dedi-cated to Pleaſure and Poetry ; the Succeſs in which gain'd her the Acquaintance and Friendſhip of the moſt ſenſible Men of the Age, and the Love of not a few of dif-ferent Characters ; for tho' a Sot have no Portion of Wit of his own, he yet, like old Age, covets what he cannot enjoy. I can't allow a Fool to be touch'd with the Charms of Wit, but the Reputation that is gain'd by Wit ; which being a Thing beyond his Reach, he is fond of it, becauſe it pleaſes others, not himſelf. Our *Aſtrea* had many of theſe, who profeſs'd not a little Love for her, and whom ſhe us'd as Fools ſhould be us'd, for her Sport, and the Diverſion of her Acquaintance. I went to viſit her one Day, and found with her a young brisk pert Fop very gaily dreſs'd, and who after an abundance of Impertinence left us. His Figure was ſo extraordinary, that I could not but enquire into his Name, and more particular Character, which *Aſtrea* gave me in the following Manner.

This is a young vain Coxcomb, but newly come from the Univerſity, and full of the impudent Self-Opinion and Pride of that Place, takes the common Privilege

lege of being very impertinent in all Company, efpecially among Women, and Men that underftand not the Jargon of the Schools. He's of a good Family, and was left a pretty good paternal Eftate, which he endeavour'd to encreafe by marrying a rich Aunt he had in the Country, who had Occafion for juft fuch a Fop; for tho' he has not been two Years from *Oxford*, he has met with feveral uncommon Adventures, and among the reft, his Addreffes to me fhall not be the leaft confiderable for all our Diverfions.

Going down to take Poffeffion of his paternal Eftate, and full of no very good Thoughts of wronging his Brothers, he lay at his Aunt's; who, tho' none of the youngeft, was not old enough yet to have given off all Thoughts of Love, or to be exempted from the Effects of Enjoyment: for after a long Intrigue with the Steward of her Eftate, fhe was, or imagin'd at leaft that fhe was, with Child; and tho' fhe lik'd him well enough for a Gallant, fhe could by no Means think him fit for a Husband, either becaufe her Pride would not permit her to think of her Servant for her Mafter, or that fhe fear'd to give him a Power over her Conduct, who had been a Witnefs how weak a Guard of Virtue fhe had to fecure the conjugal Duty he might expect from her as her Husband.

C 3

But

But whatever was the Motive, the Arrival of her Nephew gave her other Thoughts, finding him a fit Coxcomb for her Ends; for you find, that a little Converſation will let you into his Character, at leaſt ſo far as to diſcover him to be a very ſelf-conceited Fool, and one on whom by conſequence Flattery would have no ſmall Effect. His Aunt having made this Diſcovery, took Care to detain him ſome Days longer than he intended, and by all the cunning Arts of a deſigning Woman, gave him Cauſe to believe that his Suit would not be very unſuccefsful, if he ſhould make his Addreſſes to her. He naturally thought well of himſelf, and fir'd with ſo many Advances that his Aunt made to him, he was reſolv'd to try if he could gain her.

She was a Woman that had yet a Reſt of Beauty, improv'd too by the Help of Art, that ſhe might pretend, without Vanity, to a Conqueſt where no brighter or more youthful Faces interpos'd; to this ſhe had an engaging Air, and a ſprightly Converſation: but that which compleated the Victory over our young Spark, was her Eſtate; that was exceeding beautiful, becauſe very great, and join'd with her other Charms, was not to be refiſted by a Man who was poſſeſs'd with the contrary Vices of Avarice and Prodigality. For

he

he had ftill a Thirft of Wealth, which he perpetually fquander'd ; being incapable of doing a generous Action, tho' he would do many foolifh ones, which feem'd to him worthy that Name ; as particularly that which I'm juft going to relate after his Marriage with his Aunt, for there ended this Amour.

Some fmall Time after the Confummation of the Nuptials, finding her Fears of being with Child vain, and quite tired of the Fool her Husband, fhe perpetually was contriving how to get handfomely rid of him ; for tho' he feem'd to love her well enough for a Wife, yet he was too watchful of her Motions to give her Opportunity of thofe Pleafures fhe had fo long taken with Liberty. This made her very ill-humour'd and crofs ; which he endeavour'd, by pleafing her all the Ways he could think of, to remove : But all in vain ; unlefs he could remove himfelf, and his legal Right to her Eftate, all his Careffes and Complaifance fignified nothing. In fhort, after fhe had acted this Part fometime, and made him very earneft in the Enquiry into the Caufe of her Chagrin, fhe informed him that fhe was very fenfible the chief Motive that engaged him to make Love to her, was her Eftate, and that all his Profeffions of Love were only falfe Baits to delude her too credulous Heart, and catch her Eftate ; that fhe could never forgive herfelf, being over-reached by fo unexperienced a Youth, or ever have Patience to fupport the Afflic- tion this gave her.

He ufed all the Arguments he could think of to convince her of her Error, and that he loved her with a fincere and tender Paffion, without any Regard to her Eftate, which fhe was as entirely Miftrefs of as before. In vain was all he faid, fhe turned it to a contrary End to what he meant it ; told him 'twas eafy profeffing his Love fincere, when he was in Poffeffion of the Fruits of his paft Diffimulation, and that fhe could never believe her For- tune had no Share in his Affections, as long as he was Mafter of it, whether fhe would or not : that fhe muft defpair, be- ing fo much older than him, of long be- ing able fo much as of a cold Civility, when it was out of her Power to give him any more. He, out of a foolifh Fan- cy of Generofity, or exceffive good Opi- nion of his own Charms and Power over her, tells her he has now thought of a Way to fatisfy her Doubts, and by a convincing Proof of his Love, remove all thofe Anxieties that gave her fo much Pain, and robbed him of his Reft and Satisfac- tion ; for to fhew her that it was her Perfon, and that alone, which he efteemed,

he

he would immediately put her Fortune into her own Poſſeſſion again, and keep no other Right he had to any Thing he had of her's but her Perſon, which was the Treaſure he only coveted a quiet Enjoyment of.

· This was the Point ſhe had all this While been labouring to gain, and you may imagine ſhe loſt not the lucky Minute of the Fool's ridiculous Fondneſs. The Writings were made, and ſhe put in abſolute Poſſeſſion of all her Fortune, and had therefore no farther Need of a longer Diſſimulation; nay, the Curb that had been ſet on her unruly Will for the ſhort Time of their Marriage, provoked her to obſerve no Meaſures with him, whom ſhe could not forgive the many Pleaſures he had diſappointed her of. He was firſt tormented with freſh Proofs every Day of his being a notorious Cuckold, to which were added the Affronts of the Servants, and the Contempt of the Miſtreſs; and when none, of theſe would rid her Hands of him, whoſe Sight ſhe loath'd, having taken particular Care to have him well beaten, ſhe thruſt him out of Doors, to provide for himſelf. His late Treatment made him unwilling to return, for Fear of a worſe Reception; and ſince he had found all Means ineffectual to reclaim her, he concluded to paſs on to his own Eſtate,

and

and from thence to *London*, out of the
hearing himself the perpetual Difcourfe of
the Country.

He had not long been in Town, when
one Day walking in the Park in a very
mean Condition (his own Eftate being then
feized by his Brothers, for the Repay-
ment of what he had wronged them of)
he fees his Wife alone, and tho' mask'd,
knows her : his Neceffities prompted him
at leaft to try if the making himfelf Mafter of her Perfon, and playing the Tyrant in his Turn, would not furnifh him
with a prefent Supply, if not recover him
the Poffeffion of her Eftate, by cancelling
the Deed that put it into her Power to
abufe him.   She was very well drefs'd, and
he fomething fhabby ; he feizes her, ufes
all the Arguments he could to perfuade
her Reformation, and Re-union to a Man
that yet had a Value for her ; but all in
vain.   He told her plainly he would keep
her Perfon, tho' he had nothing to do with
her Eftate.   'Twas in vain for her to
ftruggle, fo fhe went with him to the
Horfe-Guards, contriving all the Way how
to get rid of him : and being come there,
on fome Occafion there happen'd to be a
great Concourfe of People ; this gave her
a lucky Hint, and ftarting from him, fhe
fought the Protection of the Mob, affuring them he was a paultry Scoundrel,

that

that would needs pretend to feduce her to
his Ends, but on Denial, had on his Threats
prevailed with her to go quietly to that
Place, where fhe hoped her Refcue. He
affur'd them he was her Hufband, and
that he only meant to reclaim her from
her evil Courfes, and carry her home.
She with all the Affurance imaginable,
laughing at his Affertion, defired them to
confider if that Man looked like her Hufband. Her Drefs and Mein had engaged
a Gentleman of the Guards to efpoufe her
Quarrel, who preventing the Decifion of
the Mob, declared his Opinion in the Lady's Favour, and propofed the giving him
the Civility of the Horfe-pond, which
fuiting with the brutal Pleafure of the
Mob, prevail'd ; and fo the poor Knight
was carry'd to the Enchanted Caftle, and
the Lady fet free, for more agreeable En-
counters : for fhe was not ungrateful to her
Deliverer.

This unlucky Adventure was no fmall
Check to his Hopes, and Opinion of his
own Conduct and Judgment ; yet about
half a Year after, being now more gay,
by the Recovery of his Eftate, and walking in the Park again, he meets his treacherous Spoufe, and full of the Injury he had
laft received from her, and out of Fear
of the like Misfortune, his Drefs being
now anfwerable to her's, he upbraids her

with what was paſt, and aſſures her nothing ſhall now deliver her from him; and ſo endeavouring to force her out again at the *Horſe-Guards*, where ſhe enter'd, and near which he met her, ſhe by her Cunning and ſeeming Sorrow for what had paſs'd, prevail'd with him to go out at *St. James*'s ; and being got out of the Gate, ſhe makes to the firſt Coach very peaceably with him, where he found three Gentlemen who waited ready for her, and on her Approach came out, deliver'd her from her Husband, and without much Difficulty carried her off.

Being thus again out-witted by her, and ſeeing no Help for his deſperate Condition, he gave over all Thoughts of her, and ſets his Mind on ſome freſh Amour, to wear off the uneaſy Remembrance of his paſt Adventures. Among the reſt that were doom'd to ſuffer his Addreſſes, it has been my Fate of late to ſhare the ill Luck ; tho' I have the Advantage of a great deal of good Company to atone for the impertinent Moments he taxes me with, his Converſation diverting ſometimes ſome of my beſt Friends, and his Letters myſelf : they are ſo affectedly ridiculous, that I will ſhew you one of them, extraordinary in its Kind.

To

SHOU'D I make a Palinode for the Aggreffions of my Paffion, I fhould difappoint the Juftice of your Expectations : for without any periodical Flourifhes, you know your Wit has irrefiftible Charms ; and that we can no more refift the Defire of imparting our Pain when the Paroxyfm approaches, than a fick Man in a Fever the Defire of Water. The Horofcope of my Love for the bright *Aftrea* rofe under a very noxious Influence, if its Stars ordain it abortive. You, Madam, that are Miftrefs of the Encyclopedy of the Sciences, who have the whole Galaxy of the Mufes to attend you, that have the Corufcations of the Night in your Eyes, *Jove's* Bolts and Lightning in your Frowns, and the Sheers of the three fatal Sifters in your Anger, fhould alfo have the Commiferation of the Gods in the Tribunal of your Heart, to preponderate to the Severity of your Juftice. The wife Ancients, among their Hieroglyphicks, made *Juftice* blind, that fhe might fee and difcover the feveral Shares and Proportions due to the feveral Pretenders to her Favour : You, Madam,

· are

are the Portraiture, and admirable *Icon* of that Juftice whofe Name you bear.

Terras Aftrea reliquit : that is,

" 'Tis full well known,
" That Juftice is flown.

Yet, moft ferene Fair One, fhe poffeffes your Breaft ; there fhe nidificates, there fhe erects her Bower, and there I hope to have her declare in the Favour of, Madam,

Your moft Oblequious Humble Servant,

and Non-pareil Admirer, &c.

This indeed is the Soul of a mere Academy, that is, of one whom Learning, ill underftood, has fitted for a publick · Coxcomb, and of whom there is fcarce any one fo ignorant, as to have a good Opinion. You have indeed, reply'd I, a moft extraordinary Lover of him, but whofe Folly is too grofs to be fo long entertaining as he fhall think fit to be impertinent : for like common Beggars they are not to be deny'd ; and are fo far Courtiers, to think perpetual Importunities Merit : So that if you have no Way of ridding your Hands of him but laughing at him, 'twill never do ; for a Fool follows you the more for laughing at
him.

him, as a Spaniel does for beating of him.

Why truly (reply'd *Aſtrea*) he is grown ſo troubleſome now, that I ſhall be forced to uſe him as bad as his Wife has done, in my own Defence; and that I intend to put in Execution the more ſpeedily, ſince I find my *Lyſander* grows uneaſy at his Addreſſes, which can never move any Thing but Laughter: however I ſhall eaſily ſacrifice ſo trifling a Sport to the Quiet of the Man I love, in which you muſt aſſiſt me; for *Lyſander* ſhall have no Hand in it, both to ſecure him from a Quarrel, and myſelf the Pleaſure of revenging him on a Fop that could hope where he had Poſſeſſion.

I promiſed to give her all the Aſſiſtance I was capable of, to gratify ſo reaſonable a Revenge; for if one Man affronts another by his Rudeneſs, the Perſon affronted muſt be looked upon as a Coward, if he take not Satisfaction. I can imagine no Reaſon in the World, why a Woman of Wit, that is affronted with the ſaucy impertinent Love of a Fool that will not be deny'd, ſhould not puniſh his Inſolence according to her Power. *Wit* is the Weapon ſhe had to fight with, and that ſhe was to make Uſe of in her Satisfaction, to which, as a Second, I was very willing to contribute; tho' the Part ſhe afterwards engaged me to play, was not ſo agreeable

to

to me as I at firft imagined : for to give a conceited Coxcomb any Reafon to believe he has an Afcendant over a Woman, and then allow him the leaft Opportunity, is to put herfelf in a manifeft Hazard of her Honour and Satisfaction. But this I did not much confider, being willing to free my Friend from the Importunities of one fhe could no more fuffer, than know how to be handfomely rid of.

And upon her Perfuafion, I took the Opportunity of his next Vifit to give him all the Reafon imaginable to make him think me extremely taken with his Perfon : which Interview *Aftrea* took Care to improve on my Departure, and to let him know, that I was a Perfon of no lefs Fortune than Quality, which would repair the Lofs of an unfaithful Wife. Flattery, as it has fome Power on the moft fenfible, fo it is of fuch Force with a Fool, that no Confideration can withftand it. He foon thought the Purfuit of me more eligible, (where he imagined his Perfections had made fuch an Impreffion, that I could no more refift the Charm) than the Barren Paffion he had hitherto entertain'd for *Aftrea*. In fhort, fhe came to a perfect Underftanding, and the Affignation was made, and fome Friends provided to be in Readinefs to difappoint him, when he moft thought me his own. - But the Gentlemen

tlemen retired to the Balcony to fee fome fudden Hubbub in the Street; and my Lover, full of himfelf, and the Opinion of my being wholly at his Devotion, prefs'd fo hard for the Victory, that when nothing elfe would fecure me, I was forced to cry out: on which the Gentlemen approach'd, and he believing one of 'em my Hufband, was in a moft dreadful Fright, and foon difcover'd the Bafenefs of his Spirit; for in Hopes to get clear off himfelf, he accufed me to him he fuppofed my Hufband: But this not availing, he was handfomely tofs'd in a Blanket, wafh'd, and turn'd out of Doors. All which Misfortunes he diffembled to *Aftrea*, and renew'd his Suit to her, till, by Appointment, I and the two Gentlemen enter'd the Room, and expofed the Truth of the Story; which he could not deny: and confounded with the Reproaches of *Aftrea*, and the whole Company's laughing at him, he never after troubled her with a Vifit.

This was the End of this ridiculous Amour; but that which touch'd her Heart, could not be fo eafily difpofed of. I have already mention'd *Lyfander*, as a Lover fhe valued; and fhe having contributed her Letters to him, to the laft Impreffion, I fhall fay no more of it than what thofe difcover, which I have now inferted in their Order.

LOVE-

LOVE-LETTERS

TO A

GENTLEMAN

By Mrs. *A. BEHN.*

Printed from the Original Letters.

LETTER I.

YOU bid me write, and I wiſh it were only the Effect of Complaiſance that makes me obey you. I ſhould be very angry with myſelf and you, if I thought it were any other Motive: I hope it is not, and will not have you believe otherwiſe. I cannot help however wiſhing you no Mirth, nor any Content in your Dancing-Deſign; and this unwonted Malice in me I do not like, and would have concealed it if I could, leſt you ſhould take it for ſomething which I am not, nor will believe myſelf guilty.

of

of.   May your Women be all ugly, ill-natur'd, ill-drefs'd, ill-fafhion'd, and un-converfable ; and, for your greater Difap-pointment, may every Moment of your Time there be taken up with Thoughts of me (a fufficient Curfe) and yet you will be better entertain'd than me, who poffibly am, and fhall be uneafy with Thoughts not fo good. Perhaps you had eas'd me of fome Trouble, if you had let me feen you, or known you had been well; but thefe are Favours for better Friends, and I'll endeavour not to refent the Lofs, or rather the Mifs of 'em. It may be, fince I have fo eafily granted this Defire of your's, in writing to you, you will fear you have pulled a Trouble on —— but do not. I do by this fend for you —— You know what you gave your Hand upon ; the Date of Banifhment is already out, and I could have wifhed you had been fo good-natur'd as to have difobey'd me. Pray take Notice therefore I am better natur'd than you. I am profoundly melancholy fince I faw you, I know not why : and fhould be glad to fee you when your Occafions will permit you to vifit

ASTREA.

LET-

L E T T E R II.

YOU may tell me a thoufand Years, my dear *Lycidas*, of your unbounded Friend-fhip ; but after fo unkind a Departure as that laft Night, give me Leave (when ferious) to doubt it ; nay 'tis paft Doubt, I know you rather hate me. What elfe could hurry you from me, when you faw me furrounded with all the neceffary Impoffibilities of fpeaking to you ? I made as broad Signs as one could do who durft not fpeak, both for your Sake and my own. I acted even imprudently to make my Soul underftood, that was then (if I may fay fo) in real Agonies for your Departure. 'Tis a Wonder a Woman fo violent in all her Paffions as I, did not (forgetting all Prudence, all Confiderations) fly out into abfolute Commands, or at leaft Entreaties, that you would give me a Moment's Time longer. I burft to fpeak with you to know a thoufand Things ; but particularly, how you came to be fo barbarous, as to carry away all that could make my Satisfaction. You carry'd away my Letter, and you carry'd away *Lycidas* : I will not call him mine, becaufe he has fo unkindly taken himfelf back. 'Twas with

that

that Defign you came; for I faw all Night with what Reluctancy you fpoke, how coldly you entertain'd me, and with what Pain and Uneafinefs you gave me the only Converfation I value in the World.   I am afhamed to tell you this; I know your peevifh Virtue will mifinterpret me.   But take it how you will, think of it as you pleafe; I am undone, and will be free; I will tell you, you did not ufe me well: I am ruined, and will rail at you —— Come then, I conjure you, this Evening, that after it I may fhut thofe Eyes that have been too long waking.   I have committed a thoufand Madneffes in this; but you muft pardon the Faults you have created.   Come and do fo; for I muft fee you To-night, and that in better Humour than you were laft Night.   No more; obey me as you have that Friendfhip for me you profefs: and affure yourfelf to find a very welcome Reception from (*Lycidas*)

Your A S T R E A.

LETTER III.

WHEN ſhall we underſtand one another? For I thought, dear *Ly-cidas*, you had been a Man of your Parole. I will as ſoon believe you will forget me, as that you have not remember'd the Pro-miſe you made me. Confeſs you are the teazingeſt Creature in the World, rather than ſuffer me to think you neglect me, or would put a Slight upon me, that have choſen you from all the whole Creation to give my entire Eſteem to. This I had aſſured you Yeſterday, but that I dreaded the Effects of your Cenſure To-day : and tho' I ſcorn to guard my Tongue, as hope-ing it will never offend willingly, yet I can with much Ado hold it, when I have a great Mind to ſay a thouſand Things I know will be taken in an ill Senſe. Poſſi-bly you will wonder what compels me to write ; what moves me to ſend where I find ſo little Welcome ; nay, where I meet with ſuch Returns : it may be, I wonder too. You ſay I am changed ; I had rather almoſt juſtify an Ill than repent ; main-tain falſe Arguments, than yield I am i'th' Wrong. In fine, charming Friend *Lycidas*,

whatever

whatever I was fince you knew me, believe I am ftill the fame in Soul and Thought; but that is what fhall never hurt you. what fhall never be but to ferve you, Why then did you fay you would not fit near me ; Was that, my Friend, was that the Efteem you profefs ? Who grows cold firft ? Who is changed ? And who the Aggreffor ? 'Tis I was firft in Friendfhip, and fhall be laft in Conftancy. You by Inclination, and not for want of Friends, have I placed higheft in my Efteem ; and for that Reafon your Converfation is the moft acceptable and agreeable of any in the World—and for this Reafon you fhun mine. Take your Courfe ; be a Friend like a Foe, and continue to impofe upon me, that you efteem me when you fly me. Renounce your falfe Friendfhip, or let me fee you give it entire to

A S T R E A·

LETTER IV.

I HAD rather, dear *Lycidas*, fet myfelf to write to any Man on Earth than you ; for I fear your fevere Prudence and Difcretion, fo nice, may make an ill Judgment of what I fay : Yet you bid me not diffem-

diffemble ; and you need not have caution'd me, who fo naturally hate thofe little Arts of my Sex, that I often run on Freedoms that may well enough bear a Cenfure from People fo fcrupulous as *Lycidas.* Nor dare I follow all my Inclinations neither, nor tell all the little Secrets of my Soul: why I write them, I can give no Account; tis but fooling myfelf, perhaps, into an Undoing. I do but (by this foft Entertainment) look in my Heart, like a young Gamefter, to make it venture its laft Stake : this I fay may be the Danger ; I may come off unhurt, but cannot be a Winner : why then fhould I throw an uncertain Caft, where I hazard all, and you nothing? Your ftanch Prudence is Proof againft Love, and all the Bank's on my Side. Your are fo unreafonable, you would have me pay where I have contracted no Debt ; you would have me give, and you like a Mifer would diftribute nothing. Greedy *Lycidas !* Unconfcionable and Ungenerous! You would not be in Love for all the World, yet wifh I were fo. Uncharitable! —— Would my Fever cure you? or a Curfe on me make you blefs'd? Say, *Lycidas,* will it ? I have heard, when two Souls kindly meet 'tis a vaft Pleafure, as vaft as the Curfe muft be, when Kindnefs is not equal ; and why fhould you believe that neceffary for me,

that

that will be fo very incommode for you?
Will you, dear *Lycidas*, allow then, that
you have lefs Good-Nature than I? Pray
be juft, till you can give fuch Proofs of the
.contrary, as I fhall be Judge of; or give
me a Reafon for your Ill-nature. So much
for loving.

Now, as you are my Friend, I conjure
you to confider what Refolution I took
up, when I faw you laft (which methinks
is a long Time) of feeing no Man till I
faw your Face again; and when you remember that, you will poffibly be fo kind
as to make what Hafte you can to fee me
again. Till then have Thoughts as much
in Favour of me as you can; for when
you know me better, you will believe I
merit all. May you be impatient and uneafy 'till you fee me again: and, bating
that, may all the Bleffings of Heaven and
Earth light on you, is the continued Prayers
of (dear *Lycidas*)

Your true ASTREA.

LETTER V.

THOUGH it be very late, I cannot
go to Bed, but I muft tell thee I have
been very good ever fince I faw thee, and

have been a writing, and have feen no Face
of Man, or other Body, fave my own
People.   I am mightily pleas'd with your
Kindnefs to me To-night; and 'twas, I
hope and believe, very innocent and undif-
turbing on both Sides.   My *Lycidas* fays,
He can be foft and dear when he pleafes to
put off his haughty Pride, which is only
affum'd to fee how far I dare love him un-
united.   Since then my Soul's Delight you
are, and may be ever affur'd I am, and ever
will be your's, befal me what will; and
that all the Devils of Hell fhall not prevail
againft thee: fhew then, I fay, my deareft
Love, thy native fweet Temper: fhew me
all the Love thou haft undiffembled. Then,
and never till then, fhall I believe you love;
and deferve my Heart, for God's Sake, to
keep me well: and if thou haft Love (as
I fhall never doubt, if thou art always as
To-night) fhew that Love, I befeech thee;
there being nothing fo grateful to God, and
Mankind, as Plain-dealing. 'Tis too late
to conjure thee farther: I will be purchas'd
with Softnefs, and dear Words, and kind
Expreffions, fweet Eyes, and a low Voice.

Farewel; I love thee dearly, paffionately
and tenderly, and am refolved to be eternally
(My only Dear Delight,
and Joy of my Life)
Thy *ASTREA.*

LET-

LETTER VI.

SINCE you, my deareft *Lycidas*, have prefcrib'd me Laws and Rules, how I fhall behave myfelf to pleafe and gain you; and that one of thefe is not Lying or Diffembling; and that I had To-night promis'd you fhould never have a tedious Letter from me more: I will begin to keep my Word, and ftint my Heart and Hand. I promis'd tho' to write; and tho' I have no great Matter to fay more, than the Affurance of my Eternal Love to you, yet to obey you, and not only fo, but to oblige my own impatient Heart, I muft, late as 'tis, fay fomething to thee.

I ftay'd after thee To-night, 'till I had read a whole Act of my new Play; and then he led me over all the Way, faying, Gad you were the Man: And beginning fome rallying Love-Difcourfe after Supper, which he fancy'd was not fo well receiv'd as it ought, he faid you were not handfome, and call'd *Philly* to own it; but he did not, but was of my Side, and faid you were handfome: fo he went on a While, and all ended that concern'd you. And this, upon my Word, is all.

D 2

Your

Your Articles I have read over, and do not like them; you have broke one, even before you have fworn or feal'd 'em; that is, they are wrote with Referve. I muſt have a better Account of your Heart To-morrow, when you come. I grow defperate fond of you, and would fain be us'd well; if not, I will march off: But I will believe you mean to keep your Word, as I will for ever do mine. Pray make Haſte to fee me To-morrow; and if I am not at home when you come, fend for me over the Way, where I have engaged to dine, there being an Entertainment on purpoſe To-morrow for me.

For God's Sake make no more Niceties and Scruples than need, in your Way of living with me; that is, do not make me believe this Diſtance is to eaſe you, when indeed 'tis meant to eaſe us both of Love; and for God's Sake, do not mifinterpret my Exceſs of Fondneſs; and if I forget myſelf, let the Check you give be fufficient to make me defiſt. Believe me, dear Creature, 'tis more out of Humour and Jeſt, than any Inclination on my Side; for I could fit eternally with you, without that Part of Diſturbance: Fear me not, for you are (from that) as fafe as in Heaven itſelf. Believe me, dear *Lycidas,* this Truth, and truſt me. 'Tis late, farewel; and come, for God's Sake, betimes

To-

To-morrow, and put off your foolifh Fears
and Niceties, and do not fhame me with
your perpetual ill Opinion; my Nature is
proud and infolent, and cannot bear it: I
I will be ufed fomething better, in fpite of
all your Apprehenfions falfely grounded.
Adieu, keep me as I am ever your's,

ASTREA.

By this Letter, one would think I were
the nicefl Thing on Earth; yet I know a
dear Friend goes far beyond me in that un-
neceffary Fault.

LETTER VII.

My Charming Unkind,

I WOULD have engag'd my Life you
could not have left me fo coldly, fo un-
concerned as you did; but you are refolv'd
to give me Proofs of your No Love. Your
Counfel, which was given you To-night,
has wrought the Effects which it ufually
does in Hearts like yours. Tell me no
more you love me; for 'twill be hard to
make me think it, tho' it be the only Bleffing I afk on Earth: But if Love can merit

D 3   a Heart,

a Heart, I know who ought to claim your's. My Soul is ready to burſt with Pride and Indignation ; and at the ſame Time, Love, with all his Softneſs, aſſails me, and will make me write : ſo that between one and the other, I can expreſs neither as I ought. What ſhall I do to make you know I do not uſe to condeſcend to ſo much Submiſ-ſion, nor to tell my Heart ſo freely ? Tho' you think it Uſe, methinks I find my Heart ſwell with Diſdain at this Minute, for my be-ing ready to make Aſſeverations of the con-trary, and to aſſure you I do not, nor never did love, or talk at the Rate I do to you, ſince I was born : I ſay, I would ſwear this, but ſomething rolls up my Boſom, and checks my very Thought as it riſes. You ought, Oh Faithleſs, and infinitely Adorable *Lycidas !* to know and gueſs my Tender-neſs ; you ought to ſee it grow, and daily increaſe upon your Hands. If it be trouble-ſome, 'tis becauſe I fancy you leſſen, whilſt I encreaſe, in Paſſion ; or rather, that by your ill Judgment of mine, you never had any in your Soul for me. Oh unlucky, oh vexatious Thought ! Either let me never ſee that charming Face, or eaſe my Soul of ſo tormenting an Agony, as the cruel Thought of not being belov'd. Why, my lovely Dear, ſhould I flatter you ? Or, why make more Words of my Tenderneſs, than another Woman, that loves as well, would

do,

do, as once you faid? No, you ought rather to believe that I fay more, becaufe I
have more than any Woman can be capable
of: My Soul is form'd of no other Material
than Love; and all that Soul of Love was
form'd for my dear, faithlefs *Lycidas* ——
Methinks I have a Fancy, that fomething
will prevent my going To-morrow Morning: However I conjure thee, if poffible,
to come To-morrow about feven or eight
at Night, that I may tell you in what a
deplorable Condition you left me To-night.
I cannot defcribe it; but I feel it, and wifh
you the fame Pain, for going fo inhumanly:
But oh! you went to Joys, and left me to
Torments! You went to Love alone, and
left me Love and Rage, Fevers and Calen-
tures, even Madnefs itfelf! Indeed, indeed,
my Soul! I know not to what Degree I
love you; let it fuffice I do moft paffionately, and can have no Thoughts of any other
Man, whilft I have Life. No! reproach
me, defame me, lampoon me, curfe me,
and kill me, when I do, and let Heaven do
fo too.

Farewel —— I love you more and more
every Moment of my Life. Know it, and
Good-night. Come To-morrow, being
Wednefday, to, my Adorable *Lycidas*, your

ASTREA.

❈❈❈❈❈❈❈❈❈❈❈❈❈❈❈

LETTER VIII.

WHY, my deareſt Charmer, do you
disturb that Repoſe I had reſolved to purſue, by taking it unkindly that
I did not write? I cannot diſobey you, becauſe indeed I would not, tho' 'twere better much for both I had been for ever ſilent: I prophefy ſo, but at the ſame
Time cannot help my Fate, and know not
what Force or Credit there is in the
Virtue we both profeſs; but I am ſure
'tis not good to tempt it: I think I am
ſure, and I think my *Lycidas* juſt. But
oh! to what Purpoſe is all this fooling?
You have often wiſely conſidered it; but
I never ſtay'd to think till 'twas too late;
and whatever Reſolutions I make in the
Abſence of my lovely Friend, one ſingle
Sight turns me all Woman, and all his.
Take Notice then, my *Lycidas*, I will
henceforth never be wiſe more; never
make any Vows againſt my Inclinations,
or the little wing'd Deity. I own I have
neither the Coldneſs of *Lycidas*, nor the
Prudence; I cannot either not love, or
have a thouſand Arts of hiding it; I
have nobody to fear, and therefore may

have

have fomebody to love : But if you are
deftin'd to be he, the Lord have Mercy
on me ; for I'm fure you'll have none. I
expect a Reprimand for this plain Confeffion ; but I muft juftify it, and I will,
becaufe I cannot help it : I was born to
ill Luck ; and this Lofs of my Heart, is,
poffibly, not the leaft Part on't. Do not
let me fee you difapprove it, I may one
Day grow afham'd on't, and reclaim ; but
never, whilft you blow the Flame, tho'
perhaps againft your Will. I expect now
a very wife Anfwer ; and, I believe, with
abundance of Difcretion, you will caution
me to avoid this Danger that threatens.
Do fo, if you have a Mind to make me
launch farther into the main Sea of Love :
Rather deal with me as with a right Woman ; make me believe myfelf infinitely
belov'd. I may chance, from the natural
Inconftancy of my Sex, to be as falfe as
you would wifh, and leave you in Quiet :
For as I am fatisfied I love in vain, and
without Return, I'm fatisfied that nothing,
but the Thing that hates me, could treat
me as *Lycidas* does ; and 'tis only the Vanity of being belov'd by me, can make
you countenance a Softnefs fo difpleafing
to you. How could any Thing, but the
Man that hates me, entertain me fo unkindly ? Witnefs your excellent Opinion
of me, of loving others ; witnefs your

paffing

paſſing by the End of the Street where I
live, and ſquandring away your Time at any
Coffee-houſe, rather than allow me what
you know in your Soul is the greateſt Bleffing of my Life, your dear, *dull*, melancholy
Company ; I call it dull, becauſe you can
never be gay or merry where *Aſtrea* is.
How could this Indifference poſſefs you,
when your malicious Soul knew I was lan-
guiſhing for you ? I died, I fainted, and
panted for an Hour of what you laviſh'd
out, regardleſs of me, and without ſo
much as thinking on me ! What can you
ſay, that Judgment may not paſs ? that
you may not be condemn'd for the worſt-
natur'd, incorrigible Thing in the World ?
Yield, and at leaſt ſay, My honeſt Friend
Aſtrea, I neither do love thee, nor can, nor
ever will ; at leaſt let me ſay, you were
generous, and told me plain blunt Truth :
I know it ; nay, worſe, you impudently
(but truly) told me your Buſineſs would
permit you to come every Night, but your
Inclinations would not: At leaſt this was
honeſt, but very unkind, and not over-civil.
Not you, my amiable *Lycidas*, know I
would purchaſe your Sight at any Rate ?
Why this Neglect then ? Why keeping
Diſtance ? But as much as to ſay, *Aſtrea,*
truly you will make me love, you will make
me be fond of you, you will pleaſe and delight
me with your Converſation, and I am a Fellow
that

that do not defire to be pleas'd, therefore be not fo civil to me, for I do not defire civil Company, nor Company that diverts me. A pretty Speech this! and yet if I do obey, defift being civil, and behave myfelf very rudely, as I have done, you fay, thefe two or three Days —— then, Oh *Aftrea !* where is your Profeffion ? Where your Love fo boafted ? Your Good-Nature, *&c. ?* Why truly, my dear *Lycidas,* where it was, and ever will be, fo long as you have invincible Charms, and fhew your Eyes, and look fo dearly ; tho' you may, by your prudent Counfel, and your wife Conduct of Abfence, and marching by my Door without calling in, oblige me to ftay my Hand, and hold my Tongue. I can conceal my Kindnefs, tho' not diffemble one : I can make you think I am wife, if I lift ; but when I tell you I have Friendfhip, Love, and Efteem for you, you may pawn your Soul upon it : believe 'tis true, and fatisfy yourfelf you have, my dear *Lycidas,* in your *Aftrea* all fhe profeffes. I fhould be glad to fee you as foon as poffible (you fay *Thurfday*) you can : I beg you will, and fhall with Impatience expect you betimes. Fail me not, as you would have me think you have any Value for

A S T R E A.

D 6

I beg

I beg you will not fail to let me hear from you To-day, being *Wednesday*, and see you at Night, if you can.

HERE I muft draw to an End: for tho' confiderable Trufts were repos'd in her, yet they were of that Import, that I muft not prefume here to infert 'em; but fhall conclude with her Death, occafion'd by an unskilful Phyfician, on the 16th of *April*, 1689. She was buried in the Cloyfters of *Weftmifter-Abby*, cover'd only with a plain Marble Stone, with two wretched Verfes on it, made, as I'm inform'd, by a very ingenious Gentleman, tho' no Poet: the very Perfon, whom the Envious of our Sex, and the Malicious of the other, would needs have the Author of moft of her's; which, to my Knowledge, were her own Product, without the Affiftance of any Thing but Nature, which fhews itfelf indeed without the Embarraffments of Art in every Thing fhe has wrote.

She was of a generous and open Temper, fomething paffionate, very ferviceable to her Friends in all that was in her Power; and could fooner forgive an injury, than do one. She had Wit, Honour, Good-humour, and Judgment. She was Miftrefs of all the pleafing Arts of Converfation, but us'd 'em not to any but thofe who love Plain-

dealing.

dealing. She was a Woman of Senfe, and by Confequence a Lover of Pleafure, as indeed all, both Men and Women, are ; but only fome would be thought to be above the Conditions of Humanity, and place their chief Pleafure in a proud vain Hypocrify. For my Part, I knew her intimately, and never faw aught unbecoming the juft Modefty of our Sex, tho' more gay and free than the Folly of the Precife will allow. She was, I'm fatisfy'd, a greater Honour to our Sex, than all the Canting Tribe of Diffemblers, that die with the falfe Reputation of Saints. This I may venture to fay, becaufe I'm unknown, and the revengeful Cenfures of my Sex will not reach me, fince they will never be able to draw the Veil, and difcover the Speaker of thefe bold Truths. If I have done my dead Friend any Manner of Juftice, I'm fatisfy'd, having obtain'd my End : If not, the Reader muft remember that there are few *Aftrea*'s arife in our Age, and 'till fuch a one does appear, all our Endeavours in Encomiums on the laft muft be vain and impotent.

T H E

THE
HISTORY
OF THE
ROYAL SLAVE.

I DO not pretend, in giving you the History of this *ROYAL SLAVE,* to entertain my Reader with the Adventures of a feign'd *Hero,* whofe Life and Fortunes Fancy may manage at the Poet's Pleafure; nor in relating the Truth, defign to adorn it with any Accidents, but fuch as arrived in earneft to him: And it fhall come fimply into the World, recommended by its own proper Merits, and natural Intrigues; there being enough of Reality to fupport it, and to render

it

it diverting, without the Addition of Invention.

I was myself an Eye-witnefs to a great Part of what you will find here fet down; and what I could not be Witnefs of, I receiv'd from the Mouth of the chief Actor in this Hiftory, the *Hero* himfelf, who gave us the whole Tranfactions of his Youth: And I fhall omit, for Brevity's Sake, a thoufand little Accidents of his Life, which, however pleafant to us, where Hiftory was fcarce, and Adventures very rare, yet might prove tedious and heavy to my Reader, in a World where he finds Diverfions for every Minute, new and ftrange. But we who were perfectly charm'd with the Character of this great Man, were curious to gather every Circumftance of his Life.

The Scene of the laft Part of his Adventures lies in a Colony in *America*, called *Surinam*, in the *Weft-Indies*.

But before I give you the Story of this *Gallant Slave*, 'tis fit I tell you the Manner of bringing them to thefe new *Colonies;* thofe they make Ufe of there, not being *Natives* of the Place: for thofe we live with in perfect Amity, without daring to command 'em; but, on the contrary, carefs 'em with all the brotherly and friendly Affection in the World; trading with them for their Fifh, Venifon,

Buffaloes

Buffaloes Skins, and little Rarities ; as *Marmosets*, a fort of Monkey, as big as a Rat or Weafel, but of a marvellous and delicate Shape, having Face and Hands like a Human Creature ; and *Coufheries*, a little Beaft in the Form and Fafhion of a Lion, as big as a Kitten, but fo exactly made in all Parts like that Noble Beaft, that it is it in *Miniature :* Then for little *Paraketocs*, great *Parrots*, *Muckaws* and a thoufand other Birds and Beafts of wonderful and furprizing Forms, Shapes, and Colours : For Skins of prodigious Snakes, of which there are fome three-fcore Yards in Length ; as is the Skin of one that may be feen at his Majefty's *Antiquary's ;* where are alfo fome rare Flies, of amazing Forms and Colours, prefented to 'em by myfelf : fome as big as my Fift, fome lefs ; and all of various Excellencies, fuch as Art cannot imitate. Then we trade for Feathers, which they order into all Shapes, make themfelves little fhort Habits of 'em, and glorious Wreaths for their Heads, Necks, Arms and Legs, whofe Tinctures are un-conceïvable. I had a Set of thefe prefented to me, and I gave 'em to the *King's Theatre ;* it was the Drefs of the *Indian Queen*, infinitely admir'd by Perfons of Quality ; and was inimitable. Befides thefe, a thoufand little Knacks, and Rari-

ties

ties in Nature; and fome of Art, as their
Baskets, Weapons, Aprons, &c. We
dealt with 'em with Beads of all Colours,
Knives, Axes, Pins and Needles, which
they us'd only as Tools to drill Holes
with in their Ears, Nofes and Lips,
where they hang a great many little
Things; as long Beads, Bits of Tin, Brafs
or Silver beat thin, and any fhining Trin-
ket. The Beads they weave into Aprons
about a Quarter of an Ell long, and of the
fame Breadth; working them very pretti-
ly in Flowers of feveral Colours; which
Apron they wear juft before 'em, as *Adam*
and *Eve* did the Fig-leaves; the Men
wearing a long Stripe of Linen, which
they deal with us for. They thread thefe
Beads alfo on long Cotton-threads, and
make Girdles to tie their Aprons to,
which come twenty times, or more, about
the Wafte, and then crofs, like a Shoul-
der-belt, both Ways, and round their
Necks, Arms and Legs. This Adorn-
ment, with their long black Hair, and
the Face painted in little Specks or
Flowers here and there, makes 'em a
wonderful Figure to behold. Some of
the Beauties, which indeed are finely
fhap'd, as almoft all are, and who have
pretty Features, are charming and novel;
for they have all that is called Beauty,
except the Colour, which is a reddifh
                                    Yellow;

Yellow; or after a new Oiling, which they often ufe to themfelves, they are of the Colour of a new Brick, but fmooth, foft and fleek. They are extreme modeft and bafhful, very fhy, and nice of being touch'd. And tho' they are all thus naked, if one lives for ever among 'em, there is not to be feen an indecent Action, or Glance: and being continually us'd to fee one another fo unadorn'd, fo like our firft Parents before the Fall, it feems as if they had no Wifhes, there being nothing to heighten Curiofity: but all you can fee, you fee at once, and every Moment fee; and where there is no Novelty, there can be no Curiofity. Not but I have feen a handfome young *Indian*, dying for Love of a very beautiful young *Indian* Maid; but all his Courtfhip was, to fold his Arms, purfue her with his Eyes, and Sighs were all his Language: Whilft fhe, as if no fuch Lover were prefent, or rather as if fhe defired none fuch, carefully guarded her Eyes from beholding him; and never approach'd him, but fhe look'd down with all the blufhing Modefty I have feen in the moft Severe and Cautious of our World. And thefe People reprefented to me an abfolute *Idea* of the firft State of Innocence, before Man knew how to fin: And 'tis moft evident and plain, that fimple Nature is the moft harmlefs, in-

offenfive

offenfive and virtuous Miftrefs. 'Tis fhe alone, if fhe were permitted, that better inftructs the World, than all the Inventions of Man: Religion would here but deftroy that Tranquillity they poffefs by Ignorance; and Laws would but teach 'em to know Offences, of which now they have no Notion. They once made Mourning and Fafting for the Death of the *Englifh* Governor, who had given his Hand to come on fuch a Day to 'em, and neither came nor fent; believing, when a Man's Word was paft, nothing but Death could or fhould prevent his keeping it: And when they faw he was not dead, they ask'd him what Name they had for a Man who promis'd a Thing he did not do? The Governor told them, Such a Man was a *Lyar*, which was a Word of Infamy to a Gentleman. Then one of 'em reply'd, *Governor, you are a Lyar, and guilty of that Infamy.* They have a native Juftice, which knows no Fraud; and they underftand no Vice, or Cunning, but when they are taught by the *White* Men. They have Plurality of Wives; which, when they grow old, ferve thofe that fucceed 'em, who are young, but with a Servitude eafy and refpected; and unlefs they take Slaves in War, they have no other Attendants.

Thofe

Thofe on that *Continent* where I was, had no King ; but the oldeft War-Captain was obey'd with great Refignation.

A War-Captain is a Man who has led them on to Battle with Conduct and Succefs ; of whom I fhall have Occafion to fpeak more hereafter, and of fome other of their Cuftoms and Manners, as they fall in my Way.

With thefe People, as I faid, we live in perfect Tranquillity, and good Underftanding, as it behoves us to do ; they knowing all the Places where to feek the beft Food of the Country, and the Means of getting it ; and for very fmall and unvaluable Trifles, fupplying us with what 'tis almoft impoffible for us to get : for they do not only in the Woods, and over the *Sevana's,* in Hunting, fupply the Parts of Hounds, by fwiftly fcouring thro' thofe almoft impaffable Places, and by the mere Activity of their Feet, run down the nimbleft Deer, and other eatable Beafts ; but in the Water, one would think they were Gods of the Rivers, or Fellow-Citizens of the Deep ; fo rare an Art they have in fwimming, diving, and almoft living in Water ; by which they command the lefs fwift Inhabitants of the Floods. And then for fhooting, what they cannot take, or reach with their Hands, they do with Arrows ; and have fo admirable an

Aim,

Aim, that they will fplit almoft an Hair, and at any Diftance that an Arrow can reach: they will fhoot down Oranges, and other Fruit, and only touch the Stalk with the Dart's Point, that they may not hurt the Fruit. So that they being on all Occafions very ufeful to us, we find it abfolutely neceffary to carefs 'em as Friends, and not to treat 'em as Slaves; nor dare we do otherwife, their Numbers fo far furpaffing ours in that Continent.

Thofe then whom we make ufe of to work in our Plantations of Sugar, are *Negroes,* Black-Slaves altogether, who are tranfported thither in this Manner.

Thofe who want Slaves, make a Bargain with a Mafter, or a Captain of a Ship, and contract to pay him fo much apiece, a Matter of twenty Pound a Head, for as many as he agrees for, and to pay for 'em when they fhall be deliver'd on fuch a Plantation: So that when there arrives a Ship laden with Slaves, they who have fo contracted, go aboard, and receive their Number by Lot; and perhaps in one Lot that may be for ten, there may happen to be three or four Men, the reft Women and Children. Or be there more or lefs of either Sex, you are obliged to be contented with your Lot.

Coramantien, a Country of *Blacks* fo called, was one of thofe Places in which
they

they found the moſt advantageous Trading for theſe Slaves, and thither moſt of our great Traders in that Merchandize traffick; for that Nation is very warlike and brave: and having a continual Campaign, being always in Hoſtility with one neighbouring Prince or other, they had the Fortune to take a great many Captives: for all they took in Battle were ſold as Slaves; at leaſt thoſe common Men who could not ranſom themſelves. Of theſe Slaves ſo taken, the General only has all the Profit; and of theſe Generals our Captains and Maſters of Ships buy all their Freights.

The King of *Coramantien* was of himſelf a Man of an hundred and odd Years old, and had no Son, tho' he had many beautiful Black Wives: for moſt certainly there are Beauties that can charm of that Colour. In his younger Years he had had many gallant Men to his Sons, thirteen of whom died in Battle, conquering when they fell; and he had only left him for his Succeſſor, one Grand-child, Son to one of theſe dead Victors, who, as ſoon as he could bear a Bow in his Hand, and a Quiver at his Back, was ſent into the Field, to be train'd up by one of the oldeſt Generals to War; where, from his natural Inclination to Arms, and the Occaſions given him, with the good Conduct

of

of the old General, he became, at the Age
of feventeen, one of the moſt expert Captains, and braveſt Soldiers that ever ſaw
the Field of *Mars :* ſo that he was ador'd
as the Wonder of all that World, and the
Darling of the Soldiers. Befides, he was
adorn'd with a native Beauty, ſo tranſcend-
ing all thoſe of his gloomy Race, that he
ſtruck an Awe and Reverence, even into
thoſe that knew not his Quality ; as he did
into me, who beheld him with Surprize
and Wonder, when afterwards he arrived
in our World.

He had ſcarce arrived at his ſeven-
teenth Year, when, fighting by his Side,
the General was kill'd with an Arrow in
his Eye, which the Prince *Oroonoko* (for
ſo was this gallant *Moor* call'd) very narrowly avoided ; nor had he, if the General who ſaw the Arrow ſhot, and perceiving it aimed at the Prince, had not
bow'd his Head between, on Purpoſe to
receive it in his own Body, rather than it
ſhould touch that of the Prince, and ſo
ſaved him.

'Twas then, afflicted as *Oroonoko* was,
that he was proclaimed General in the
old Man's Place : and then it was, at
the finiſhing of that War, which had continu'd for two Years, that the Prince
came to Court, where he had hardly been
a Month together, from the Time of his

fifth

ı Year to that of feventeen : and 'twas
ızing to imagine where it was he
..l'd fo much Humanity ; or to give
... Accomplifhments a jufter Name, where
... he got that real Greatnefs of Soul,
thofe refined Notions of true Honour, that
abfolute Generofity, and that Softnefs,
that was capable of the higheft Paffions
of Love and Gallantry, whofe Objects
re almoft continually fighting Men, or
thofe mangled or dead, who heard no
Sounds but thofe of War and Groans.
Some Part of it we may attribute to the
Care of a *Frenchman* of Wit and Learning, who finding it turn to a very good
Account to be a fort of Royal Tutor to
this young Black, and perceiving him
very ready, apt, and quick of Apprehenfion, took a great Pleafure to teach him
Morals, Language and Science ; and was
for it extremely belov'd and valu'd by
him. Another Reafon was, he lov'd when
he came from War, to fee all the *Englifh*
Gentlemen that traded thither ; and did
not only learn their Language, but that of
the *Spaniard* alfo, with whom he traded
afterwards for Slaves.

I have often feen and converfed with
this Great Man, and been a Witnefs to
many of his mighty Actions ; and do
affure my Reader, the moft illuftrious
Courts could not have produced a braver

 Man,

Man, both for Greatnefs of Courage ;
Mind, a Judgment more folid, a
more quick, and a Converfation
fweet and diverting. He knew almo
much as if he had read much : He
heard of and admired the *Romans*: He
heard of the late Civil Wars in *Engla*
and the deplorable Death of our gr
Monarch ; and would difcourfe of it w
all the Senfe and Abhorrence of the
juftice imaginable. He had an extre
good and graceful Mien, and all the Ci i-
lity of a well-bred Great Man. He had
nothing of Barbarity in his Nature, but
in all Points addrefs'd himfelf as if his
Education had been in fome *European*
Court.

This great and juft Character of *Oroonoko* gave me an extreme Curiofity to fee
him, efpecially when I knew he fpoke
French and *Englifh*, and that I could talk
with him. But tho' I had heard fo much
of him, I was as greatly furprized when
I faw him, as if I had heard nothing of
him ; fo beyond all Report I found him.
He came into the Room, and addreffed
himfelf to me, and fome other Women,
with the beft Grace in the World. He
was pretty tall, but of a Shape the moft
exact that can be fancy'd : The moft famous Statuary could not form the Figure
of a Man more admirably turn'd from

Head

Head to Foot. His Face was not of that brown rusty Black which most of that Nation are, but a perfect Ebony, or polished Jet. His Eyes were the most aweful that could be seen, and very piercing; the White of 'em being like Snow, as were his Teeth. His Nose was rising and *Roman*, instead of *African* and flat : His Mouth the finest shaped that could be seen; far from those great turn'd Lips, which are so natural to the rest of the Negroes. The whole Proportion and Air of his Face was so nobly and exactly form'd, that bating his Colour, there could be nothing in Nature more beautiful, agreeable and handsome. There was no one Grace wanting, that bears the Standard of true Beauty. His Hair came down to his Shoulders, by the Aids of Art, which was by pulling it out with a Quill, and keeping it comb'd ; of which he took particular Care. Nor did the Perfections of his Mind come short of those of his Person ; for his Discourse was admirable upon almost any Subject : and whoever had heard him speak, would have been convinced of their Errors, that all fine Wit is confined to the white Men, especially to those of Christendom ; and would have confess'd that *Oroonoko* was as capable even of reigning well, and of governing as wisely, had as great a Soul,

E 2

as

as politick Maxims, and was as senfible of Power, as any Prince civiliz'd in the moft refined Schools of Humanity and Learning, or the moft illuftrious Courts.

This Prince, fuch as I have defcrib'd him, whofe Soul and Body were fo admirably adorned, was (while yet he was in the Court of his Grandfather, as I faid) as capable of Love, as 'twas poffible for a brave and gallant Man to be ; and in faying that, I have named the higheft Degree of Love : for fure great Souls are moft capable of that Paffion.

I have already faid, the old General was kill'd by the Shot of an Arrow, by the Side of this Prince, in Battle; and that *Oroonoko* was made General. This old dead Hero had one only Daughter left of his Race, a Beauty, that to defcribe her truly, one need fay only, fhe was Female to the noble Male ; the beautiful Black *Venus* to our young *Mars;* as charming in her Perfon as he, and of delicate Virtues. I have feen a hundred White Men fighing after her, and making a thoufand Vows at her Feet, all in vain and unfuccefsful. And fhe was indeed too great for any but a Prince of her own Nation to adore.

Oroonoko Coming from the Wars (which were now ended) after he had made his Court to his Grandfather, he thought in
Honour

Honour he ought to make a Visit to *Imoinda*, the Daughter of his Foster-father, the dead General; and to make some Excuses to her, because his Preservation was the Occasion of her Father's Death; and to present her with those Slaves that had been taken in this last Battle, as the Trophies of her Father's Victories. When he came, attended by all the young Soldiers of any Merit, he was infinitely surpriz'd at the Beauty of this fair Queen of Night, whose Face and Person were so exceeding all he had ever beheld, that lovely Modesty with which she receiv'd him, that Softness in her Look and Sighs, upon the melancholy Occasion of this Honour that was done by so great a Man as *Oroonoko*, and a Prince of whom she had heard such admirable Things; the Awfulness wherewith she receiv'd him, and the Sweetness of her Words and Behaviour while he stay'd, gain'd a perfect Conquest over his fierce Heart, and made him feel, the Victor could be subdu'd. So that having made his first Compliments, and presented her an hundred and fifty Slaves in Fetters, he told her with his Eyes, that he was not insensible of her Charms; while *Imoinda*, who wish'd for nothing more than so glorious a Conquest, was pleas'd to believe, she understood that silent Language of new-born Love; and, from that

E 3

Moment,

Moment, put on all her Additions to Beauty.

The Prince return'd to Court with quite another Humour than before; and tho' he did not ſpeak much of the fair *Imoinda*, he had the Pleaſure to hear all his Followers ſpeak of nothing but the Charms of that Maid, inſomuch, that, even in the Preſence of the old King, they were extolling her, and heightning, if poſſible, the Beauties they had found in her: ſo that nothing elſe was talk'd of, no other Sound was heard in every Corner where there were Whiſperers, but *Imoinda!* *Imoinda!*

'Twill be imagin'd *Oroonoko* ſtay'd not long before he made his ſecond Viſit; nor, conſidering his Quality, not much longer before he told her, he ador'd her. I have often heard him ſay, that he admir'd by what ſtrange Inſpiration he came to talk Things ſo ſoft, and ſo paſſionate, who never knew Love, nor was us'd to the Converſation of Women; but (to uſe his own Words) he ſaid, 'Moſt hap-
' pily, ſome new, and, till then, un-
' known Power inſtructed his Heart and
' Tongue in the Language of Love; and
' at the ſame Time, in Favour of him, in-
' ſpir'd *Imoinda* with a Senſe of his Paſ-
' ſion.' She was touch'd with what he ſaid, and return'd it all in ſuch Anſwers

as went to his very Heart, with a Pleafure unknown before. Nor did he ufe
thofe Obligations ill, that Love had done
him, but turn'd all his happy Moments to
the beft Advantage; and as he knew no
Vice, his Flame aim'd at nothing but Honour, if fuch a Diftinction may be made
in Love; and efpecially in that Country,
where Men take to themfelves as many
as they can maintain; and where the only
Crime and Sin againft a Woman, is, to
turn her off, to abandon her to Want,
Shame and Mifery: fuch ill Morals are
only practis'd in *Chriftian* Countries, where
they prefer the bare Name of Religion;
and, without Virtue or Morality, think
that fufficient. But *Oroonoko* was none of
thofe Profeffors; but as he had right
Notions of Honour, fo he made her fuch
Propofitions as were not only and barely
fuch; but, contrary to the Cuftom of his
Country, he made her Vows, fhe fhould
be the only Woman he would poffefs while
he liv'd; that no Age or Wrinkles fhould
incline him to change: for her Soul
would be always fine, and always young;
and he fhould have an eternal *Idea* in
his Mind of the Charms fhe now bore;
and fhould look into his Heart for that
Idea, when he could find it no longer in
her Face.

E 4   After

After a thouſand Aſſurances of his laſt-ing Flame, and her eternal Empire over him, ſhe condeſcended to receive him for her Huſband; or rather, receive him, as the greateſt Honour the Gods could do her.

There is a certain Ceremony in theſe Caſes to be obſerv'd, which I forgot to aſk how 'twas perform'd; but 'twas con-cluded on both Sides, that in Obedience to him, the Grandfather was to be firſt made acquainted with the Deſign : For they pay a moſt abſolute Reſignation to the Monarch, eſpecially when he is a Pa-rent alſo.

On the other Side, the old King, who had many Wives, and many Concubines, wanted not Court-Flatterers to inſinuate into his Heart a thouſand tender Thoughts for this young Beauty; and who repreſented her to his Fancy, as the moſt charming he had ever poſſeſs'd in all the long Race of his numerous Years. At this Character, his old Heart, like an extinguiſh'd Brand, moſt apt to take Fire, felt new Sparks of Love, and began to kindle ; and now grown to his ſecond Childhood, long'd with Impatience to behold this gay Thing, with whom, alas! he could but innocent-ly play. But how he ſhould be confirm'd ſhe was this *Wonder*, before he us'd his Power to call her to Court, (where Mai-

lens

dens never came, unless for the King's private Use) he was next to confider ; and while he was fo doing, he had Intelligence brought him, that *Imoinda* was moft certainly Miftrefs to the Prince *Oroonoko.* This gave him fome Chagrine : however, it gave him alfo an Opportunity, one Day, when the Prince was a hunting, to wait on a Man of Quality, as his Slave and Attendant, who fhould go and make a Prefent to *Imoinda,* as from the Prince ; he fhould then, unknown, fee this fair Maid, and have an Opportunity to hear what Meffage fhe would return the Prince for his Prefent, and from thence gather the State of her Heart, and Degree of her Inclination.   This was put in Execution, and the old Monarch faw, and burn'd : He found her all he had heard, and would not delay his Happinefs, but found he fhould have fome Obftacle to overcome her Heart ; for fhe exprefs'd her Senfe of the Prefent the Prince had fent her, in Terms fo fweet, fo foft and pretty, with an Air of Love and Joy that could not be diffembled, infomuch that 'twas paft Doubt whether fhe lov'd *Oroonoko* entirely. This gave the old King fome Affliction ; but he falv'd it with this, that the Obedience the People pay their King, was not at all inferior to what they paid their Gods ; and what Love would not oblige

E 5

Imoinda

Imoinda to do, Duty would compel her to.

He was therefore no sooner got into his Apartment, but he sent the Royal Veil to *Imoinda* ; that is the Ceremony of Invitation : He sends the Lady he has a Mind to honour with his Bed, a Veil, with which she is covered, and secur'd for the King's Use ; and 'tis Death to disobey ; besides, held a most impious Disobedience.

'Tis not to be imagin'd the Surprize and Grief that seiz'd the lovely Maid at this News and Sight. However, as Delays in these Cases are dangerous, and Pleading worse than Treason ; trembling, and almost fainting, she was oblig'd to suffer herself to be cover'd, and led away.

They brought her thus to Court ; and the King, who had caus'd a very rich Bath to be prepar'd, was led into it, where he sat under a Canopy, in State, to receive this long'd-for Virgin ; whom he having commanded to be brought to him, they (after disrobing her) led her to the Bath, and making fast the Doors, left her to descend. The King, without more Courtship, bad her throw off her Mantle, and come to his Arms. But *Imoinda*, all in Tears, threw herself on the Marble, on the Brink of the Bath, and besought him to

hear

hear her. She told him, as she was a Maid, how proud of the Divine Glory she should have been, of having it in her Power to oblige her King : but as by the Laws he could not, and from his Royal Goodness would not take from any Man his wedded Wife ; so she believ'd she should be the Occasion of making him commit a great Sin, if she did not reveal her State and Condition ; and tell him she was another's, and could not be so happy to be his.

The King, enrag'd at this Delay, hastily demanded the Name of the bold Man, that had married a Woman of her Degree, without his Consent. *Imoinda* seeing his Eyes fierce, and his Hands tremble, (whether with Age or Anger, I know not, but she fancy'd the last) almost repented she had said so much, for now she fear'd the Storm would fall on the Prince ; she therefore said a thousand Things to appease the raging of his Flame, and to prepare him to hear who it was with Calmness : but before she spoke, he imagin'd who she meant, but would not seem to do so, but commanded her to lay aside her Mantle, and suffer herself to receive his Caresses, or, by his Gods he swore, that happy Man whom she was going to name should die, tho' it were even *Oroonoko* himself. *Therefore* (said he) *deny this Marriage, and swear thyself a Maid. That* (reply'd *Imoinda*) *by all our Powers I do ; for I am not yet known to my Husband.* 'Tis *enough* (said the King) *'tis enough both to satisfy my Conscience and my Heart.* And rising from his Seat, he went and led her into the Bath ; it being in vain for her to resist.

In this Time, the Prince, who was return'd from Hunting, went to visit his *Imoinda*, but found her gone ; and not only so, but heard she had receiv'd the Royal Veil. This rais'd him to a Storm ; and in his Madness, they had much ado to save him from laying violent Hands on himself. Force first prevail'd, and then Reason : They urg'd all to him, that might oppose his Rage ; but nothing weigh'd so greatly with him as the King's old Age, uncapable of injuring him with *Imoinda*. He would give Way to that Hope, because it pleas'd him most, and flatter'd best his Heart. Yet this serv'd not altogether to make him cease his different Passions, which sometimes rag'd within him, and softned into Showers. 'Twas not enough to appease him, to tell him, his Grandfather was old, and could not that Way injure him, while he retain'd that awful Duty which the young Men are us'd there to pay to their grave Relations. He could not be convinc'd he had no Cause to sigh and mourn for the Loss of a Mistress, he

could

could not with all his Strength and Courage
retrieve, and he would often cry, ‘ Oh,
‘ my Friends! were fhe in wall’d Cities,
‘ or confin’d from me in Fortifications of
‘ the greateft Strength ; did Inchantments
‘ or Monfters detain her from me ; I
‘ would venture tho’ any Hazard to free
‘ her : But here, in the Arms of a feeble
‘ old Man, my Youth, my violent Love,
‘ my Trade in Arms, and all my vaft De-
‘ fire of Glory, avail me nothing. *Imoin-*
‘ *da* is as irrecoverably loft to me, as if
‘ fhe were fnatch’d by the cold Arms of
‘ Death : Oh ! fhe is never to be retriev’d.
‘ If I would wait tedious Years ; till Fate
‘ fhould bow the old King to his Grave,
‘ even that would not leave me *Imoinda*
‘ free ; but ftill that Cuftom that makes
‘ it fo vile a Crime for a Son to marry
‘ his Father’s Wives or Miftreffes, would
‘ hinder my Happinefs ; unlefs I would
‘ either ignobly fet an ill Precedent to my
‘ Succeffors, or abandon my Country, and
‘ fly with her to fome unknown World
‘ who never heard our Story.’

But it was objected to him, That his
Cafe was not the fame : for *Imoinda* being
his lawful Wife by folemn Contract, ’twas
he was the injur’d Man, and might, if he
fo pleas’d, take *Imoinda* back, the Breach
of the Law being on his Grandfather’s
Side ; and that if he could circumvent him,
and

and redeem her from the *Otan*, which is
the Palace of the King's Women, a fort of
Scraglio, it was both juft and lawful for him
fo to do.

This Reafoning had fome Force upon
him, and he fhould have been entirely
comforted, but for the Thought that fhe
was poffefs'd by his Grandfather. However, he lov'd her fo well, that he was refolv'd to believe what moft favour'd his
Hope, and to endeavour to learn from
Imoinda's own Mouth, what only fhe could
fatisfy him in, whether fhe was robb'd of
that Bleffing which was only due to his
Faith and Love. But as it was very hard
to get a Sight of the Women, (for no
Men ever enter'd into the *Otan*, but when
the King went to entertain himfelf with
fome one of his Wives or Miftreffes ; and
'twas Death, at any other Time, for any
other to go in) fo he knew not how to
contrive to get a Sight of her.

While *Oroonoko* felt all the Agonies of
Love, and fuffer'd under a Torment the
moft painful in the World, the old King
was not exempted from his Share of Affliction. He was troubled, for having been
forc'd, by an irrefiftible Paffion, to rob
his Son of a Treafure, he knew, could not
but be extremely dear to him ; fince fhe
was the moft beautiful that ever had been
feen, and had befides, all the Sweetnefs

and

and Innocence of Youth and Modefty, with a Charm of Wit furpaffing all. He found, that however fhe was forc'd to expofe her lovely Perfon to his wither'd Arms, fhe could only figh and weep there, and think of *Oroonoko* ; and oftentimes could not forbear fpeaking of him, tho' her Life were, by Cuftom, forfeited by owning her Paffion. But fhe fpoke not of a Lover only, but of a Prince dear to him to whom fhe fpoke ; and of the Praifes of a Man, who, 'till now, fill'd the old Man's Soul with Joy at every Recital of his Bravery, or even his Name. And 'twas this Dotage on our young Hero, that gave *Imoinda* a thoufand Privileges to fpeak of him without offending ; and this Condefcenfion in the old King, that made her take the Satisfaction of fpeaking of him fo very often.

Befides, he many times enquir'd how the Prince bore himfelf : And thofe of whom he ask'd, being entirely Slaves to to the Merits and Virtues of the Prince, ftill anfwer'd what they thought conduc'd beft to his Service ; which was, to make the old King fancy that the Prince had no more Intereft in *Imoinda*, and had refign'd her willingly to the Pleafure of the King ; that he diverted himfelf with his Mathematicians, his Fortifications, his Officers, and his Hunting.

This

This pleas'd the old Lover, who fail'd not to report thefe Things again to *Imoinda,* that fhe might, by the Example of her young Lover, withdraw her Heart, and reft better contented in his Arms. But, however fhe was forc'd to receive this unwelcome News, in all Appearance, with Unconcern and Content; her Heart was burfting within, and fhe was only happy when fhe could get alone, to vent her Griefs and Moans with Sighs and Tears.

What Reports of the Prince's Conduct were made to the King, he thought good to juftify, as far as poffibly he could by his Actions; and when he appear'd in the Prefence of the King, he fhew'd a Face not at all betraying his Heart: fo that in a little Time, the Old Man, being entirely convinc'd that he was no longer a Lover of *Imoinda,* he carry'd him with him, in his Train, to the *Otan,* often to banquet with his Miftreffes. But as foon as he enter'd, one Day, into the Apartment of *Imoinda,* with the King, at the firft Glance from her Eyes, notwithftanding all his determined Refolution, he was ready to fink in the Place where he ftood; and had certainly done fo, but for the Support of *Aboan,* a young Man who was next to him; which, with his Change of Countenance, had betray'd him, had the King chanc'd to look that Way. And I
have

have obferv'd, 'tis a very great Error in thofe who laugh when one fays, *A* Negro *can change Colour :* for I have feen 'em as frequently blufh, and look pale, and that as vifibly as ever I faw in the moft beautiful *White.* And 'tis certain, that both thefe Changes were evident, this Day, in both thefe Lovers. And *Imoinda,* who faw with fome Joy the Change in the Prince's Face, and found it in her own, ftrove to divert the King from beholding either, by a forc'd Carefs, with which fhe met him ; which was a new Wound in the Heart of the poor dying Prince. But as foon as the King was bufy'd in looking on fome fine Thing of *Imoinda's* making, fhe had Time to tell the Prince, with her angry, but Love-darting Eyes, that fhe refented his Coldnefs, and bemoan'd her own miferable Captivity. Nor were his Eyes filent, but anfwer'd her's again, as much as Eyes could do, inftructed by the moft tender and moft paffionate Heart that ever lov'd : And they fpoke fo well, and fo effectually, as *Imoinda* no longer doubted but fhe was the only Delight and Darling of that Soul fhe found pleading in 'em its Right of Love, which none was more willing to refign than fhe. And 'twas this powerful Language alone that in an Inftant convey'd all the Thoughts of their Souls to each other ; that they

both found there wanted but Opportunity
to make them both entirely happy. But
when he faw another Door open'd by
Onahal (a former old Wife of the King's,
who now had Charge of *Imoinda*) and
faw the Profpect of a Bed of State made
ready, with Sweets and Flowers for the
Dalliance of the King, who immediately led
the trembling Victim from his Sight, into
that prepar'd Repofe ; what Rage ! what
wild Frenzies feiz'd his Heart ! which
forcing to keep within Bounds, and to fuffer without Noife, it became the more in-
fupportable, and rent his Soul with ten
thoufand Pains. He was forc'd to retire
to vent his Groans, where he fell down
on a Carpet, and lay ftruggling a long
Time, and only breathing now and then—
Oh *Imoinda !* When *Onahal* had finifhed
her neceffary Affair within, fhutting the
Door, fhe came forth, to wait till the
King called ; and hearing fome one fighing in the other Room, fhe pafs'd on, and
found the Prince in that deplorable Condition, which fhe thought needed her Aid.
She gave him Cordials, but all in vain ;
till finding the Nature of his Difeafe, by
his Sighs, and naming *Imoinda,* fhe told
him he had not fo much Caufe as he imagined to afflict himfelf : for if he knew
the King fo well as fhe did, he would not
lofe a Moment in Jealoufy ; and that fhe
was

was confident that *Imoinda* bore, at this Minute, Part in his Affliction. *Aboan* was of the fame Opinion, and both together perfuaded him to re-affume his Courage ; and all fitting down on the Carpet, the Prince faid fo many obliging Things to *Onahal*, that he half-perfuaded her to be of his Party : and fhe promifed him, fhe would thus far comply with his juft Defires, that fhe would let *Imoinda* know how faithful he was, what he fuffer'd, and what he faid.

This Difcourfe lafted till the King called, which gave *Oroonoko* a certain Satiffaction ; and with the Hope *Onahal* had made him conceive, he affumed a Look as gay as 'twas poffible a Man in his Circumftances could do : and prefently after, he was call'd in with the reft who waited without. The King commanded Mufick to be brought, and feveral of his young Wives and Miftreffes came all together by his Command, to dance before him ; where *Imoinda* perform'd her Part with an Air and Grace fo furpaffing all the reft, as her Beauty was above 'em, and received the Prefent ordained as a Prize. The Prince was every Moment more charmed with the new Beauties and Graces he beheld in this Fair-One ; and while he gazed, and fhe danc'd, *Onahal* was retir'd to a Window with *Aboan*.

This

This *Onahal,* as I faid, was one of the Caft-Miftreffes of the old King; and 'twas thefe (now paft their Beauty) that were made Guardians or Governantees to the new and the young ones, and whofe Bufinefs it was to teach them all thofe wanton Arts of Love, with which they prevail'd and charm'd heretofore in their Turn; and who now treated the triumphing Happy-ones with all the Severity, as to Liberty and Freedom, that was poffible, in Revenge of the Honours they rob them of; envying them thofe Satisfactions, thofe Gallantries and Prefents, that were once made to themfelves, while Youth and Beauty lafted, and which they now faw pafs, as it were regardlefs by, and paid only to the Bloomings. And certainly, nothing is more afflicting to a decay'd Beauty, than to behold in itfelf declining Charms, that were once ador'd; and to find thofe Careffes paid to new Beauties, to which once fhe laid Claim; to hear them whifper, as fhe paffes by, that once was a delicate Woman. Thofe abandon'd Ladies therefore endeavour to revenge all the Defpights and Decays of Time, on thefe flourifhing Happy-ones. And 'twas this Severity that gave *Oroonoko* a thoufand Fears he fhould never prevail with *Onahal* to fee *Imoinda.* But, as I faid, fhe was now retir'd to a Window with *Aboan.*

This

This young Man was not only one of the beſt Quality, but a Man extremely well made, and beautiful ; and coming often to attend the King to the *Otan*, he had ſubdu'd the Heart of the antiquated *Onahal*, which had not forgot how pleaſant it was to be in love. And tho' ſhe had ſome Decays in her Face, ſhe had none in her Senſe and Wit ; ſhe was there agreeable ſtill, even to *Aboan*'s Youth : ſo that he took Pleaſure in entertaining her with Diſcourſes of Love. He knew alſo, that to make his Court to theſe She-favourites, was the Way to be great ; theſe being the Perſons that do all Affairs and Buſineſs at Court. He had alſo obſerved, that ſhe had given him Glances more tender and inviting than ſhe had done to others of his Quality. And now, when he ſaw that her Favour could ſo abſolutely oblige the Prince, he fail'd not to ſigh in her Ear, and look with Eyes all ſoft upon her, and gave her Hope that ſhe had made ſome Impreſſions on his Heart. He found her pleas'd at this, and making a thouſand Advances to him : but the Ceremony ending, and the King departing, broke up the Company for that Day, and his Converſation.

Aboan fail'd not that Night to tell the Prince of his Succeſs, and how advantageous the Service of *Onahal* might be to

his

his Amour with *Imoinda*. The Prince was over-joy'd with this good News, and befought him, if it were poffible, to carefs her fo, as to engage her entirely, which he could not fail to do, if he comply'd with her Defires : *For then* (faid the Prince) *her Life lying at your Mercy, fhe muft grant you the Requeft you make in my Behalf. Aboan* underftood him, and affur'd him he would make Love fo effectually, that he would defy the moft expert Miftrefs of the Art, to find out whether he diffembled it, or had it really. And 'twas with Impatience they waited the next Opportunity of going to the *Otan*.

'The Wars came on, the Time of taking the Field approached ; and 'twas impoffible for the Prince to delay his going at the Head of his Army to encounter the Enemy ; fo that every Day feem'd a tedious Year, till he faw his *Imoinda :* for he believ'd he could not live, if he were forced away without being fo happy. 'Twas with Impatience therefore that he expected the next Vifit the King would make ; and, according to his Wifh, it was not long.

The Parley of the Eyes of thefe two Lovers had not pafs'd fo fecretly, but an old jealous Lover could fpy it ; or rather, he wanted not Flatterers who told him they obferv'd it : fo that the Prince was

haften'd

haften'd to the Camp, and this was the laft Vifit he found he fhould make to the *Otan ;* he therefore urged *Aboan* to make the beft of this laft Effort, and to explain himfelf fo to *Onahal,* that fhe deferring her Enjoyment of her young Lover no longer, might make Way for the Prince to fpeak to *Imoinda.*

The whole Affair being agreed on be-tween the Prince and *Aboan,* they attend-ed the King, as the Cuftom was, to the *Otan ;* where, while the whole Company was taken up in beholding the Dancing, and Antick Poftures the Women-Royal made to divert the King, *Onahal* fingled out *Aboan,* whom fhe found moft pliable to her Wifh. When fhe had him where fhe believed fhe could not be heard, fhe figh'd to him, and foftly cry'd, ' Ah ' *Aboan !* when will you be fenfible of my ' Paffion ? I confefs it with my Mouth, ' becaufe I would not give my Eyes the ' Lye ; and you have but too much al- ' ready perceived they have confefs'd ' my Flame : nor would I have you be- ' lieve, that becaufe I am the abandon'd ' Miftrefs of a King, I efteem myfelf al- ' together divefted of Charms : No, ' *Aboan ;* I have ftill a Reft of Beauty enough ' engaging, and have learn'd to pleafe too ' well, not to be defirable. I can have ' Lovers ftill, but will have none but
' *Aboan.*

' *Aboan.* Madam, (*reply'd the half-feigning*
' *Youth*) you have already, by my Eyes,
' found you can ftill conquer; and I be-
' lieve 'tis in pity of me you condefcend
' to this kind Confeffion. But, Madam,
' Words are ufed to be fo fmall a Part
' of our Country-Courtfhip, that 'tis rare
' one can get fo happy an Opportunity as
' to tell one's Heart; and thofe few Mi-
' nutes we have, are forced to be fnatch'd
' for more certain Proofs of Love than
' fpeaking and fighing: and fuch I lan-
' guifh for.'

He fpoke this with fuch a Tone, that
fhe hoped it true, and could not forbear
believing it; and being wholly tranfported with Joy for having fubdued the fineft
of all the King's Subjects to her Defires,
fhe took from her Ears two large Pearls,
and commanded him to wear 'em in his.
He would have refufed 'em crying, *Madam thefe are not the Proofs of your Love
that I expect; 'tis Opportunity, 'tis a Lone-
Hour only, that can make me happy.* But
forcing the Pearls into his Hand, fhe
whifper'd foftly to him; *Oh! do not fear
a Woman's Invention, when Love fets her a
thinking.* And preffing his Hand, fhe
cry'd, *This Night you fhall be happy. Come
to the Gate of the Orange-Grove, behind the*
Otan, *and I will be ready about Midnight
to receive you.* 'Twas thus agreed, and
fhe

fhe left him, that no Notice might be taken of their fpeaking together.

The Ladies were ftill dancing, and the King, laid on a Carpet, with a great deal of Pleafure was beholding them, efpecially *Imoinda*, who that Day appeared more lovely than ever, being enlivened with the good Tidings *Onahal* had brought her, of the conftant Paffion the Prince had for her.   The Prince was laid on another Carpet at the other End of the Room, with his Eyes fixed on the Object of his Soul ; and as fhe turned or moved, fo did they ; and fhe alone gave his Eyes and Soul their Motions.   Nor did *Imoinda* employ her Eyes to any other Ufe, than in beholding with infinite Pleafure the Joy fhe produced in thofe of the Prince.   But while fhe was more regarding him than the Steps fhe took, fhe chanced to fall, and fo near him, as that leaping with extreme Force from the Carpet, he canght her in his Arms as fhe fell; and 'twas vifible to the whole Prefence, the Joy wherewith he received her.   He clafped her clofe to his Bofom, and quite forgot that Reverence . that was due to the Miftrefs of a King, and that Punifhment that is the Reward of a Boldnefs of this Nature. And had not the Prefence of Mind of *Imoinda* (fonder of his Safety than her own) befriended him, in making her fpring from his Arms, and fall into her Dance again, he had at that Inſtant met his Death; for the old King, jealous to the laſt Degree, roſe up in Rage, broke all the Diverſion, and led *Imoinda* to her Apartment, and ſent out Word to the Prince, to go immediately to the Camp; and that if he were found another Night in Court, he ſhould ſuffer the Death ordained for diſobedient to Offenders.

You may imagine how welcome this News was to *Oroonoko*, whoſe unſeaſonable Tranſport and Careſs of *Imoinda* was blamed by all Men that loved him: and now he perceived his Fault, yet cry'd, *That for ſuch another Moment he would be content to die.*

All the *Otan* was in Diſorder about this Accident; and *Onahal* was particularly concern'd, becauſe on the Prince's Stay depended her Happineſs; for ſhe could no longer expect that of *Aboan:* So that e'er they departed, they contrived it ſo, that the Prince and he ſhould both come that Night to the Grove of the *Otan*, which was all of Oranges and Citrons, and that there they would wait her Orders.

They parted thus with Grief enough 'till Night, leaving the King in Poſſeſſion of the lovely Maid. But nothing could appeaſe the Jealouſy of the old Lover;

he

he would not be impofed on, but would have it that *Imoinda* made a falfe Step on Purpofe to fall into *Oroonoko*'s Bofom, and that all Things looked like a Defign on both Sides; and 'twas in vain fhe protefted her Innocence: He was old and obftinate, and left her, more than half affur'd that his Fear was true.

The King going to his Apartment, fent to know where the Prince was, and if he intended to obey his Command. The Meffenger return'd, and told him, he found the Prince penfive, and altogether unprepar'd for the Campaign; that he lay negligently on the Ground, and anfwer'd very little. This confirm'd the Jealoufy of the King, and he commanded that they fhould very narrowly and privately watch his Motions; and that he fhould not ftir from his Apartment, but one Spy or other fhould be employ'd to watch him: So that the Hour approaching, wherein he was to go to the Citron-Grove; and taking only *Aboan* along with him, he leaves his Apartment, and was watched to the very Gate of the *Otan*; where he was feen to enter, and where they left him, to carry back the Tidings to the King.

Oroonoko and *Aboan* were no fooner enter'd, but *Onahal* led the Prince to the Apartment of *Imoinda*; who, not knowing any thing of her Happiness, was laid in Bed. But *Onahal* only left him in her Chamber, to make the best of his Opportunity, and took her dear *Aboan* to her own; where he shewed the Height of Complaisance for his Prnce, when, to give him an Opportunity, he suffered himself to be caressed in Bed by *Onahal*.

The Prince softly waken'd *Imoinda*, who was not a little surpriz'd with Joy to find him there; and yet she trembled with a thousand Fears. I believe he omitted saying nothing to this young Maid, that might persuade her to suffer him to seize his own, and take the Rights of Love. And I believe she was not long resisting those Arms where she so longed to be; and having Opportunity, Night, and Silence, Youth, Love, and Desire, he soon prevail'd, and ravished in a Moment what his old Grandfather had been endeavouring for so many Months.

'Tis not to be imagined the Satisfaction of these two young Lovers; nor the Vows she made him, that she remained a spotless Maid till that Night, and that what she did with his Grandfather had robb'd him of no Part of her Virgin-Honour; the Gods, in Mercy and Justice, having reserved that for her plighted Lord, to whom of Right it belonged. And 'tis impossible to express the Transports he

suffer'd,

suffer'd, while he liften'd to a Difcourfe fo charming from her loved Lips ; and clafped that Body in his Arms, for whom he had fo fong languifhed : and nothing now afflicted him, but his fudden Departure from her ; for he told her the Neceffity, and his Commands, but fhould depart fatisfy'd in this, That fince the old King had hitherto not been able to deprive him of thofe Enjoyments which only belonged to him, he believed for the future he would be lefs able to injure him ; fo that, abating the Scandal of the Veil, which was no otherwife fo, than that fhe was Wife to another, he believed her fafe, even in the Arms of the King, and innocent ; yet would he have ventur'd at the Conqueft of the World, and have given it all to have had her avoided that Honour of receiving the *Royal Vcil*. 'Twas thus, between a thoufand Careffes, that both bemoan'd the hard Fate of Youth and Beauty, fo liable to that cruel Promotion : 'Twas a Glory that could well have been fpared here, tho' defired and aim'd at by all the young Females of that Kingdom.

But while they were thus fondly employ'd, forgetting how Time ran on, and that the Dawn muft conduct him far away from his only Happinefs, they heard a great Noife in the *Otan,* and unufual

 Voices

Voices of Men; at which the Prince, ſtarting from the Arms of the frighted *Imoinda*, ran to a little Battle-Ax he uſed to wear by his Side; and having not ſo much Leiſure as to put on his Habit, he oppoſed himſelf againſt ſome who were already opening the Door : which they did with ſo much Violence, that *Oroonoko* was not able to defend it; but was forced to cry out with a commanding Voice, ‘ Whoever ye are that have the Boldneſs ‘ to attempt to approach this Apartment ‘ thus rudely; know, that I, the Prince ‘ *Oroonoko*, will revenge it with the cer- ‘ tain Death of him that firſt enters : There- ‘ fore ſtand back, and know, this Place is ‘ ſacred to Love and Me this Night; To- ‘ morrow ’tis the King’s.’

This he ſpoke with a Voice ſo reſolv’d and aſſur’d, that they ſoon retired from the Door; but cry’d, ‘ ’Tis by the King’s ‘ Command we are come; and being ſa- ‘ tisfy’d by thy Voice, O Prince, as much ‘ as if we had enter’d, we can report ‘ to the King the Truth of all his Fears, ‘ and leave thee to provide for thy own ‘ Safety, as thou art advis’d by thy ‘ Friends.’

At theſe Words they departed, and left the Prince to take a ſhort and ſad Leave of his *Imoinda*; who, truſting in the Strength of her Charms, believed ſhe

ſhould

fhould appeafe the Fury of a jealous King, by faying, fhe was furprized, and that it was by Force of Arms he got into her Apartment. All her Concern now was for his ·Life, and therefore fhe haften'd him to the Camp, and with much ado prevail'd on him to go. Nor was it fhe alone that prevail'd; *Aboan* and *Onahal* both pleaded, and both affured him of a Lye that fhould be well enough contrived to fecure *Imoinda*. So that at laft, with a Heart fad as Death, dying Eyes, and fighing Soul, *Oroonoko* departed, and took his Way to the Camp.

It was not long after, the King in Perfon came to the *Otan* ; where beholding *Imoinda*, with Rage in his Eyes, he up-braided her Wickednefs, and Perfidy ; and threatning her Royal Lover, fhe fell on her Face at his Feet, bedewing the Floor with her Tears, and imploring his Pardon for a Fault which fhe had not with her Will committed ; as *Onahal*, who was alfo proftrate with her, could tefti-fy : That, unknown to her, he had broke into her Apartment, and ravifhed her. She fpoke this much againft her Confci-ence; but to fave her own Life, 'twas ab-folutely neceffary fhe fhould feign this Fal-fity. She knew it could not injure the Prince, he being fled to an Army that would ftand by him, againft any Injuries

F 4

that

that fhould affault him. However, this laft Thought of *Imoinda's* being ravifhed, changed the Meafures of his Revenge; and whereas before he defigned to be himfelf her Executioner, he now refolved fhe fhould not die. But as it is the greateft Crime in Nature amongft them, to touch a Woman after having being poffefs'd by a Son, a Father, or a Brother, fo now he looked on *Imoinda* as a polluted thing wholly unfit for his Embrace; nor would he refign her to his Grandfon, becaufe fhe had received the *Royal Veil*: He therefore removes her from the *Otan*, with *Onahal*; whom he put into fafe Hands, with Order they fhould be both fold off as Slaves to another Country, either *Chriftian* or *Heathen*, 'twas no Matter where.

This cruel Sentence, worfe than Death, they implor'd might be reverfed; but their Prayers were vain, and it was put in Execution accordingly, and that with fo much Secrecy, that none, either without or within the *Otan*, knew any thing of their Abfence, or their Deftiny.

The old King neverthelefs executed this with a great deal of Reluctancy; but he believed he had made a very great Conqueft over himfelf, when he had once refolved, and had perform'd what he refolved. He believed now, that his Love had been unjuft; and that he could not

expect

expect the Gods, or *Captain of the Clouds* (as they call the unknown Power) would suffer a better Consequence from so ill a Cause. He now begins to hold *Oroonoko* excused; and to say, he had reason for what he did. And now every body could assure the King how passionately *Imoinda* was beloved by the Prince; even those confess'd it now, who said the contrary before his Flame was not abated. So that the King being old, and not able to defend himself in War, and having no Sons of all his Race remaining alive, but only this, to maintain him on his Throne; and looking on this as a Man disobliged, first by the Rape of his Mistress, or rather Wife, and now by depriving him wholly of her, he fear'd, might make him desperate, and do some cruel thing, either to himself or his old Grandfather the Offender, he began to repent him extremely of the Contempt he had, in his Rage, put on *Imoinda*. Besides, he consider'd he ought in Honour to have killed her for this Offence, if it had been one. He ought to have had so much Value and Consideration for a Maid of her Quality, as to have nobly put her to Death, and not to have sold her like a common Slave; the greatest Revenge, and the most disgraceful of any, and to which they a thousand times prefer Death, and

F 5 implore

implore it ; as *Imoinda* did, but could not
obtain that Honour. Seeing therefore
it was certain that *Oroonoko* would highly
refent this Affront, he thought good to
make fome Excufe for his Rafhnefs to
him ; and to that End, he fent a Meffenger to the Camp, with Orders to treat with
him about the Matter, to gain his Pardon,
and endeavour to mitigate his Grief : but
that by no Means he fhould tell him fhe
was fold, but fecretly put to Death ; for
he knew he fhould never obtain his Pardon for the other.

When the Meffenger came, he found the
Prince upon the Point of engaging with
the Enemy ; but as foon as he heard of
the Arrival of the Meffenger, he commanded him to his Tent, where he embraced him, and received him with Joy ;
which was foon abated by the down-caft
Looks of the Meffenger, who was in-
ftantly demanded the Caufe by *Oroonoko* ;
who, impatient of Delay, ask'd a thoufand Queftions in a Breath, and all concerning *Imoinda*. But there needed little
Return ; for he could almoft anfwer himfelf of all he demanded, from his Sight
and Eyes. At laft the Meffenger cafting
himfelf at the Prince's Feet, and kiffing
them with all the Submiffion of a Man
that had fomething to implore which he
dreaded to utter, befought him to hear
with

with Calmnefs what he had to deliver to him, and to call up all his noble and heroick Courage, to encounter with his Words, and defend himfelf againft the ungrateful Things he had to relate. *Oroonoko* reply'd, with a deep Sigh, and a languifhing Voice, —— *I am armed againft their worft Efforts* —— *For I know they will tell me,* Imoinda *is no more* —— *And after that, you may fpare the reft.* Then, commanding him to rife, he laid himfelf on a Carpet, under a rich Pavilion, and remained a good while filent, and was hardly heard to figh. When he was come a little to himfelf, the Meffenger asked him Leave to deliver that Part of his Embaffy which the Prince had not yet divin'd : And the Prince cry'd, *I permit thee*—— Then he told him the Affliction the old King was in, for the Rafhnefs he had committed in his Cruelty to *Imoinda;* and how he deign'd to ask Pardon for his Offence, and to implore the Prince would not fuffer that Lofs to touch his Heart too fenfibly, which now all the Gods could not reftore him, but might recompenfe him in Glory, which he begged he would purfue ; and that Death, that common Revenger of all Injuries, would foon even the Account between him and a feeble old Man.

Oroonoko bad him return his Duty to his Lord and Mafter ; and to affure him, there

was

was no Account of Revenge to be adjudged between them: If there was, he was the Aggreſſor, and that Death would be juſt, and, maugre his Age, would ſee him righted; and he was contented to leave his Share of Glory to Youths more fortunate and worthy of that Favour from the Gods: That henceforth he would never lift a Weapon, or draw a Bow, but abandon the ſmall Remains of his Life to Sighs and Tears, and the continual Thoughts of what his Lord and Grandfather had thought good to ſend out of the World, with all that Youth, that Innocence and Beauty.

After having ſpoken this, whatever his greateſt Officers and Men of the beſt Rank could do, they could not raiſe him from the Carpet, or perſuade him to Action, and Reſolutions of Life; but commanding all to retire, he ſhut himſelf into his Pavilion all that Day, while the Enemy was ready to engage: and wondring at the Delay, the whole Body of the chief of the Army then addreſs'd themſelves to him, and to whom they had much ado to get Admittance. They fell on their Faces at the Foot of his Carpet, where they lay, and beſought him with earneſt Prayers and Tears to lead them forth to Battle, and not let the Enemy take Advantages of them; and implored him to have Regard
                                        to

to his Glory, and to the World, that depended on his Courage and Conduct. But he made no other Reply to all their Supplications than this, That he had now no more Bufinefs for Glory ; and for the World, it was a Trifle not worth his Care : *Go,* (continued he, fighing) *and divide it amongft you, and reap with Joy what you fo vainly prize, and leave me to my more welcome Deftiny.*

They then demanded what they fhould do, and whom he would conftitute in his Room, that the Confufion of ambitious Youth and Power might not ruin their Order, and make them a Prey to the Enemy. He reply'd, he would not give himfelf that Trouble—— but wifhed 'em to chufe the braveft Man amongft 'em, let his Quality or Birth be what it would : ' For, Oh my Friends ! (fays he) it is not ' Titles make Men Brave or Good ; or ' Birth that beftows Courage and Gene- ' rofity, or makes the Owner Happy. ' Believe this, when you behold *Oroonoko* ' the moft wretched, and abandoned by ' Fortune, of all the Creation of the ' Gods.' So turning himfelf about, he would make no more Reply to all they could urge or implore.

The Army beholding their Officers return unfuccefsful, with fad Faces and ominous Looks, that prefaged no good

Luck,

Luck, fuffer'd a thoufand Fears to take Poffeflion of their Hearts, and the Enemy to come even upon them before they could provide for their Safety by any Defence: and tho' they were affured by fome who had a Mind to animate them, that they fhould be immediately headed by the Prince ; and that in the mean time *Aboan* had Orders to command as General; yet they were fo difmay'd for want of that great Example of Bravery, that they could make but a very feeble Refiftance ; and, at laft, down-right fled before the Enemy, who purfued 'em to the very Tents, killing 'em : Nor could all *Aboan*'s Courage, which that Day gained him immortal Glory, fhame 'em into a manly Defence of themfelves. The Guards that were left behind about the Prince's Tent, feeing the Soldiers flee before the Enemy, and fcatter themfelves all over the Plain, in great Diforder, made fuch Out-cries, as rouz'd the Prince from his amorous Slumber, in which he had re-mained buried for two Days, without per-mitting any Suftenance to approach him. But, in Spite of all his Refolutions, he had not the Conftancy of Grief to that Degree, as to make him infenfible of the Danger of his Army ; and in that Inftant he leap-ed from his Couch, and cry'd— ' Come, ' if we muft die, let us meet Death the ' nobleft Way ; and 'twill be more like

' Oroo-

' *Oroonoko* to encounter him at an Army's
' Head, oppofing the Torrent of a con-
' quering Foe, than lazily on a Couch,
' to wait his lingering Pleafure, and die
' every Moment by a thoufand racking
' Thoughts ; or be tamely taken by an
' Enemy, and led a whining, love-fick
' Slave to adorn the Triumphs of *Jamoan*,
' that young Victor, who already is en-
' ter'd beyond the Limits I have prefcrib'd
' him.'

While he was fpeaking, he fuffer'd his
People to drefs him for the Field ; and
fallying out of his Pavilion, with more
Life and Vigour in his Countenance than
ever he fhew'd, he appear'd like fome Divine Power defcended to fave his Country
from Deftruction : And his People had
purpofely put him on all Things that
might make him fhine with moft Splendor,
to ftrike a reverend Awe into the Beholders. He flew into the thickeft of thofe
that were purfuing his Men ; and being
animated with Defpair, he fought as if
he came on Purpofe to die, and did fuch
Things as will not be believed that human Strength could perform ; and fuch,
as foon infpir'd all the reft with new Courage, and new Ardor. And now it was
that they began to fight indeed ; and fo,
as if they would not be out-done even by
their ador'd Hero ; who turning the Tide
of

of the Victory, changing abfolutely the Fate of the Day, gain'd an entire Conqueft: And *Oroonoko* having the good Fortune to fingle out *Jamoan*, he took him Prifoner with his own Hand, having wounded him almoft to Death.

This *Jamoan* afterwards became very dear to him, being a Man very gallant, and of excellent Graces, and fine Parts ; fo that he never put him amongft the Rank of Captives as they ufed to do, without Diftinction, for the common Sale, or Market, but kept him in his own Court, where he retain'd nothing of the Prifoner but the Name, and returned no more into his own Country ; fo great an Affection he took for *Oroonoko,* and by a thoufand Tales and Adventures of Love and Gallantry, flatter'd his Difeafe of Melancholy and Languifhment ; which I have often heard him fay, had certainly kill'd him, but for the Converfation of this Prince and *Aboan,* and the *French* Governor he had from his Childhood, of whom I have fpoken before, and who was a Man of admirable Wit, great Ingenuity and Learning ; all which he had infufed into his young Pupil. This *Frenchman* was banifhed out of his own Country for fome Heretical Notions he held ; and tho' he was a Man of very little Religion, yet he had admirable Morals, and a brave Soul.

After

After the total Defeat of *Jamoan*'s Army, which all fled, or were left dead upon the Place, they spent some Time in the Camp; *Oroonoko* chusing rather to remain a While there in his Tents, than to enter into a Palace, or live in a Court where he had so lately suffer'd so great a Loss, the Officers therefore, who saw and knew his Cause of Discontent, invented all sorts of Diversions and Sports to entertain their Prince: So that what with those Amusements abroad, and others at home, that is, within their Tents, with the Persuasions, Arguments, and Care of his Friends and Servants that he more peculiarly priz'd, he wore off in Time a great Part of that Chagrin, and Torture of Despair, which the first Efforts of *Imoinda*'s Death had given him; insomuch, as having received a thousand kind Embassies from the King, and Invitation to return to Court, he obey'd, tho' with no little Reluctancy; and when he did so, there was a visible Change in him, and for a long Time he was much more melancholy than before. But Time lessens all Extremes, and reduces 'em to Mediums, and Unconcern; but no Motives of Beauties, tho' all endeavour'd it, could engage him in any sort of Amour, tho' he had all the Invitations to it, both from his own Youth, and other Ambitions and Designs.

Oroo-

Oroonoko was no sooner return'd from this last Conquest, and received at Court with all the Joy and Magnificence that could be expres'd to a Young Victor, who was not only return'd Triumphant, but belov'd like a Deity, than there arriv'd in the Port an *English* Ship.

The Master of it had often before been in these Countries, and was very well known to *Oroonoko*, with whom he had traffick'd for Slaves, and had us'd to do the same with his Predeceffors.

This Commander was a Man of a finer fort of Addrefs and Converfation, better bred, and more engaging, than moft of that fort of Men are ; fo that he feem'd rather never to have been bred out of a Court, than almoft all his Life at Sea. This Captain therefore was always better receiv'd at Court, than moft of the Traders to thofe Countries were ; and efpecially by *Oroonoko*, who was more civiliz'd, according to the *European* Mode, than any other had been, and took more Delight in the *White* Nations ; and, above all, Men of Parts and Wit. To this Captain he fold abundance of his Slaves ; and for the Favour and Efteem he had for him, made him many Prefents, and oblig'd him to ftay at Court as long as poffibly he could. Which the Captain feem'd to take as a very great Honour done him, entertaining

ing the Prince every Day with Globes and Maps, and Mathematical Difcourfes and Inftruments ; eating, drinking, hunting, and living with him with fo much Familiarity, that it was not to be doubted but he had gain'd very greatly upon the Heart of this gallant young Man. And the Captain, in Return of all thefe mighty Favours, befought the Prince to honour his Veffel with his Prefence fome Day or other at Dinner, before he fhould fet fail; which he condefcended to accept, and appointed his Day. The Captain, on his Part, fail'd not to have all Things in a Readinefs, in the moft magnificent Order he could poffibly ; And the Day being come, the Captain, in his Boat, richly adorn'd with Carpets and Velvet Cufhions, rowed to the Shore, to receive the Prince; with another Long-boat, where was plac'd all his Mufick and Trumpets, with which *Oroonoko* was extremely delighted ; who met him on the Shore, attended by his *French* Governor, *Jamoan*, *Aboan*, and about an Hundred of the nobleft of the Youths of the Court ; And after they had firft carried the Prince on Board, the Boats fetch'd the reft off ; where they found a very fplendid Treat, with all Sorts of fine Wines ; and were as well entertain'd, as 'twas poffible in fuch a Place to be.

The

The Prince having drank hard of Punch, and several Sorts of Wine, as did all the rest, (for great Care was taken they should want nothing of that Part of the Entertainment) was very merry, and in great Admiration of the Ship, for he had never been in one before ; so that he was curious of beholding every Place where he decently might descend. The rest, no less curious, who were not quite overcome with drinking, rambled at their Pleasure *Fore* and *Aft,* as their Fancies guided 'em: So that the Captain, who had well laid his Design before, gave the Word, and seiz'd on all his Guests ; they clapping great Irons suddenly on the Prince, when he was leap'd down into the Hold, to view that Part of the Vessel ; and locking him fast down, secur'd him. The same Treachery was us'd to all the rest ; and all in one Instant, in several Places of the Ship, were lash'd fast in Irons, and betray'd to Slavery. That great Design over, they set all Hands at Work to hoist Sail ; and with as treacherous as fair a Wind they made from the Shore with this innocent and glorious Prize, who thought of nothing less than such an Entertainment.

Some have commended this Act, as brave in the Captain ; but I will spare my Sense of it, and leave it to my Reader to judge as he pleases. It may be easily guess'd,

guefs'd, in what Manner the Prince refented this Indignity, who may be beft
refembled to a Lion taken in a Toil; fo
he raged, fo he ftruggled for Liberty, but
all in vain: And they had fo wifely managed his Fetters, that he could not ufe a
Hand in his Defence, to quit himfelf of a
Life that would by no Means endure Slavery; nor could he move from the Place
where he was ty'd, to any folid Part of
the Ship, againft which he might have beat
his Head, and have finifh'd his Difgrace
that Way. So that being deprived of all
other Means, he refolv'd to perifh for want
of Food; and pleas'd at laft with that
Thought, and toil'd and tir'd by Rage and
Indignation, he laid himfelf down, and
fullenly refolv'd upon dying, and refufed
all Things that were brought him.

This did not a little vex the Captain,
and the more fo, becaufe he found almoft
all of 'em of the fame Humour; fo that
the Lofs of fo many brave Slaves, fo tall
and goodly to behold, would have been
very confiderable: He therefore order'd
one to go from him (for he would not be
feen himfelf) to *Oroonoko*, and to affure
him, he was afflicted for having rafhly
done fo unhofpitable a Deed, and which
could not be now remedied, fince they
were far from Shore; but fince he refented
it in fo high a Nature, he affur'd him he
would

would revoke his Refolution, and fet both him and his Friends afhore on the next Land they fhould touch at ; and of this the Meffenger gave him his Oath, provided he would refolve to live. And *Oroonoko*, whofe Honour was fuch, as he never had violated a Word in his Life himfelf, much lefs a folemn Affeveration, believ'd in an Inftant what this Man faid ; but reply'd, He expected, for a Confirmation of this, to have his fhameful Fetters difmifs'd. This Demand was carried to the Captain; who return'd him Anfwer, That the Offence had been fo great which he had put upon the Prince, that he durft not truft him with Liberty while he remain'd in the Ship, for fear, left by a Valour natural to him, and a Revenge that would animate that Valour, he might commit fome Outrage fatal to himfelf, and the King his Mafter, to whom the Veffel did belong. To this *Oroonoko* reply'd, He would engage his Honour to behave himfelf in all friendly Order and Manner, and obey the Command of the Captain, as he was Lord of the King's Veffel, and General of thofe Men under his Command.

This was deliver'd to the ftill doubting Captain, who could not refolve to truft a Heathen, he faid, upon his Parole, a Man that had no Senfe or Notion of the God that he worfhipp'd. *Oroonoko* then

reply'd,

reply'd, He was very forry to hear that the Captain pretended to the Knowledge and Worfhip of any Gods, who had taught him no better Principles, than not to credit as he would be credited. But they told him, the Difference of their Faith occafion'd that Diftruft : for the Captain had protefted to him upon the Word of a Chriftian, and fworn in the Name of a great God ; which if he fhould violate, he muft expect eternal Torments in the World to come. ' Is that all the Obligations he ' has to be juft to his Oath ? (reply'd *Oroo-* ' *noko*) Let him know, I fwear by my ' Honour ; which to violate, would not ' only render me contemptible and de- ' fpifed by all brave and honeft Men, and ' fo give my felf perpetual Pain, but it ' would be eternally offending and dif- ' pleafing to all Mankind ; harming, betray- ' ing circumventing, and outraging all ' Men. But Punifhments hereafter are ' fuffer'd by one's felf ; and the World ' takes no Cognizance whether this God ' has reveng'd 'em or not, 'tis done fo ' fecretly, and deferr'd fo long ; while ' the Man of no Honour fuffers every Mo- ' ment the Scorn and Contempt of the ' honefter World, and dies every Day ig- ' nominioufly in his Fame, which is more ' valuable than Life. I fpeak not this to ' move Belief, but to fhew you how you
' miftake,

'miſtake, when you imagine, that he
'who will violate his Honour, will keep
'his Word with his *Gods.*' So, turning
from him with a diſdainful Smile, he re-
fuſed to anſwer him, when he urged him
to know what Anſwer he ſhould carry back
to his Captain ; ſo that he departed without ſaying any more.

The Captain pondering and conſulting
what to do, it was concluded, that nothing but *Oroonoko*'s Liberty would encourage any of the reſt to eat, except the
Frenchman, whom the Captain could not
pretend to keep Priſoner, but only told
him, he was ſecur'd, becauſe he might act
ſomething in Favour of the Prince ; but
that he ſhould be freed as ſoon as they
came to Land. So that they concluded
it wholly neceſſary to free the Prince from
his Irons, that he might ſhew himſelf to
the reſt ; that they might have an Eye upon him, and that they could not fear a ſingle Man.

This being reſolved, to make the Obligation the greater, the Captain himſelf
went to *Oroonoko* ; where, after many
Compliments, and Aſſurances of what
he had already promis'd, he receiving from
the Prince his Parole, and his Hand, for
his good Behaviour, diſmiſs'd his Irons,
and brought him to his own Cabin ;
where, after having treated and repos'd
him

him a While, (for he had neither eat nor flept in four Days before) he befought him to vifit thofe obftinate People in Chains, who refufed all manner of Suftenance ; and intreated him to oblige 'em to eat, and affure 'em of their Liberty the firft Opportunity.

Oroonoko, who was too generous not to give Credit to his Words, fhew'd himfelf to his People, who were tranfported with Excefs of Joy at the Sight of their darling Prince ; falling at his Feet, and kiffing and embracing 'em ; believing, as fome divine Oracle, all he affur'd 'em. But he befought 'em to bear their Chains with that Bravery that became thofe whom he had feen act fo nobly in Arms ; and that they could not give him greater Proofs of their Love and Friendfhip, fince 'twas all the Security the Captain (his Friend) could have againft the Revenge, he faid,. they might poffibly juftly take for the Injuries fuftained by him. And they all, with one Accord, affur'd him, that they could not fuffer enough, when it was for his Repofe and Safety.

After this, they no longer refus'd to eat, but took what was brought 'em, and were pleas'd with their Captivity, fince by it they hoped to redeem the Prince, who, all the reft of the Voyage, was treated with all the Refpect due to his

Birth, tho' nothing could divert his Melancholy ; and he would often figh for *Imoinda,* and think this a Punifhment due to his Misfortune, in having left that noble Maid behind him, that fatal Night, in the *Otan,* when he fled to the Camp.

Poffefs'd with a thoufand Thoughts of paft Joys with this fair young Perfon, and a Thoufand Griefs for her eternal Lofs, he endur'd a tedious Voyage, and at laft arriv'd at the Mouth of the River of *Surinam,* a Colony belonging to the King of *England,* and where they were to deliver fome Part of their Slaves. There the Merchants and Gentlemen of the Country going on Board, to demand thofe Lots of Slaves they had already agreed on ; and, amongft thofe, the Overfeers of thofe Plantations where I then chanc'd to be : The Captain, who had given the Word, order'd his Men to bring up thofe noble Slaves in Fetters, whom I have fpoken of ; and having put 'em, fome in one, and fome in other Lots, with Women and Children, (which thy call *Pickaninies*) they fold 'em off, as Slaves to feveral Merchants and Gentlemen ; not putting any two in one Lot, becaufe they would feparate 'em far from each other ; nor daring to truft 'em together, left Rage and Courage fhould put 'em upon contriving

triving fome great Action, to the Ruin of the Colony.

Oroonoko was firft feiz'd on, and fold to our Overfeer, who had the firft Lot, with feventeen more of all Sorts and Sizes, but not one of Quality with him. When he faw this, he found what they meant; for, as I faid, he underftood *Englifh* pretty well; and being wholly unarm'd and defencelefs, fo as it was in vain to make any Refiftance, he only beheld the Captain with a Look all fierce and difdainful, upbraiding him with Eyes that forc'd Blufhes on his guilty Cheeks, he only cry'd in paffing over the Side of the Ship; *Farewel, Sir, 'tis worth my Sufferings to gain fo true a Knowledge, both of you, and of your Gods, by whom you fwear.* And defiring thofe that held him to forbear their Pains, and telling 'em he would make no Refiftance, he cry'd, *Come, my Fellow-Slaves, let us defcend, and fee if we can meet with more Honour and Honefty in the next World we fhall touch upon.* So he nimbly leapt into the Boat, and fhewing no more Concern, fuffer'd himfelf to be row'd up the River, with his feventeen Companions.

The Gentlemen that brought him, was a young *Cornifh* Gentleman, whofe Name was *Trefry;* a Man of great Wit, and fine Learning, and was carried into thofe Parts by the Lord —— Governor, to

manage

manage all his Affairs. He reflecting·on the laſt Words of *Oroonoko* to the Captain, and beholding the Richneſs of his Veſt, no ſooner came into the Boat, but he fix'd his Eyes on him ; and finding ſomething ſo extraordinary in his Face, his Shape and Mein, a Greatneſs of Look, and Haughtineſs in his Air, and finding he ſpoke *Engliſh*, had a great Mind to be enquiring into his Quality and Fortune ; which, though *Oroonoko* endeavour'd to hide, by only confeſſing he was above the Rank of common Slaves, *Trefry* ſoon found he was yet ſomething greater than he confeſs'd ; and from that Moment began to conceive ſo vaſt an Eſteem for him, that he ever after lov'd him as his deareſt Brother, and ſhew'd him all the Civilities due to ſo great a Man.

Trefry was a very good Mathematician, and a Linguiſt ; could ſpeak *French* and *Spaniſh* ; and in the three Days they remain'd in the Boat, (for ſo long were they going from the Ship to the Plantation) he entertain'd *Oroonoko* ſo agreeably with his Art and Diſcourſe, that he was no leſs pleas'd with *Trefry*, than he was with the Prince ; and he thought himſelf, at leaſt, fortunate in this, that ſince he was a Slave, as long as he would ſuffer himſelf to remain ſo, he had a Man of ſo excellent Wit and Parts for a Maſter.

So

So that before they had finifh'd their Voyage up the River, he made no Scruple of declaring to *Trefry* all his Fortunes, and moft Part of what I have here related, and put himfelf wholly into the Hands of his new Friend, who he found refented all the Injuries were done him, and was charm'd with all the Greatneffes of his Actions; which were recited with that Modefty, and delicate Senfe, as wholly vanquifh'd him, and fubdu'd him to his Intereft. And he promis'd him, on his Word and Honour, he would find the Means to re-conduct him to his own Country again; affuring him, he had a perfect Abhorrence of fo difhonourable an Action; and that he would fooner have dy'd, than have been the Author of fuch a Perfidy. He found the Prince was very much concerned to know what became of his Friends, and how they took their Slavery; and *Trefry* promifed to take Care about the enquiring after their Condition, and that he fhould have an Account of 'em.

Tho', as *Oroonoko* afterwards faid, he had little Reafon to credit the Words of a *Backearary;* yet he knew not why, but he faw a kind of Sincerity, and aweful Truth in the Face of *Trefry;* he faw Honefty in his Eyes, and he found him wife and witty enough to underftand Honour : for it was one of his Maxims, *A Man of Wit could not be a Knave or Villain.*

G 3

In

In their Paffage up the River, they put in at feveral Houfes for Refrefhment; and ever when they landed, Numbers of People would flock to behold this Man: not but their Eyes were daily entertain'd with the Sight of Slaves; but the Fame of *Oroonoko* was gone before him, and all People were in Admiration of his Beauty. Befides, he had a rich Habit on, in which he was taken, fo different from the reft, and which the Captain could not ftrip him of, becaufe he was forc'd to furprize his Perfon in the Minute he fold him. When he found his Habit made him liable, as he thought, to be gazed at the more, he begged *Trefry* to give him fomething more befitting a Slave, which he did, and took off his Robes: Neverthelefs, he fhone thro' all, and his *Ofenbrigs* (a fort of brown *Holland* Suit he had on) could not conceal the Graces of his Looks and Mein; and he had no lefs Admirers than when he had his dazling Habit on: The Royal Youth appear'd in fpite of the Slave, and People could not help treating him after a different Manner, without defigning it. As foon as they approached him, they venerated and efteemed him; his Eyes infenfibly commanded Refpect, and his Behaviour infinuated it into every Soul. So that there was nothing talked of but this young and gallant Slave, even by thofe who yet knew not that he was a Prince.   I

I ought to tell you that the Chriſtians never buy any Slaves but they give 'em ſome Name of their own, their native ones being likely very barbarous, and hard to pronounce ; ſo that Mr. *Trefry* gave *Oroonoko* that of *Cæſar ;* which Name will live in that Country as long as that (ſcarce more) glorious one of the great *Roman :* for 'tis moſt evident he wanted no Part of the perſonal Courage of that *Cæſar*, and acted Things as memorable, had they been done in ſome Part of the World repleniſh-ed with People and Hiſtorians, that might have given him his Due.   But his Misfor-tune was, to fall in an obſcure World, that afforded only a Female Pen to celebrate his Fame ; tho' I doubt not but it had lived from others Endeavours, if the *Dutch*, who immediately after his Time took that Country, had not killed, baniſhed and diſperſed all thoſe that were capable of giving the World this great Man's Life, much better than I have done.   And Mr. *Trefry*, who deſign'd it, died before he be-gan it, and bemoan'd himſelf for not having undertook it in Time.

For the future therefore I muſt call *Oroonoko Cæſar ;* ſince by that Name only he was known in our Weſtern World, and by that Name he was received on Shore at *Parham-Houſe,* where he was de-ſtin'd a Slave.   But if the King himſelf

G 4

(God

(God blefs him) had come afhore, there could not have been greater Expectation by all the whole Plantation, and thofe neighbouring ones, than was on ours at that Time: and he was received more like a Governor than a Slave : Notwithftanding, as the Cuftom was, they affigned him his Portion of Land, his Houfe and his Bufinefs up in the Plantation.   But as it was more for Form, than any Defign to put him to his Tafk, he endured no more of the Slave but the Name, and remain'd fome Days in the Houfe, receiving all Vifits that were made him, without ftirring towards that Part of the Plantation where the *Negroes* were.

At laft, he would needs go view his Land, his Houfe, and the Bufinefs affign'd him.   But he no fooner came to the Houfes of the Slaves, which are like a little Town by itfelf, the *Negroes* all having left Work, but they all came forth to behold him, and found he was that Prince who had, at feveral Times, fold moft of 'em to thefe Parts ; and from a Veneration they pay to great Men, efpecially if they know 'em, and from the Surprize and Awe they had at the Sight of him, they all caft them-felves at his Feet, crying out, in their Language, *Live, O King! Long live, O King!* and kiffing his Feet, paid him even Divine Homage.

Several

Several *English* Gentlemen were with him, and what Mr. *Trefry* had told 'em was here confirm'd ; of which he himfelf before had no other Witnefs than *Cæfar* himfelf: But he was infinitely glad to find his Grandeur confirmed by the Adoration of all the Slaves.

Cæfar, troubled with their Over-Joy, and Over-Ceremony, befought 'em to rife, and to receive him as their Fellow-Slave ; affuring them he was no better. At which they fet up with one Accord a moft terrible and hideous Mourning and Condoling, which he and the *English* had much ado to appeafe: but at laft they prevailed with 'em, and they prepared all their barbarous Mufick, and every one kill'd and drefs'd fomething of his own Stock (for every Family has their Land apart, on which, at their Leifure-times, they breed all eatable Things) and clubbing it together, made a moft magnificent Supper, inviting their *Grandee Captain*, their *Prince*, to honour it with his Prefence ; which he did, and feveral *English* with him, where they all waited on him, ·fome playing, others dancing before him all the Time, according to the Manners of their feveral Nations, and with unwearied Induftry endeavouring to pleafe and delight him.

While they fat at Meat, Mr. *Trefry* told *Cæfar*, that moft of thefe young Slaves

were

were undone in Love with a fine She-
Slave, whom they had had about fix Months
on their Land; the Prince, who never
heard the Name of *Love* without a Sigh,
nor any Mention of it without the Curiofity of examining further into that
Tale, which of all Difcourfes was moft
agreeable tô him, asked, how they came
to be fo unhappy, as to be all undone for
one fair Slave? *Trefry*, who was naturally
amorous, and delighted to talk of Love as
well as any Body, proceeded to tell him,
they had the moft charming Black that
ever was beheld on their Plantation,
about fifteen or fixteen Years old, as he
guefs'd; that for his Part he had done
nothing but figh for her ever fince fhe
came; and that all the White Beauties he
had feen, never charm'd him fo abfolutely
as this fine Creature had done; and that
no Man, of any Nation, ever beheld her,
that did not fall in love with her; and
that fhe had all the Slaves perpetually at her Feet; and the whole Country
refounded with the Fame of *Clemene*, for
fo (faid he) we have chriften'd her: but
fhe denies us all with fuch a noble Difdain, that 'tis a Miracle to fee, that fhe
who can give fuch eternal Defires, fhould
herfelf be all Ice and all Unconcern.   She
is adorn'd with the moft graceful Modefty
that ever beautify'd Youth; the fofteft
Sigher

Sigher —— that, if she were capable of Love, one would swear she languished for some absent happy Man; and so retired, as if she fear'd a Rape even from the God of Day, or that the Breezes would steal Kisses from her delicate Mouth. Her Task of Work, some sighing Lover every Day makes it his Petition to perform for her; which she accepts blushing, and with Reluctancy, for Fear he will ask her a Look for a Recompence, which he dares not presume to hope; so great an Awe she strikes into the Hearts of her Admirers. ' I do not wonder (*reply'd the Prince*) that ' *Clemene* should refuse Slaves, being, as ' you say, so beautiful; but wonder how ' she escapes those that can entertain her ' as you can do; or why, being your ' Slave, you do not oblige her to yield? ' I confess (*said* Trefry) when I have, ' against her Will, entertained her with ' Love so long, as to be transported with ' my Passion even above Decency, I have ' been ready to make Use of those Advan- ' tages of Strength and Force Nature has ' given me: But Oh; she disarms me with ' that Modesty and Weeping, so ten- ' der and so moving, that I retire, and ' thank my Stars she overcame me.' The Company laugh'd at his Civility to a Slave, and *Cæsar* only applauded the Nobleness of his Passion and Nature, since that Slave .

G 6

might

might be noble, or, what was better, have true Notions of Honour and Virtue in her. Thus paffed they this Night, after having received from the Slaves all imaginable Refpect and Obedience.

The next Day, *Trefry* ask'd *Cæfar* to walk when the Heat was allay'd, and defignedly carried him by the Cottage of the fair Slave; and told him fhe whom he fpoke of laft Night lived there retir'd: *But* (fays he) *I would not wifh you to approach; for I am fure you will be in Love as foon as you behold her.* *Cæfar* affured him, he was Proof againft all the Charms of that Sex; and that if he imagined his Heart could be fo perfidious to love again after *Imoinda,* he believed he fhould tear it from his Bofom. They had no fooner fpoke, but a little Shock-Dog, that *Clemene* had prefented her, which fhe took great Delight in, ran out; and fhe, not knowing any Body was there, ran to get it in again, and bolted out on thofe who were juft fpeaking of her: when feeing them, fhe would have run in again, but *Trefry* caught her by the Hand, and cry'd, Clemene, *however you fly a Lover, you ought to pay fome Refpect to this Stranger,* (pointing to *Cæfar.*) But fhe, as if fhe had refolved never to raife her Eyes to the Face of a Man again, bent 'em the more to the Earth, when he fpoke, and gave
the

the Prince the Leifure to look the more
at her. There needed no long gazing,
or Confideration, to examine who this
fair Creature was ; he foon faw *Imoinda*
all over her ; in a Minute he faw her Face,
her Shape, her Air, her Modefty, and all
that call'd forth his Soul with Joy at his
Eyes, and left his Body deftitute of almoft
Life : it ftood without Motion, and for a
Minute knew not that it had a Being ;
and, I believe, he had never come to himfelf, fo opprefs'd he was with Over-joy,
if he had not met with this Allay, that
he perceived *Imoinda* fall dead in the Hands
of *Trefry*. This awaken'd him, and he
ran to her Aid, and caught her in his
Arms, where .by Degrees fhe came to her
felf ; and 'tis needlefs to tell with what
Tranfports, what Extafies of Joy, they
both a While beheld each other, without
fpeaking ; then fnatched each other to
their Arms ; then gaze again, as if they
ftill doubted whether they poffefs'd the
Bleffing they grafped : but when they
recover'd their Speech, 'tis not to be imagined what tender Things they exprefs'd
to each other ; wondring what ftrange
Fate had brought them again together. They foon inform'd each other
of their Fortunes, and equally bewail'd
their Fate ; but at the fame Time they
mutually

mutually protefted, that even Fetters and Slavery were foft and eafy, and would be fupported with Joy and Pleafure, while they could be fo happy to poffefs each other, and to be able to make good their Vows. *Cæfar* fwore he difdained the Empire of the World, while he could behold his *Imoinda;* and fhe defpifed Grandeur and Pomp, thofe Vanities of her Sex, when fhe could gaze on *Oroonoko.* He ador'd the very Cottage where fhe refided, and faid, That little Inch of the World would give him more Happinefs than all the Univerfe could do; and fhe vow'd it was a Palace, while adorned with the Prefence of *Oroonoko.*

Trefry was infinitely pleafed with this Novel, and found this *Clemene* was the fair Miftrefs of whom *Cæfar* had before fpoke; and was not a little fatisfy'd, that Heaven was fo kind to the Prince as to fweeten his Misfortunes by fo lucky an Accident; and leaving the Lovers to themfelves, was impatient to come down to *Parham-Houfe* (which was on the fame Plantation) to give me an Account of what had happened. I was as impatient to make thefe Lovers a Vifit, having already made a Friendfhip with *Cæfar,* and from his own Mouth learned what I have related; which was confirmed by his *Frenchman,*
who

who was fet on fhore to feek his Fortune, and of whom they could not make a Slave, becaufe a Chriftian ; and he came daily to *Parham-Hill* to fee and pay his Refpects to his Pupil Prince.   So that concerning and interefting myfelf in all that related to *Cæfar,* whom I had affured of Liberty as foon as the Governour arrived, I hafted prefently to the Place where thefe Lovers were, and was infinitely glad to find this beautiful young Slave (who had already gain'd all our Efteems, for her Modefty and extraordinary Prettinefs) to be the fame I had heard *Cæfar* fpeak fo much of.   One may imagine then we paid her a treble Refpect ; and tho' from her being carved in fine Flowers and Birds all over her Body, we took her to be of Quality before, yet when we knew *Clemene* was *Imoinda,* we could not enough admire her.

I had forgot to tell you, that thofe who are nobly born of that Country, are fo delicately cut and raifed all over the Fore-part of the Trunk of their Bodies, that it looks as if it were japan'd, the Works being raifed like high Point round the Edges of the Flowers.   Some are only carved with a little Flower, or Bird, at the Sides of the Temples, as was *Cæfar ;* and thofe who are fo carved over the Body, refemble our antient *Picts* that are

figur'd

figur'd in the Chronicles, but thefe Carvings are more delicate.

From that happy Day *Cæfar* took *Clemene* for his Wife, to the general Joy of all People; and there was as much Magnificence as the Country could afford at the Celebration of this Wedding: and in a very fhort Time after fhe conceived with Child, which made *Cæfar* even adore her, knowing he was the laft of his great Race. This new Accident made him more impatient of Liberty, and he was every Day treating with *Trefrey* for his and *Clemene*'s Liberty, and offer'd either Gold, or a vaft Quantity of Slaves, which fhould be paid before they let him go, provided he could have any Security that he fhould go when his Ranfom was paid. They fed him from Day to Day with Promifes, and delay'd him till the Lord-Governor fhould come; fo that he began to fufpect them of Falfhood, and that they would delay him till the Time of his Wife's Delivery, and make a Slave of the Child too; for all the Breed is theirs to whom the Parents belong. This Thought made him very uneafy, and his Sullennefs gave them fome Jealoufies of him; fo that I was obliged, by fome Perfons who fear'd a Mutiny (which is very fatal fometimes in thofe Colonies that abound fo with Slaves, that they exceed the Whites in vaft Numbers)

bers) to difcourfe with *Cæfar*, and to give him all the Satisfaction I poffibly could : They knew he and *Clemene* were fcarce an Hour in a Day from my Lodgings ; that they eat with me, and that I oblig'd them in all Things I was capable. I entertained them with the Lives of the *Romans*, and great Men, which charmed him to my Company ; and her, with teaching her all the pretty Works that I was Miftrefs of, and telling her Stories of Nuns, and endeavouring to bring her to the Knowledge of the true God : But of all Difcourfes, *Cæfar* liked that the worft, and would never be reconciled to our Notions of the Trinity, of which he ever made a Jeft ; it was a Riddle he faid would turn his Brain to conceive, and one could not make him underftand what Faith was. However, thefe Converfations fail'd not altogether fo well to divert him, that he liked the Company of us Women much above the Men, for he could not drink, and he is but an ill Companion in that Country that cannot. So that obliging him to love us very well, we had all the Liberty of Speech with him, efpecially my felf, whom he call'd his *Great Miftrefs* ; and indeed my Word would go a great Way with him. For thefe Reafons I had Opportunity to take Notice of him, that he was not well pleafed of late, as he

11ufed

ufed to be ; was more retired and thoughtful ; and told him, I took it ill he fhould fufpect we would break our Words with him, and not permit both him and *Clemene* to return to his own Kingdom, which was not fo long a Way, but when he was once on his Voyage he would quickly arrive there. He made me fome Anfwers that fhew'd a Doubt in him, which made me afk, what Advantage it would be to doubt? It would but give us a Fear of him, and poffibly compel us to treat him fo as I fhould be very loth to behold ; that is, it might occafion his Confinement. Perhaps this was not fo luckily fpoke of me, for I perceiv'd he refented that Word, which I ftrove to foften again in vain : However, he affur'd me, that whatfoever Refolutions he fhould take, he would act nothing upon the *White* People ; and as for myfelf, and thofe upon that *Plantation* where he was, he would fooner forfeit his eternal Liberty, and Life itfelf, than lift his Hand againft his greateft Enemy on that Place. He befought me to fuffer no Fears upon his Account, for he could do nothing that Honour fhould not dictate ; but he accufed himfelf for having fuffer'd Slavery fo long ; yet he charg'd that Weaknefs on Love alone, who was capable of making him neglect even Glory itfelf ;

and,

and, for which, now he reproaches himself every Moment of the Day. Much
more to this Effect he spoke, with an Air
impatient enough to make me know he
would not be long in Bondage ; and tho'
he suffer'd only the Name of a Slave, and
had nothing of the Toil and Labour of
one, yet that was sufficient to render him
uneasy ; and he had been too long idle,
who us'd to be always in Action, and in
Arms. He had a Spirit all rough and
fierce, and that could not be tam'd to
lazy Rest : And tho' all Endeavours were
us'd to exercise himself in such Actions
and Sports as this World afforded, as
Running, Wrestling, Pitching the Bar,
Hunting and Fishing, Chasing and Kiiling
Tygers of a monstrous Size, which this
Continent affords in abundance ; and wonderful *Snakes*, such as *Alexander* is reported to have encounter'd at the River of
Amazons, and which *Cæsar* took great
Delight to overcome ; yet these were not
Actions great enough for his large Soul,
which was still panting after more renown'd
Actions.

Before I parted that Day with him, I
got, with much ado, a Promise from him
to rest yet a little longer with Patience,
and wait the Coming of the Lord Governour, who was every Day expected on our
Shore : He assur'd me he would, and this

Pro-

Promife he defired me to know was given perfectly in Complaifance to me, in whom he had an entire Confidence.

After this, I neither thought it convenient to truft him much out of our View, nor did the Country, who fear'd him; but with one Accord it was advis'd to treat him fairly, and oblige him to remain within fuch a Compafs, and that he fhould be permitted, as feldom as could be, to go up to the Plantations of the *Negroes*; or, if he did, to be accompany'd by fome that fhould be rather, in Appearance, Attendants than Spies. This Care was for fome time taken, and *Cæfar* look'd upon it as a Mark of extraordinary Refpect, and was glad his Difcontent had oblig'd 'em to be more obfervant to him; he received new Affurance from the Overfeer, which was confirmed to him by the Opinion of all the Gentlemen of the Country, who made their Court to him. During this Time that we had his Company more frequently than hitherto we had had, it may not be unpleafant to relate to you the Diverfions we entertain'd him with, or rather he us.

My Stay was to be fhort in that Country; becaufe my Father dy'd at Sea, and never arriv'd to poffefs the Honour defign'd him, (which was Lieutenant-General of fix and thirty Iflands, befides the
Continent

Continent of *Surinam*) nor the Advantages he hop'd to reap by them : So that though we were oblig'd to continue on our Voyage, we did not intend to ſtay upon the Place. Though, in a Word, I muſt ſay thus much of it ; That certainly had his late. Majeſty, of ſacred Memory, but ſeen and known what a vaſt and charming World he had been Maſter of in that Continent, he would never have parted ſo eaſily with it to the *Dutch.* 'Tis a Continent, whoſe vaſt Extent was never yet known, and may contain more noble Earth than all the Univerſe beſide ; for, they ſay, it reaches from Eaſt to Weſt one Way as far as *China,* and another to *Peru :* It affords all Things, both for Beauty and Uſe ; 'tis there eternal Spring, always the very Months of *April, May,* and *June*; the Shades are perpetual, the Trees bearing at once all Degrees of Leaves, and Fruit, from blooming Buds to ripe Autumn·: Groves of Oranges, Lemons Citrons, Figs, Nutmegs, and noble Aromaticks, continually bearing their Fragrancies : The Trees appearing all like Noſegays, adorn'd with Flowers of different Kinds ; ſome are all White, ſome Purple, ſome Scarlet, ſome Blue, ſome Yellow ; bearing at the ſame Time ripe Fruit, and blooming young, or producing every Day new. The very Wood of
all

all thefe Trees has an intrinfic Value, above common Timber ; for they are, when cut, of different Colours, glorious to behold, and bear a Price confiderable, to inlay withal. Befides this, they yield rich Balm, and Gums ; fo that we make our Candles of fuch an aromatic Sub-ftance, as does not only give a fufficient Light, but as they burn, they caft their Perfumes all about. Cedar is the common Firing, and all the Houfes are built with it. The very Meat we eat, when fet on the Table, if it be native, I mean of the Country, perfumes the whole Room ; efpecially a little Beaft call'd an *Armadillo,* a Thing which I can liken to nothing fo well as a *Rhinoceros ;* 'tis all in white Ar-mour, fo jointed, that it moves as well in it, as if it had nothing on : This Beaft is about the Bignefs of a Pig of fix Weeks old. But it were endlefs to give an Account of all the divers wonderful and ftrange Things that Country affords, and which he took a great Delight to go in Search of ; tho' thofe Adventures are often-times fatal, and at leaft dangerous : But while we had *Cæfar* in our Company on thefe Defigns, we fear'd no Harm, nor fuffer'd any.

As foon as I came into the Country, the beft Houfe in it was prefented me, call'd *St. John's Hill :* It ftood on a vaft

Rock

Rock of white Marble, at the Foot of which, the River ran a vaſt Depth down, and not to be deſcended on that Side; the little Waves ſtill daſhing and waſhing the Foot of this Rock, made the ſofteſt Murmurs and Purlings in the World; and the oppoſite Bank was adorn'd with ſuch vaſt Quantities of different Flowers eternally blowing, and every Day and Hour new, fenc'd behind 'em with lofty Trees of a thouſand rare Forms and Colours, that the Proſpect was the moſt raviſhing that Fancy can create. On the Edge of this white Rock, towards the River, was a Walk, or Grove, of Orange and Lemon-Trees, about half the Length of the *Mall* here, whoſe flowery and Fruit-bearing Branches met at the Top, and hinder'd the Sun, whoſe Rays are very fierce there, from entring a Beam into the Grove; and the cool Air that came from the River, made it not only fit to entertain People in, at all the hotteſt Hours of the Day, but refreſh the ſweet Bloſſoms, and made it always ſweet and charming; and ſure, the whole Globe of the World cannot ſhew ſo delightful a Place as this Grove was: Not all the Gardens of boaſted *Italy* can produce a Shade to out-vie this, which Nature has join'd with Art to render ſo exceeding fine; and 'tis a Marvel to ſee how ſuch vaſt Trees, as

big

big as *English* Oaks, could take Footing on so solid a Rock, and in so little Earth as cover'd that Rock: But all Things by Nature there are rare, delightful, and wonderful.   But to our Sports.

Sometimes we would go surprising, and in Search of young *Tygers* in their Dens, watching when the old ones went forth to forage for Prey: and oftentimes we have been in great Danger, and have fled apace for our Lives, when surpriz'd by the Dams.   But once, above all other Times, we went on this Design, and *Cæsar* was with us; who had no sooner stoln a young *Tyger* from her Nest, but going off, we encounter'd the Dam, bearing a Buttock of a Cow, which she had torn off with her mighty Paw, and going with it towards her Den: We had only four Women, *Cæsar*, and an *English* Gentleman, Brother to *Harry Martin* the great *Oliverian;* we found there was no escaping this enraged and ravenous Beast.   However, we Women fled as fast as we could from it; but our Heels had not saved our Lives, if *Cæsar* had not laid down her *Cub*, when he found the *Tyger* quit her Prey to make the more Speed towards him; and taking Mr. *Martin*'s Sword, desired him to stand aside, or follow the Ladies. He obey'd him; and *Cæsar* met this monstrous Beast of mighty Size, and vast Limbs, who came with

open

open Jaws upon him; and fixing his aweful ftern Eyes full upon thofe of the Beaft, and putting himfelf into a very fteady and good aiming Pofture of Defence, ran his Sword quite through his Breaft, down to his very Heart, home to the Hilt of the Sword: The dying Beaft ftretch'd forth her Paw, and going to grafp his Thigh, furpriz'd with Death in that very Moment, did him no other Harm than fixing her long Nails in his Flefh very deep, feebly wounded him, but could not grafp the Flefh to tear off any. When he had done this, he hallow'd to us to return; which, after fome Affurance of his Victory, we did, and found him lugging out the Sword from the Bofom of the *Tyger*, who was laid in her Blood on the Ground. He took up the *Cub*, and with an Unconcern that had nothing of the Joy or Gladnefs of Victory, he came and laid the Whelp at my Feet. We all extremely wonder'd at his daring, and at the Bignefs of the Beaft, which was about the Height of an Heifer, but of mighty great and ftrong Limbs.

Another time, being in the Woods, he kill'd a *Tyger*, that had long infefted that Part, and born away abundance of Sheep and Oxen, and other Things, that were for the Support of thofe to whom they belong'd. Abundance of People affail'd this Beaft, fome affirming they had fhot

her with feveral Bullets quite through the Body at feveral times; and fome fwearing they fhot her through the very Heart; and they believed fhe was a Devil, rather than a mortal Thing. *Cæfar* had often faid, he had a Mind to encounter this Monfter, and fpoke with feveral Gentlemen who had attempted her; one crying, I fhot her with fo many poifon'd Arrows, another with his Gun in this Part of her, and another in that; fo that he remarking all the Places where fhe was fhot, fancy'd ftill he fhould overcome her, by giving her another Sort of a Wound than any had yet done; and one Day faid (at the Table) 'What Trophies and Gar-
' lands, Ladies, will you make me, if I
' bring you home the Heart of this ra-
' venous Beaft, that eats up all your
' Lambs and Pigs?' We all promis'd he fhould be rewarded at our Hands. So taking a Bow, which he chofe out of a great many, he went up into the Wood, with two Gentlemen, where he imagin'd this Devourer to be. They had not pafs'd very far into it, but they heard her Voice, growling and grumbling, as if fhe were pleas'd with fomething fhe was doing. When they came in View, they found her muzzling in the Belly of a new ravifh'd Sheep, which fhe had torn open; and feeing herfelf approach'd, fhe took faft hold

of

of her Prey with her fore Paws, and set
a very fierce raging Look on *Cæsar*, without offering to approach him, for Fear at
the same Time of loosing what she had in
Possession: So that *Cæsar* remain'd a good
while, only taking Aim, and getting an
Opportunity to shoot her where he design'd. 'Twas some Time before he could
accomplish it; and to wound her, and not
kill her, would but have enrag'd her the
more, and endanger'd him. He had a
Quiver of Arrows at his Side, so that if
one fail'd, he could be supply'd: At last,
retiring a little, he gave her Opportunity
to eat, for he found she was ravenous, and
fell to as soon as she saw him retire, being
more eager of her Prey, than of doing
new Mischiefs; when he going softly to
one Side of her, and hiding his Person behind certain Herbage, that grew high and
thick, he took so good Aim, that, as he
intended, he shot her just into the Eye,
and the Arrow was sent with so good a
Will, and so sure a Hand, that it stuck
in her Brain, and made her caper, and
become mad for a Moment or two; but
being seconded by another Arrow, she
fell dead upon the Prey. *Cæsar* cut her
open with a Knife, to see where those
Wounds were that had been reported to
him, and why she did not die of 'em.
But I shall now relate a Thing that, possibly,

H 2

will

will find no Credit among Men ; becaufe 'tis a Notion commonly receiv'd with us, That nothing can receive a Wound in the Heart, and live : But when the Heart of this courageous Animal was taken out, there were feven Bullets of Lead in it, the Wound feam'd up with great Scars, and fhe liv'd with the Bullets a great While, for it was long fince they were fhot : This Heart the Conqueror brought up to us, and 'twas a very great Curio-fity, which all the Country came to fee ; and which gave *Cæfar* Occafion of many fine Difcourfes of Accidents in War, and ftrange Efcapes.

At other times he would go a Fifhing ; and difcourfing on that Diverfion, he found we had in that Country a very ftrange Fifh, call'd a *Numb-Eel*, (an *Eel* of which I have eaten) that while it is alive, it has a Quality fo cold, that thofe who are angling, tho' with a Line of ever fo great a Length, with a Rod at the End of it, it fhall in the fame Minute the Bait is touch'd by this *Eel*, feize him or her that holds the Rod with a Numb-nefs, that fhall deprive 'em of Senfe for a While ; and fome have fallen into the Water, and other's drop'd, as dead, on the Banks of the Rivers where they ftood, as foon as this Fifh touches the Bait. *Cæ-far* us'd to laugh at this, and believ'd it

im-

impoffible a Man could lofe his Force at
the Touch of a Fifh ; and could not underftand that Philofophy, that a cold Quality fhould be of that Nature ; however, he
had a great Curiofity to try whether it
would have the fame Effect on him it had
on others, and often try'd, but in vain.
At laft, the fought-for Fifh came to the
Bait, as he ftood angling on the Bank ; and
inftead of throwing away the Rod, or giving it a fudden Twitch out of the Water,
whereby he might have caught both the
Eel, and have difmifs'd the Rod, before it
could have too much Power over him ; for
Experiment-fake, he grafp'd it but the
harder, and fainting, fell into the River ;
and being ftill poffefs'd of the Rod, the
Tide carry'd him, fenfelefs as he was, a
great Way, till an *Indian* Boat took him
up ; and perceiv'd, when they touch'd
him, a Numbnefs feize them, and by that
knew the Rod was in his Hand ; which
with a Paddle, (that is a fhort Oar) they
ftruck away, and fnatch'd it into the Boat,
Eel and all. If *Cæfar* was almoft dead, with
the Effect of this Fifh, he was more fo with
that of the Water, where he had remain'd
the Space of going a League, and they
found they had much ado to bring him
back to Life ; but at laft they did, and
brought him home, where he was in a few
Hours well recover'd and refrefh'd, and not

H 3

a lit-

a little afham'd to find he fhould be overcome by an *Eel*, and that all the People,
who heard his Defiance, would laugh at
him.   But we chear'd him up ; and he being convinc'd, we had the *Eel* at Supper,
which was a quarter of an Ell about, and
moft delicate Meat ; and was of the more
Value, fince it coft fo dear as almoft the
Life of fo gallant a Man.

About this Time we were in many mortal Fears, about fome Difputes the *Englifh*
had with the *Indians ;* fo that we could
fcarce truft our felves, without great
Numbers, to go to any *Indian* Towns, or
Place where they abode, for fear they
fhould fall upon us, as they did immediately after my coming away ; and the Place
being in the Poffeffion of the *Dutch*, they
us'd them not fo civilly as the *Englifh ;* fo
that they cut in Pieces all they could take,
getting into Houfes, and hanging up the
Mother, and all her Children about her ;
and cut a Footman, I left behind me, all
in Joints, and nail'd him to Trees.

This Feud began while I was there ; fo
that I loft half the Satisfaction I propos'd,
in not feeing and vifiting the *Indian* Towns.
But one Day, bemoaning of our Misfortunes upon this Account, *Cæfar* told us, we
need not fear, for if we had a Mind to go,
he would undertake to be our Guard.
Some would, but moft would not venture :

About

About eighteen of us refolv'd, and took Barge; and after eight Days, arriv'd near an *Indian* Town: But approaching it, the Hearts of fome of our Company fail'd, and they would not venture on Shore; fo we poll'd, who would, and who would not. For my Part, I faid, if *Cæfar* would, I would go. He refolv'd; fo did my Brother, and my Woman, a Maid of good Courage. Now none of us fpeaking the Language of the People, and imagining we fhould have a half Diverfion in gazing only; and not knowing what they faid, we took a Fifherman that liv'd at the Mouth of the River, who had been a long Inhabitant there, and oblig'd him to go with us: But becaufe he was known to the *Indians,* as trading among 'em, and being, by long living there, become a perfect *Indian* in Colour, we, who had a Mind to furprize 'em, by making them fee fomething they never had feen, (that is, *White* People) refolv'd only my felf, my Brother and Woman fhould go: So *Cæfar,* the Fifherman, and the reft, hiding behind fome thick Reeds and Flowers that grew in the Banks, let us pafs on towards the Town, which was on the Bank of the River all along. A little diftant from the Houfes, or Huts, we faw fome dancing, others bufy'd in fetching and carrying of Water from the River. They had no fooner fpy'd us, but

H 4   they

they set up a loud Cry, that frighted us at first; we thought it had been for those that should kill us, but it seems it was of Wonder and Amazement. They were all naked; and we were dress'd, so as is most commode for the hot Countries, very glittering and rich; so that we appear'd extremely fine; my own Hair was cut short, and I had a Taffety Cap, with black Feathers on my Head; my Brother was in a Stuff-Suit, with Silver Loops and Buttons, and abundance of green Ribbon. This was all infinitely surprising to them; and because we saw them stand still till we approach'd 'em, we took Heart and advanc'd, came up to 'em, and offer'd 'em our Hands; which they took, and look'd on us round about, calling still for more Company; who came swarming out, all wondering, and crying out *Tepeeme;* taking their Hair up in their Hands, and spreading it wide to those they call'd out to; as if they would say (as indeed it signify'd) *Number-less Wonders,* or not to be recounted, no more than to number the Hair of their Heads. By Degrees they grew more bold, and from gazing upon us round, they touch'd us, laying their Hands upon all the Features of our Faces, feeling our Breasts and Arms, taking up one Petticoat, then wondering to see another; admiring our Shoes and Stockings, but more our Gar-

ters,

ters, which we gave 'em, and they ty'd
about their Legs; being lac'd with Silver
Lace at the Ends; for they much efteem
any fhining Things.   In fine, we fuffer'd
'em to furvey us as they pleas'd, and we
thought they would never have done admiring us.   When *Cæfar,* and the reft,
faw we were receiv'd with fuch Wonder,
they came up to us; and finding the *Indian*
Trader whom they knew, (for 'tis by thefe
Fifherman, call'd *Indian* Traders, we hold
a Commerce with 'em; for they love not
to go far from home, and we never go to
them) when they faw him therefore, they
fet up a new Joy, and cry'd in their Language, *Oh, here's our* Tiguamy, *and we
fhall know whether thofe Things can fpeak.* So
advancing to him, fome of 'em gave him
their Hands, and cry'd, *Amora Tiguamy;*
which is as much as, *How do you do?* or,
Welcome Friend; and all, with one din, began to gabble to him, and afk'd, if we
had Senfe and Wit?   If we could talk of
Affairs of Life and War, as they could do?
If we could hunt, fwim, and do a thoufand Things they ufe?   He anfwer'd 'em,
We could.   Then they invited us into
their Houfes, and drefs'd Venifon and Buf-
falo for us; and going out, gather'd a Leaf
of a Tree, called a *Sarumbo* Leaf, of fix
Yards long, and fpread it on the Ground
for a Table-Cloth; and cutting another in

Pieces, inftead of Plates, fet us on little low *Indian* Stools, which they cut out of one entire Piece of Wood, and paint in a fort of Japan-Work. They ferve every one their Mefs on thefe Pieces of Leaves ; and it was very good, but too high-feafon'd with Pepper. When we had eat, my Brother and I took out our Flutes, and play'd to 'em, which gave 'em new Wonder ; and I foon perceiv'd, by an Admiration that is natural to thefe People, and by the extreme Ignorance and Simplicity of 'em, it were not difficult to eftablifh any unknown or extravagant Religion among them, and to impofe any Notions or Fictions upon 'em. For feeing a Kinfman of mine fet fome Paper on Fire with a Burning-Glafs, a Trick they had never before feen, they were like to have ador'd him for a God, and begg'd he would give 'em the Characters or Figures of his Name, that they might oppofe it againft Winds and Storms: which he did, and they held it up in thofe Seafons, and fancy'd it had a Charm to conquer them, and kept it like a holy Relique. They are very fuperftitious, and call'd him the Great *Peeie*, that is, *Prophet.* They fhewed us their *Indian Peeie*, a Youth of about fixteen Years old, as handfome as Nature could make a Man. They confecrate a beautiful Youth from his Infancy, and all Arts are ufed to compleat him in

the

the fineſt Manner, both in Beauty and Shape : He is bred to all the little Arts and Cunning they are capable of ; to all the legerdemain Tricks, and Slight of Hand whereby he impoſes on the Rabble ; and is both a Doctor in Phyſick and Divinity : And by theſe Tricks makes the Sick believe he ſometimes eaſes their Pains, by drawing from the afflicted Part little Serpents, or odd Flies, or Worms, or any ſtrange Thing ; and though they have beſides undoubted good Remedies for almoſt all their Diſeaſes, they cure the Patient more by Fancy than by Medicines, and make themſelves feared, loved, and reverenced. This young *Pœie* had a very young Wife, who ſeeing my Brother kiſs her, came running and kiſs'd me. After this they kiſs'd one another, and made it a very great Jeſt, it being ſo novel ; and new Admiration and Laughing went round the Multitude, that they never will forget that Ceremony, never before us'd or known. *Cæſar* had a Mind to ſee and talk with their War-Captains, and we were conducted to one of their Houſes, where we beheld ſeveral of the great Captains, who had been at Council : But ſo frightful a Viſion it was to ſee 'em, no Fancy can create ; no ſad Dreams can repreſent ſo dreadful a Spectacle. For my Part, I took 'em for Hobgoblins, or Fiends, rather than Men : But

how-

however their Shapes appear'd, their Souls were very humane and noble; but some wanted their Noses, some their Lips, some both Noses, and Lips, some their Ears, and others cut through each Cheek, with long Slashes, through which their Teeth appear'd: They had several other formidable Wounds and Scars, or rather Dismembrings. They had *Comitia's*, or little Aprons before them; and Girdles of Cotton, with their Knives naked stuck in it; a Bow at their Back, and a Quiver of Arrows on their Thighs; and most had Feathers on their Heads of divers Colours. They cry'd *Amora Tiguamy* to us, at our Entrance, and were pleas'd we said as much to them: They seated us, and gave us Drink of the best Sort, and wonder'd as much as the others had done before, to see us. *Cæsar* was marvelling as much at their Faces, wondring how they should be all so wounded in War; he was impatient to know how they all came by those frightful Marks of Rage or Malice, rather than Wounds got in noble Battle: They told us by our Interpreter, That when any War was waging, two Men, chosen out by some old Captain whose Fighting was past, and who could only teach the Theory of War, were to stand in Competition for the Generalship, or great War-Captain; and being brought before the old

Judges,

Judges, now paſt Labour, they are ask'd, What they dare do, to ſhew they are worthy to lead an Army? When he who is firſt aſk'd, making no Reply, cuts off his Noſe, and throws it contemptibly on the Ground ; and the other does ſomething to himſelf that he thinks ſurpaſſes him, and perhaps deprives himſelf of Lips and an Eye : So they ſlaſh on 'till one gives out, and many have dy'd in this Debate. And it's by a paſſive Valour they ſhew and prove their Activity ; a ſort of Courage too brutal to be applauded by our *Black* Hero ; neverthelefs, he exprefs'd his Eſteem of 'em.

In this Voyage *Cæſar* begat ſo good an Underſtanding between the *Indians* and the *Engliſh*, that there were no more Fears or Heart-burnings during our Stay, but we had a perfect, open, and free Trade with 'em. Many Things remarkable, and worthy reciting, we met with in this ſhort Voyage; becauſe *Cæſar* made it his Buſineſs to ſearch out and provide for our Entertainment, eſpecially to pleaſe his dearly ador'd *Imoinda*, who was a Sharer in all our Adventures ; we being refolv'd to make her Chains as eafy as we could, and to compliment the Prince in that Manner that moſt oblig'd him.

As we were coming up again, we met with ſome *Indians* of ſtrange Aſpects ; that

is,

is, of a larger Size, and other fort of Features, than thofe of our Country. Our *Indian Slaves*, that row'd us, afk'd 'em fome Queftions; but they could not underftand us, but fhew'd us a long Cotton String, with feveral Knots on it, and told us, they had been coming from the Mountains fo many Moons as there were Knots: they were habited in Skins of a ftrange Beaft, and brought along with 'em Bags of Gold-Duft; which, as well as they could give us to underftand, came ftreaming in little fmall Channels down the high Mountains, when the Rains fell; and offer'd to be the Convoy to any Body, or Perfons, that would go to the Mountains. We carry'd thefe Men up to *Parham,* where they were kept 'till the Lord-Governor came: And becaufe all the Country was mad to be going on this Golden Adventure, the Governor, by his Letters, commanded (for they fent fome of the Gold to him) that a Guard fhould be fet at the Mouth of the River of *Amazons* (a River fo call'd, almoft as broad as the River of *Thames)* and prohibited all People from going up that River, it conducting to thofe Mountains of Gold. But we going off for *England* before the Project was further profecuted, and the Governor being drown'd in a Hurricane, either the Defign died, or the *Dutch* have the Advantage

tage

tage of it : And 'tis to bemoan'd what his Majesty loft, by losing that Part of *America.*

Though this Digreflion is a little from my Story, however, since it contains some Proofs of the Curiofity and Daring of this great Man, I was content to omit nothing of his Character.

It was thus for some Time we diverted him ; but now *Imoinda* began to shew she was with Child, and did nothing but sigh and weep for the Captivity of her Lord, herself, and the Infant yet unborn ; and believ'd, if it were so hard to gain the Liberty of two, 'twould be more difficult to get that for three. Her Griefs were so many Darts in the great Heart of *Cæfar*, and taking his Opportunity, one *Sunday*, when all the *Whites* were overtaken in Drink, as there were abundance of several Trades, and *Slaves* for four Years, that inhabited among the *Negro* Houses ; and *Sunday* being their Day of Debauch, (otherwife they were a sort of Spies upon *Cæfar)* he went, pretending out of Goodnefs to 'em, to feaft among 'em, and sent all his Mufick, and order'd a great Treat for the whole Gang, about three hundred *Negroes,* and about an hundred and fifty were able to bear Arms, such as they had, which were fufficient to do Execution, with Spirits accordingly : For the *Englifh* had none but rufty

Swords,

Swords, that no Strength could draw from a Scabbard ; except the People of particular Quality, who took Care to oil 'em, and keep 'em in good Order : The Guns also, unless here and there one, or those newly carried from *England*, would do no Good or Harm ; for 'tis the Nature of that Country to rust and eat up Iron, or any Metals but Gold and Silver. And they are very expert at the Bow, which the *Negroes* and *Indians* are perfect Masters of.

Cæsar, having singled out these Men from the Women and Children, made an Harangue to 'em, of the Miseries and Ignominies of Slavery ; counting up all their Toils and Sufferings, under such Loads, Burdens and Drudgeries, as were fitter for Beasts than Men ; senseless Brutes, than human Souls. He told 'em, it was not for Days, Months or Years, but for Eternity ; there was no End to be of their Misfortunes : They suffer'd not like Men, who might find a Glory and Fortitude in Oppression ; but like Dogs, that lov'd the Whip and Bell, and fawn'd the more they were beaten : That they had lost the divine Quality of Men, and were become insensible Asses, fit only to bear : Nay, worse ; an Ass, or Dog, or Horse, having done his Duty, could lie down in Retreat, and rise to work again, and while he did his Duty, endur'd no Stripes ; but Men,
vil-

villanous, senseless Men, such as they, toil'd on all the tedious Week 'till *Black Friday*; and then, whether they work'd or not, whether they were faulty or meriting, they, promiscuously, the Innocent with the Guilty, suffer'd the infamous Whip, the sordid Stripes, from their Fellow-Slaves, 'till their Blood trickled from all Parts of their Body; Blood, whose every Drop ought to be revenged with a Life of some of those Tyrants that impose it. 'And why *(said he)* my dear Friends 'and Fellow-sufferers, should we be Slaves 'to an unknown People? Have they vanquished us nobly in Fight? Have they won us in Honourable Battle? And 'are we by the Chance of War become 'their Slaves? This would not anger a 'noble Heart; this would not animate a 'Soldier's Soul: No, but we are bought 'and sold like Apes or Monkeys, to be 'the Sport of Women, Fools and Cowards; 'and the Support of Rogues and Runagades, that have abandoned their own 'Countries for Rapine, Murders, Theft 'and Villanies. Do you not hear every 'Day how they upbraid each other with 'Infamy of Life, below the wildest Sal'vages? And shall we render Obedience 'to such a degenerate Race, who have no 'one human Virtue left, to distinguish
'them

‘ them from the vileſt Creatures? Will you,
‘ I ſay, ſuffer the Laſh from ſuch Hands?
‘ *They all reply'd with one Accord,* No, No,
‘ No; *Cæſar* has ſpoke like a great Cap-
‘ tain, like a great King.’
After this he would have proceeded,
but was interrupted by a tall *Negro*, of
ſome more Quality than the reſt, his Name
was *Tuſcan;* who bowing at the Feet of
Cæſar, cry'd, ‘ My Lord, we have liſten'd
‘ with Joy and Attention to what you
‘ have ſaid; and, were we only Men,
‘ would follow ſo great a Leader through
‘ the World: But O! conſider we are
‘ Huſbands and Parents too, and have
‘ Things more dear to us than Life; our
‘ Wives and Children, unfit for Travel in
‘ thoſe unpaſſable Woods, Mountains and
‘ Bogs. We have not only difficult Lands
‘ to overcome, but Rivers to wade, and
‘ Mountains to encounter; ravenous Beaſts
‘ of Prey,’——*To this* Cæſar *reply'd,*
‘ That Honour was the firſt Principle in
‘ Nature, that was to be obey'd; but
‘ as no Man would pretend to that, with-
‘ out all the Acts of Virtue, Compaſſion,
‘ Charity, Love, Juſtice and Reaſon, he
‘ found it not inconſiſtent with that, to
‘ take equal Care of their Wives and Chil-
‘ dren as they would of themſelves; and
‘ that he did not deſign, when he led
‘ them to Freedom, and glorious Liberty,
                              ‘ that

‘ that they fhould leave that better Part of
‘ themfelves to perifh by the Hand of the
‘ Tyrant's Whip : But if there were a
‘ Woman among them fo degenerate from
‘ Love and Virtue, to chufe Slavery be-
‘ fore the Purfuit of her Hufband, and
‘ with the Hazard of her Life, to fhare
‘ with him in his Fortunes; that fuch a one
‘ ought to be abandoned, and left as a Prey
‘ to the common Enemy.’

To which they all agreed—— and bow-
ed. After this, he fpoke of the impaffable Woods and Rivers; and convinced
them, the more Danger the more Glory.
He told them, that he had heard of one
Hannibal, a great Captain, had cut his Way
through Mountains of folid Rocks ; and
fhould a few Shrubs oppofe them, which
they could fire before 'em ? No, 'twas a
trifling Excufe to Men refolved to die, or
overcome. As for Bogs, they are with a
little Labour filled and harden'd ; and the
Rivers could be no Obftacle, fince they
fwam by Nature, at leaft by Cuftom, from
the firft Hour of their Birth : That when
the Children were weary, they muft carry
them by Turns, and the Woods and their
own Induftry would afford them Food. To
this they all affented with Joy.

Tufcan then demanded, what he would
do : He faid he would travel towards the
Sea, plant a new Colony, and defend it
by

by their Valour; and when they could find a Ship, either driven by Strefs of Weather, or guided by Providence that Way, they would feize it, and make it a Prize, till it had tranfported them to their own Countries: at leaft they fhould be made free in his Kingdom, and be efteem'd as his Fellow-Sufferers, and Men that had the Courage and the Bravery to attempt, at leaft, for Liberty; and if they died in the Attempt, it would be more brave, than to live in perpetual Slavery.

They bow'd and kifs'd his Feet at this Refolution, and with one Accord vow'd to follow him to Death; and that Night was appointed to begin their March. They made it known to their Wives, and directed them to tie their Hamocks about their Shoulders, and under their Arms, like a Scarf and to lead their Children that could go, and carry thofe that could not. The Wives, who pay an entire Obedience to their Husbands, obey'd, and ftay'd for 'em where they were appointed: The Men ftay'd but to furnifh themfelves with what defenfive Arms they could get; and all met at the Rendezvouz, where *Cæfar* made a new encouraging Speech to 'em and led 'em out.

But as they could not march far that Night, on *Monday* early, when the Overfeers went to call 'em all together, to go

to

to work, they were extremely furprized, to find not one upon the Place, but all fled with what Baggage they had. You may imagine this News was not only fuddenly fpread all over the Plantation, but foon reached the neighbouring ones ; and we had by Noon about 600 Men, they call the Militia of the Country, that came to affift us in the Purfuit of the Fugitives : But never did one fee fo comical an Army march forth to War. The Men of any Fafhion would not concern themfelves, tho' it were almoft the Common Caufe ; for fuch Revoltings are very ill Examples, and have very fatal Confequences often-times, in many Colonies : But they had a Refpect for *Cæfar*, and all Hands were againft the *Parhamites* (as they called thofe of *Parham-Plantation*) becaufe they did not in the firft Place love the Lord-Gover-nor ; and fecondly, they would have it, that *Cæfar* was ill ufed, and baffled with : and 'tis not impoffible but fome of the beft in the Country was of his Council in this Flight, and depriving us of all the Slaves ; fo that they of the better Sort would not meddle in the Matter. The Deputy-Gover-nor, of whom I have had no great Occafion to fpeak, and who was the moft fawning fair-tongu'd Fellow in the World, and one that pretended the moft Friendfhip to *Cæfar*, was now the only violent Man

againft

againſt him ; and though he had nothing, and ſo need fear nothing, yet talked and looked bigger than any Man. He was a Fellow, whoſe Character is not fit to be mentioned with the worſt of the Slaves : This Fellow would lead his Army forth to meet *Cæſar*, or rather to purſue him. Moſt of their Arms were of thoſe Sort of cruel Whips they call *Cat with nine Tails ;* ſome had ruſty uſeleſs Guns for Shew ; others old Basket Hilts, whoſe Blades had never ſeen the Light in this Age ; and others had long Staffs and Clubs. Mr. *Trefry* went along, rather to be a Mediator than a Conqueror in ſuch a Battle ; for he foreſaw and knew, if by fighting they put the *Negroes* into Deſpair, they were a ſort of ſullen Fellows, that would drown or kill themſelves before they would yield; and he advis'd that fair Means was beſt : But *Byam* was one that abounded in his own Wit, and would take his own Meaſures.

It was not hard to find theſe Fugitives ; for as they fled, they were forced to fire and cut the Woods before 'em : So that Night or Day they purſu'd 'em by the Light they made, and by the Path they had cleared. But as ſoon as *Cæſar* found he was purſu'd, he put himſelf in a Poſture of Defence, placing all the Women and Children in the Rear ; and himſelf, with *Tuſcan* by his Side, or next to him, all pro-
miſing

mifing to die or conquer.   Encouraged
thus, they never ftood to parley, but fell
on pell-mell upon the *Englifh*, and killed
fome, and wounded a great many ; they
having Recourfe to their Whips, as the
beft of their Weapons.   And as they ob-
ferved no Order, they perplexed the Enemy fo forely, with lafhing 'em in the
Eyes ; and the Women and Children feeing their Husbands fo treated, being of
fearful and cowardly Difpofitions, and
hearing the *Englifh* cry out, *Yield, and
Live! Yield, and be Pardon'd!* they all ran
in amongft their Husbands and Fathers,
and hung about them, crying out, *Yield !
Yield! and leave* Cæfar *to their Revenge* :
that by Degrees the Slaves abandon'd *Cæfar*,
and left him only *Tufcan* and his Heroick
Imoinda, who grown as big as fhe was,
did neverthelefs prefs near her Lord,
having a Bow and a Quiver full of poifoned
Arrows, which fhe managed with fuch
Dexterity, that fhe wounded feveral, and
fhot the Governor into the Shoulder ; of
which Wound he had liked to have died,
but that an *Indian* Woman, his Miftrefs,
fucked the Wound, and cleans'd it from
the Venom : But however, he ftir'd not
from the Place till he had parly'd with
Cæfar, who he found was refolved to die
fighting, and would not be taken ; no
more would *Tufcan* or *Imoinda*.   But he,

more

more thirſting after Revenge of another
Sort, than that of depriving him of Life,
now made uſe of all his Art of Talking and
Diſſembling, and beſought *Cæſar* to yield
himſelf upon Terms which he himſelf
ſhould propoſe, and ſhould be ſacredly aſ-
ſented to, and kept by him. He told
him, It was not that he any longer fear'd
him, or could believe the Force of two
Men, and a young Heroine, could over-
throw all them, and with all the Slaves
now on their Side alſo; but it was the vaſt
Eſteem he had for his Perſon, the Deſire
he had to ſerve ſo gallant a Man, and to hinder himſelf from the Reproach hereafter, of
having been the Occaſion of the Death of
a Prince, whoſe Valour and Magnanimity
deſerved the Empire of the World. He
proteſted to him, he looked upon his Action as gallant and brave, however tending
to the Prejudice of his Lord and Maſter,
who would by it have loſt ſo conſiderable
a Number of Slaves; that this Flight of
his ſhould be look'd on as a Heat of
Youth, and a Raſhneſs of a too forward
Courage, and an unconſider'd Impatience
of Liberty, and no more; and that he labour'd in vain to accompliſh that which
they would effectually perform as ſoon as
any Ship arrived that would touch on his
Coaſt: 'So that if you will be pleaſed
' *(continued he)* to ſurrender yourſelf, all
' ima-

' imaginable Refpect fhall be paid you ;
' and your Self, your Wife and Child, if
' it be born here, fhall depart free out of
' our Land.'   But *Cæfar* would hear of no
Compofition ; though *Byam* urged, if he
purfued and went on in his Defign, he
would inevitably perifh, either by great
Snakes, wild Beafts or Hunger ; and he
ought to have Regard to his Wife, whofe
Condition requir'd Eafe, and not the Fa-
tigues of tedious Travel, where fhe could
not be fecured from being devoured.   But
Cæfar told him, there was no Faith in the
White Men, or the Gods they ador'd ;
who inftructed them in Principles fo falfe,
that honeft Men could not live amongft
them ; though no People profefs'd fo
much, none perform'd fo little : That he
knew what he had to do when he dealt
with Men of Honour ; but with them a
Man ought to be eternally on his Guard,
and never to eat and drink with Chriftians,
without his Weapon of Defence in his
Hand ; and, for his own Security, never
to credit one Word they fpoke.   As for
the Rafhnefs and Inconfideratenefs of his
Action, he would confefs the Governor is
in the right ; and that he was afhamed of
what he had done, in endeavouring to
make thofe free, who were by Nature
Slaves, poor wretched Rogues, fit to be
ufed as Chriftians Tools ; Dogs, treache-

rous and cowardly, fit for such Masters; and they wanted only but to be whipped into the Knowledge of the Christian Gods, to be the vilest of all creeping Things; to learn to worship such Deities as had not Power to make them just, brave, or honest: In fine, after a thousand Things of this Nature, not fit here to be recited, he told *Byam,* He had rather die, than live upon the same Earth with such Dogs. But *Trefry* and *Byam* pleaded and protested together so much, that *Trefry* believing the Governor to mean what he said, and speaking very cordially himself, generously put himself into *Cæsar*'s Hands, and took him aside, and persuaded him, even with Tears, to live, by surrendring himself, and to name his Conditions. *Cæsar* was overcome by his Wit and Reasons, and in Consideration of *Imoinda;* and demanding what he desired, and that it should be ratify'd by their Hands in Writing, because he had perceived that was the common Way of Contract between Man and Man amongst the Whites; all this was performed, and *Tuscan*'s Pardon was put in, and they surrender'd to the Governor, who walked peaceably down into the Plantation with them, after giving Order to bury their Dead. *Cæsar* was very much toil'd with the Bustle of the Day, for he had fought like a Fury; and what

Mis-

Mifchief was done, he and *Tufcan* performed alone; and gave their Enemies a fatal Proof, that they durft do any Thing, and fear'd no mortal Force.

But they were no fooner arrived at the Place where all the Slaves receive their Punifhments of Whipping, but they laid Hands on *Cæfar* and *Tufcan*, faint with Heat and Toil; and furprizing them, bound them to two feveral Stakes, and whipped them in a moft deplorable and inhuman Manner, rending the very Flefh from their Bones, efpecially *Cæfar*, who was not perceived to make any Moan, or to alter his Face, only to roll his Eyes on the faithlefs Governor, and thofe he believed Guilty, with Fiercenefs and Indignation; and to complete his Rage, he faw every one of thofe Slaves who but a few Days before ador'd him as fomething more than Mortal, now had a Whip to give him fome Lafhes, while he ftrove not to break his Fetters; tho' if he had, it were impoffible: but he pronounced a Woe and Revenge from his Eyes, that darted Fire, which was at once both aweful and terrible to behold.

When they thought they were fufficiently revenged on him, they unty'd him, almoft fainting with Lofs of Blood, from a thoufand Wounds all over his Body; from which they had rent his Clothes, and led

him

him bleeding and naked as he was, and
loaded him all over with Irons; and then
rubb'd his Wounds, to complete their
Cruelty, with *Indian* Pepper, which had
like to have made him raving mad ; and,
in this Condition made him fo faft to the
Ground, that he could not ftir, if his Pains
and Wounds would have given him Leave.
They fpared *Imoinda*, and did not let her fee
this Barbarity committed towards her Lord,
but carried her down to *Parham*, and fhut
her up ; which was not in Kindnefs to her,
but for Fear fhe fhould die with the Sight,
or mifcarry, and then they fhould lofe a
young Slave, and perhaps the Mother.

You muft know, that when the News
was brought on *Monday* Morning, that
Cæfar had betaken himfelf to the Woods,
and carry'd with him all the *Negroes*, we
were poffefs'd with extreme Fear, which
no Perfuafions could diffipate, that he
would fecure himfelf till Night, and then
would come down and cut all our Throats.
This Apprehenfion made all the Females
of us fly down the River, to be fecured ;
and while we were away, they acted this
Cruelty ; for I fuppofe I had Authority
and Intereft enough there, had I fufpected
any fuch Thing, to have prevented it : but
we had not gone many Leagues, but the
News overtook us, that *Cæfar* was taken
and whipped like a common Slave. We
met

met on the River with Colonel *Martin*, a Man of great Gallantry, Wit, and Goodnefs, and whom I have celebrated in a Character of my new Comedy, by his own Name, in Memory of fo brave a Man: He was wife and eloquent, and, from the Finenefs of his Parts, bore a great Sway over the Hearts of all the Colony: He was a Friend to *Cæfar*, and refented this falfe Dealing with him very much. We carried him back to *Parham*, thinking to have made an Accommodation; when he came, the firft News we heard, was, That the Governor was dead of a Wound *Imoinda* had given him; but it was not fo well. But it feems, he would have the Pleafure of beholding the Revenge he took on *Cæfar*; and before the cruel Ceremony was finifhed, he dropt down; and then they perceived the Wound he had on his Shoulder was by a venom'd Arrow, which, as I faid, his *Indian* Miftrefs healed, by fucking the Wound.

We were no fooner arrived, but we went up to the Plantation to fee *Cæfar*; whom we found in a very miferable and unexpreffible Condition; and I have a thoufand Times admired how he lived in fo much tormenting Pain. We faid all Things to him, that Trouble, Pity and Good-Nature could fuggeft, protefting our Innocency of the Fact, and our Abhor-

I 3

rence

rence of such Cruelties ; making a thousand Professions and Services to him, and
begging as many Pardons for the Offenders, till we said so much, that he believed we had no Hand in his ill Treatment ; but told us, He could never pardon *Byam* ; as for *Trefry*, he confess'd he
saw his Grief and Sorrow for his Suffering, which he could not hinder, but was
like to have been beaten down by the
very Slaves, for speaking in his Defence :
But for *Byam*, who was their Leader,
their Head —— and should, by his Justice
and Honour, have been an Example to
'em —— for him, he wished to live to
take a dire Revenge of him ; and said,
*It had been well for him, if he had sacrificed
me, instead of giving me the contemptible
Whip.* He refused to talk much ; but begging us to give him our Hands, he took
them, and protested never to lift up his
to do us any Harm. He had a great Respect for Colonel *Martin,* and always took
his Counsel like that of a Parent ; and
assured him, he would obey him in any
Thing, but his Revenge on *Byam :* ‘ There-
‘ fore *(said he)* for his own Safety, let
‘ him speedily dispatch me ; for if I could
‘ dispatch myself, I would not, till that
‘ Justice were done to my injured Person,
‘ and the Contempt of a Soldier: No, I
‘ would not kill myself, even after a
‘ Whip-

' Whipping, but will be content to live
' with that Infamy, and be pointed at by
' every grinning Slave, till I have com-
' pleted my Revenge ; and then you fhall
' fee, that *Oroonoko* fcorns to live with the
' Indignity that was put on *Cæfar.*' All
we could do, could get no more Words
from him ; and we took Care to have him
put immediately into a healing Bath, to
rid him of his Pepper, and ordered a Chirurgeon to anoint him with healing Balm,
which he fuffer'd, and in fome Time he began to be able to walk and eat. We failed
not to vifit him every Day, and to that
End had him brought to an Apartment at
Parham.

The Governor had no fooner recover'd,
and had heard of the Menaces of *Cæfar,*
but he called his Council, who (not to difgrace them, or burlefque the Government
there) confifted of fuch notorious Villains as
Newgate never tranfported ; and, poffibly,
originally were fuch who underftood neither the Laws of God or Man, and had
no fort of Principles to make them worthy the Name of Men ; but at the very
Council-Table would contradict and fight
with one another, and fwear fo bloodily,
that 'twas terrible to hear and fee 'em.
(Some of 'em were afterwards hanged,
when the *Dutch* took Poffeffion of the
Place, others fent off in Chains.) But

I 4

calling

calling thefe fpecial Rulers of the Nation
together, and requiring their Counfel in
this weighty Affair, they all concluded,
that (damn 'em) it might be their own
Cafes ; and that *Cæfar* ought to be made
an Example to all the *Negroes*, to fright
'em from daring to threaten their Betters,
their Lords and Mafters ; and at this Rate
no Man was fafe from his own Slaves ; and
concluded, *nemine contradicente*, That *Cæfar* fhould be hanged.

Trefry then thought it Time to ufe his
Authority, and told *Byam*, his Command
did not extend to his Lord's Plantation ;
and that *Parham* was as much exempt from
the Law as *White-Hall* ; and that they
ought no more to touch the Servants of
the Lord —— (who there reprefented the
King's Perfon) than they could thofe
about the King himfelf ; and that *Parham*
was a Sanctuary ; and tho' his Lord were
abfent in Perfon, his Power was ftill in
being there, which he had entrufted with
him, as far as the Dominions of his particular Plantations reached, and all that belonged to it ; the reft of the Country, as
Byam was Lieutenant to his Lord, he
might exercife his Tyranny upon. *Trefry*
had others as powerful, or more, that
interefted themfelves in *Cæfar*'s Life, and
abfolutely faid, he fhould be defended.
So turning the Governor, and his wife

Coun-

Council, out of Doors, (for they fat at *Parham-Houfe)* we fet a Guard upon our Lodging-Place, and would admit none but thofe we called Friends to us and *Cæfar.*

The Governor having remain'd wounded at *Parham,* till his Recovery was completed, *Cæfar* did not know but he was ftill there, and indeed for the moft Part, his Time was fpent there: for he was one that loved to live at other Peoples Expence, and if he were a Day abfent, he was ten prefent there; and us'd to play, and walk, and hunt, and fifh with *Cæfar :* So that *Cæfar* did not at all doubt, if he once recover'd Strength, but he fhould find an Opportunity of being revenged on him; though, after fuch a Revenge, he could not hope to live: for if he efcaped the Fury of the *Englifh* Mobile, who perhaps would have been glad of the Occafion to have killed him, he was refolved not to furvive his Whipping; yet he had fome tender Hours, a repenting Softnefs, which he called his Fits of Cowardice, wherein he ftruggled with Love for the Victory of his Heart, which took Part with his charming *Imoinda* there; but for the moft Part, his Time was pafs'd in melancholy Thoughts, and black Defigns. He confider'd, if he fhould do this Deed, and die either in the Attempt, or after it, he left his lovely *Imoinda* a Prey, or at beft a Slave to the

I 5

en-

enraged Multitude; his great Heart could not endure that Thought: *Perhaps* (said he) *she may be first ravish'd by every Brute; expos'd first to their nasty Lusts, and then a shameful Death:* No, he could not live a Moment under that Apprehension, too insupportable to be borne. These were his Thoughts, and his silent Arguments with his Heart, as he told us afterwards: So that now resolving not only to kill *Byam*, but all those he thought had enraged him; pleasing his great Heart with the fancy'd Slaughter he should make over the whole Face of the Plantation; he first resolved on a Deed, (that however horrid it first appear'd to us all) when we had heard his Reasons, we thought it brave and just. Being able to walk, and, as he believed, fit for the Execution of his great Design, he begg'd *Trefry* to trust him into the Air, believing a Walk would do him good; which was granted him; and taking *Imoinda* with him, as he used to do in his more happy and calmer Days, he led her up into a Wood, where (after with a thousand Sighs, and long gazing silently on her Face, while Tears gush'd, in spite of him, from his Eyes) he told her his Design, first of killing her, and then his Enemies, and next himself, and the Impossibility of escaping, and therefore he told her the Necessity of dying. He found the heroick

roick Wife faster pleading for Death, than he was to propose it, when she found his fix'd Resolution; and, on her Knees, besought him not to leave her a Prey to his Enemies. He (grieved to Death) yet pleased at her noble Resolution, took her up, and embracing of her with all the Passion and Languishment of a dying Lover, drew. his Knife to kill this Treasure of his Soul, this Pleasure of his Eyes; while Tears trickled down his Cheeks, hers were smiling with Joy she should die by so noble a Hand, and be sent into her own Country (for that's their Notion of the next World) by him she so tenderly loved, and so truly ador'd in this: For Wives have a Respect for their Husbands equal to what any other People pay a Deity; and when a Man finds any Occasion to quit his Wife, if he love her, she dies by his Hand; if not, he sells her, or suffers some other to kill her. It being thus, you may believe the Deed was soon resolv'd on; and 'tis not to be doubted, but the parting, the eternal Leave-taking of two such Lovers, so greatly born, so sensible, so beautiful, so young, and so fond, must be very moving, as the Relation of it was to me afterwards.

All that Love could say in such Cases, being ended, and all the intermitting Irresolutions being adjusted, the lovely, young and ador'd Victim lays herself down be-

        fore

fore the Sacrificer ; while he, with a Hand
refolved, and a Heart-breaking within,
gave the fatal Stroke, firft cutting her
Throat, and then fevering her yet fmiling
Face from that delicate Body, pregnant as it
was with the Fruits of tendereft Love.   As
foon as he had done, he laid the Body decently on Leaves and Flowers, of which
he made a Bed, and conceal'd it under the
fame Cover-lid of Nature ; only her Face
he left yet bare to look on : But when he
found fhe was dead, and paft all Retrieve,
never more to blefs him with her Eyes,
and foft Language, his Grief fwell'd up to
Rage ; he tore, he rav'd, he roar'd like
fome Monfter of the Wood, calling on the
lov'd Name of *Imoinda.*   A thoufand
Times he turned the fatal Knife that did
the Deed toward his own Heart, with a
Refolution to go immediately after her ;
but dire Revenge, which was now a thoufand Times more fierce in his Soul than before, prevents him ; and he would cry out,
' No, fince I have facrific'd *Imoinda* to my
' Revenge, fhall I lofe that Glory which I
' have purchafed fo dear, as at the Price
' of the faireft, deareft, fofteft Creature
' that ever Nature made ? No, no !' Then
at her Name Grief would get the Afcendant of Rage, and he would lie down by
her Side, and water her Face with Showers
of Tears, which never were wont to fall

from

from thofe Eyes; and however bent he was on his intended Slaughter, he had not Power to ftir from the Sight of this dear Object, now more beloved, and more ador'd than ever.

He remained in this deplorable Condition for two Days, and never rofe from the Ground where he had made her fad Sacrifice; at laft rouzing from her Side, and accufing himfelf with living too long, now *Imoinda* was dead, and that the Deaths of thofe barbarous Enemies were deferred too long, he refolved now to finifh the great Work: but offering to rife, he found his Strength fo decay'd, that he reeled to and fro, like Boughs affailed by contrary Winds; fo that he was forced to lie down again, and try to fummon all his Courage to his Aid. He found his Brains turned round, and his Eyes were dizzy, and Objects appear'd not the fame to him they were wont to do; his Breath was fhort, and all his Limbs furpriz'd with a Faintnefs he had never felt before. He had not eat in two Days, which was one Occafion of his Feeblenefs, but Excefs of Grief was the greateft; yet ftill he hoped he fhould recover Vigour to act his Defign, and lay expecting it yet fix Days longer; ftill mourning over the dead Idol of his Heart, and ftriving every Day to rife, but could not.

In

In all this time you may believe we were in no little Affliction for *Cæsar* and his Wife; some were of Opinion he was escaped, never to return; others thought some Accident had happened to him: But however, we fail'd not to send out a hundred People several Ways, to search for him. A Party of about forty went that Way he took, among whom was *Tuscan,* who was perfectly reconciled to *Byam:* They had not gone very far into the Wood, but they smelt an unusual Smell, as of a dead Body; for Stinks must be very noisom, that can be distinguish'd among such a Quantity of natural Sweets, as every Inch of that Land produces: so that they concluded they should find him dead, or some body that was so; they pass'd on towards it, as loathsom as it was, and made such rustling among the Leaves that lie thick on the Ground, by continual falling, that *Cæsar* heard he was approach'd; and though he had, during the Space of these eight Days, endeavour'd to rise, but found he wanted Strength, yet looking up, and seeing his Pursuers, he rose, and reel'd to a neighbouring Tree, against which he fix'd his Back; and being within a dozen Yards of those that advanc'd and saw him, he call'd out to them, and bid them approach no nearer, if they would be safe. So that they stood still, and hardly believing

ing their Eyes, that would perfuade them that it was *Cæfar* that fpoke to them, fo much he was alter'd ; they afk'd him, what he had done with his Wife, for they fmelt a Stink that almoft ftruck them dead ? He pointing to the dead Body, fighing, cry'd, *Behold her there.* They put off the Flowers that cover'd her, with their Sticks, and found fhe was kill'd, and cry'd out, *Oh, Monfter ! thou haft murder'd thy Wife.* Then asking him, why he did fo cruel a Deed ? He reply'd, He had no Leifure to anfwer impertinent Queftions : ‘ You may go back *(continued he)* and tell ‘ the faithlefs Governor, he may thank ‘ Fortune that I am breathing my laft ; ‘ and that my Arm is too feeble to obey ‘ my Heart, in what it had defign'd him : But his Tongue faultering, and trembling, he could fcarce end what he was faying. The *Englifh* taking Advantage by his Weaknefs, cry'd, *Let us take him alive by all Means.* He heard 'em ; and, as if he had reviv'd from a Fainting, or a Dream, he cried out, ‘ No, Gentlemen, you are de- ‘ ceived ; you will find no more *Cæfars* to ‘ be whipt ; no more find a Faith in me : ‘ Feeble as you think me, I have Strength ‘ yet left to fecure me from a fecond In- ‘ dignity.’ They fwore all anew ; and he only fhook his Head, and beheld them with Scorn. Then they cry'd out, *Who*

will

will venture on this single Man? Will nobo-
dy?   They ſtood all ſilent, while *Cæſar* replied, *Fatal will be the Attempt of the firſt*
Adventurer, let him aſſure himſelf (and, at.
that Word, held up his Knife in a mena-
cing Poſture :) *Look ye, ye faithleſs Crew,*
ſaid he, *'tis not Life I ſeek, nor am I afraid*
of dying, (and at that Word, cut a Piece
of Fleſh from his own Throat, and threw
it at 'em) *yet ſtill I would live if I could,*
till I had perfected my Revenge : But, oh!
it cannot be ; I feel Life gliding from my
Eyes and Heart ; and if I make not haſte, I
ſhall fall a Victim to the ſhameful Whip. At
that, he rip'd up his own Belly, and took
his Bowels and pull'd 'em out, with what
Strength he could ; while ſome, on their
Knees imploring, beſought him to hold
his Hand.   But when they ſaw him totter-
ing, they cry'd out, *Will none venture on*
him ?   A bold *Engliſhman* cry'd, *Yes, if he*
were the Devil, (taking Courage when he
ſaw him almoſt dead) and ſwearing a horrid Oath for his farewel to the World, he
ruſh'd on him.   *Cæſar* with his arm'd
Hand, met him ſo fairly, as ſtuck him to
the Heart, and he Fell dead at his feet.
Tuſcan ſeeing that, cry'd out, *I love thee,*
O Cæſar ! *and therefore will not let thee die,*
if poſſible ; and running to him, took him
in his Arms ; but, at the ſame time, ward-
ing a Blow that *Cæſar* made at his Boſom,

fom, he receiv'd it quite through his Arm ;
and *Cæfar* having not Strength to pluck the
Knife forth, tho' he attempted it, *Tufcan*
neither pull'd it out himfelf, nor fuffer'd
it to be pull'd out, but came down with
it fticking in his Arm ; and the Reafon he
gave for it, was, becaufe the Air fhould
not get into the Wound.   They put their
Hands a-crofs, and carry'd *Cæfar* between
fix of 'em, fainting as he was, and they
thought dead, or juft dying ; and they
brought him to *Parham*, and laid him on a
Couch, and had the Chirurgeon immediately to him, who dreft his Wounds,
and fow'd up his Belly, and us'd Means to
bring him to Life, which they effected.
We ran all to fee him ; and, if before we
thought him fo beautiful a Sight, he was
now fo alter'd, that his Face was like a
Death's-Head black'd over, nothing but
Teeth and Eye-holes : For fome Days we
fuffer'd no Body to fpeak to him, but caufed Cordials to be poured down his Throat ;
which fuftained his Life, and in fix or
feven Days he recovered his Senfes : For,
you muft know, that Wounds are almoft
to a Miracle cur'd in the *Indies*; unlefs
Wounds in the Legs, which they rarely
ever cure.

When he was well enough to fpeak, we
talk'd to him, and ask'd him fome Queftions about his Wife, and the Reafons

why

why he kill'd her; and he then told us what I have related of that Refolution, and of his Parting, and he befought us we would let him die, and was extremely afflicted to think it was poffible he might live: He affur'd us, if we did not difpatch him, he would prove very fatal to a great many. We faid all we could to make' him live, and gave him new Affurances; but he begg'd we would not think fo poorly of him, or of his Love to *Imoinda,* to imagine we could flatter him to Life again: But the Chirurgeon affur'd him he could not live, and therefore he need not fear. We were all (but *Cæfar*) afflicted at this News, and the Sight was ghaftly: His Difcourfe was fad; and the earthy Smell about him fo ftrong, that I was perfuaded to leave the Place for fome time, (being my felf but fickly, and very apt to fall into Fits of dangerous Illnefs upon any extraordinary Melancholy.) The Servants, and *Trefry,* and the Chirurgeons, promis'd all to take what poffible Care they could of the Life of *Cæfar;* and I, taking Boat, went with other Company to Colonel *Martin's,* about three Days Journey down the River. But I was no fooner gone, than the Governor taking *Trefry,* about fome pretended earneft Bufinefs, a Day's Journey up the River, having communicated his Defign to one *Banifter,* a

wild

wild *Irish* Man, one of the Council, a Fellow of abſolute Barbarity, and fit to execute any Villany, but rich; he came up to *Parham*, and forcibly took *Cæſar*, and had him carried to the ſame Poſt where he was whipp'd; and cauſing him to be ty'd to it, and a great Fire made before him, he told him, he ſhould die like a Dog, as he was. *Cæſar* replied, This was the firſt Piece of Bravery that ever *Baniſter* did, and he never ſpoke Senſe till he pronounc'd that Word; and if he would keep it, he would declare, in the other World, that he was the only Man, of all the *Whites*, that ever he heard ſpeak Truth. And turning to the Men that had bound him, he ſaid, *My Friends, am I to die, or to be whipt?* And they cry'd, *Whipt! no, you ſhall not eſcape ſo well.* And then he reply'd, ſmiling, *A Bleſſing on thee*; and aſſured them they need not tie him, for he would ſtand fix'd like a Rock, and endure Death ſo as ſhould encourage them to die: *But if you whip me* (ſaid he) *be ſure you tie me faſt.*

He had learn'd to take Tobacco; and when he was aſſur'd he ſhould die, he deſir'd they would give him a Pipe in his Mouth, ready lighted; which they did: And the Executioner came, and firſt cut off his Members, and threw them into the Fire; after that, with an ill-favour'd Knife, they cut off his Ears and his Noſe,

and

and burn'd them; he ftill fmoak'd on, as if nothing had touch'd him; then they hack'd off one of his Arms, and ftill he bore up and held his Pipe; but at the cutting off the other Arm, his Head funk, and his Pipe dropt, and he gave up the Ghoft, without a Groan, or a Reproach. My Mother and Sifter were by him all the While, but not fuffer'd to fave him; fo rude and wild were the Rabble, and fo inhuman were the Juftices who ftood by to fee the Execution, who after paid dear enough for their Infolence. They cut *Cæfar* into Quarters, and fent them to feveral of the chief Plantations: One Quarter was fent to Colonel *Martin*; who refus'd it, and fwore, he had rather fee the Quarters of *Banifter*, and the Governor himfelf, than thofe of *Cæfar*, on his Plantations; and that he could govern his *Negroes*, without terrifying and grieving them with frightful Spectacles of a mangled King.

Thus died this great Man, worthy of a better Fate, and a more fublime Wit than mine to write his Praife: Yet, I hope, the Reputation of my Pen is confiderable enough to make his glorious Name to furvive to all Ages, with that of the brave, the beautiful and the conftant *Imoinda.*

T H E

J. Pine inv. et sculp. 1722.

THE

FAIR JILT:

OR, THE

AMOURS

OF

Prince *Tarquin* and *Miranda.*

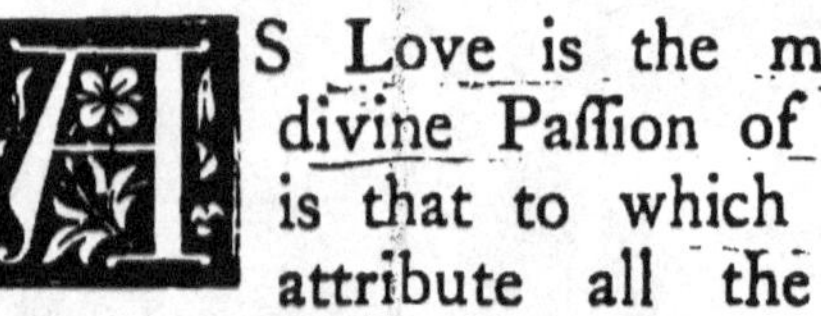

AS Love is the moſt noble and divine Paſſion of the Soul, ſo it is that to which we may juſtly attribute all the real Satisfactions of Life ; and without it Man is unfiniſh'd and unhappy.

There are a thouſand things to be ſaid of the Advantages this generous Paſſion brings to thoſe, whoſe Hearts are capable

of

of receiving its soft Impressions; for 'tis not every one that can be sensible of its tender Touches. How many Examples, from History and Observation, could I give of its wondrous Power; nay, even to a Degree of Transmigration! How many Idiots has it made wise! How many Fools eloquent! How many home-bred Squires accomplish'd! How many Cowards brave! And there is no sort of Species of Mankind on whom it cannot work some Change and Miracle, if it be a noble well-grounded Passion, except on the Fop in Fashion, the harden'd incorrigible Fop; so often wounded, but never reclaim'd: For still, by a dire Mistake, conducted by vast Opiniatrety, and a greater Portion of Self-love, than the rest of the Race of Man, he believes that Affectation in his Mein and Dress, that Mathematical Movement, that Formality in every Action, that a Face manag'd with Care, and soften'd into Ridicule, the languishing Turn, the Toss, and the Back-shake of the Periwig, is the direct Way to the Heart of the fine Person he adores; and instead of curing Love in his Soul, serves only to advance his Folly; and the more he is enamour'd, the more industriously he assumes (every Hour) the Coxcomb. These are Love's Play-things, a sort of Animals with whom he sports; and whom he never

wounds,

wounds, but when he is in good Humour,
and always fhoots laughing. 'Tis the
Diverfion of the little God, to fee what a
Fluttering and Buftle one of thefe Sparks,
new-wounded, makes ; to what fantaftick
Fooleries he has Recourfe : The Glafs is
every Moment call'd to counfel, the Valet
confulted and plagu'd for new Invention
of Drefs, the Footman and Scrutore perpetually employ'd ; *Billet-doux* and *Ma-*
drigals take up all his Mornings, till Play-
time in drefling, till Night in gazing ;
ftill, like a Sun-flower, turn'd towards
the Beams of the fair Eyes of his *Cælia*,
adjufting himfelf in the moft amorous
Pofture he can affume, his Hat under his
Arm, while the other Hand is put care-
lefly into his Bofom, as if laid upon his
panting Heart ; his Head a little bent to
one Side, fupported with a World of Cra-
vat-ftring, which he takes mighty Care
not to put into Diforder ; as one may guefs
by a never-failing and horrid Stiffnefs
in his Neck ; and if he had any Occafion
to look afide, his whole Body turns at
the fame Time, for Fear the Motion of
the Head alone fhould incommode the
Cravat or Periwig : And fometimes the
Glove is well manag'd, and the white
Hand difplay'd. Thus, with a thoufand
other little Motions and Formalities, all
in the common Place or Road of Foppery,
he

he takes infinite Pains to fhew himfelf to the
Pit and Boxes, a moft accomplifh'd Afs.
This is he, of all human Kind, on whom
Love can do no Miracles, and who can
no where, and upon no Occafion, quit one
Grain of his refin'd Foppery, unlefs in a
Duel, or a Battle, if ever his Stars fhould
be fo fevere and ill-manner'd, to reduce
him to the Neceffity of either: Fear then
would ruffle that fine Form he had fo long
preferv'd in niceft Order, with Grief con-
fidering, that an unlucky Chance-wound
in his Face, if fuch a dire Misfortune
fhould befal him, would fpoil the Sale of
it for ever.

Perhaps it will be urg'd, that fince
no Metamorphofis can be made in a Fop
by Love, you muft confider him one of
thofe that only talks of Love, and thinks
himfelf that happy Thing, a Lover; and
wanting fine Senfe enough for the real
Paffion, believes what he feels to be it.
There are in the Quiver of the God a
great many different Darts; fome that
wound for a Day, and others for a Year;
they are all fine, painted, glittering Darts,
and fhew as well as thofe made of the
nobleft Metal; but the Wounds they
make reach the Defire only, and are
cur'd by poffeffing, while the fhort-liv'd
Paffion betrays the Cheat. But 'tis that
refin'd and illuftrious Paffion of the Soul,

whofe

whofe Aim is Virtue, and whofe End is Honour, that has the Power of changing Nature, and is capable of performing all thofe heroick Things, of which Hiftory is full.

How far diftant Paffions may be from one another, I fhall be able to make appear in thefe following Rules. I'll prove to you the ftrong Effects of Love in fome unguarded and ungovern'd Hearts ; where it rages beyond the Infpirations of *a God all foft and gentle*, and reigns more like *a Fury from Hell.*

I do not pretend here to entertain you with a feign'd Story, or any Thing piec'd together with romantick Accidents ; but every Circumftance, to a Tittle, is Truth. To a great Part of the Main I myfelf was an Eye-witnefs ; and what I did not fee, I was confirm'd of by Actors in the Intrigue, Holy Men, of the Order of St. *Francis :* But for the Sake of fome of her Relations, I fhall give my *Fair Jilt* a feign'd Name, that of *Miranda ;* but my Hero muft retain his own, it being too illuftrious to be conceal'd.

You are to underftand, that in all the Catholick Countries, where Holy Orders are eftablifh'd, there are abundance of differing Kinds of Religious, both of Men and Women. Amongft the Women, there are thofe we call *Nuns,* that make folemn Vows of perpetual Chaftity; There are others who make but a fimple Vow, as for five or ten Years, or more or lefs; and that time expir'd, they may contract anew for longer time, or marry, or dif- pofe of themfelves as they fhall fee good; and thefe are ordinarily call'd *Galloping Nuns*: Of thefe there are feveral Orders; as *Canoneffes, Begines, Quefts, Swart-Sifters,* and *Jefuiteffes*, with feveral others I have forgot. Of thofe of the *Begines* was our *Fair Votrefs.*

Thefe Orders are taken up by the beft Perfons of the Town, young Maids of Fortune, who live together, not inclos'd, but in Palaces that will hold about fifteen hundred or two thoufand of thefe *Filles Devotes;* where they have a regulated Go- vernment, under a fort of *Abbefs*, or *Prio- refs*, or rather a *Governante*. They are oblig'd to a Method of Devotion, and are under a fort of Obedience. They wear a Habit much like our Widows of Quality in *England*, only without a *Bando;* and their Veil is of a thicker Crape than what we have here, thro' which one cannot fee the Face; for when they go abroad, they cover themfelves all over with it; but they put 'em up in the Churches, and lay 'em by in the Houfes. Every one of thefe have a Confeffor, who is to 'em a fort of Steward: For, you muft know,

they

they that go into thefe Places, have the
Management of their own Fortunes, and
what their Parents defign 'em. Without ·
the Advice of this Confeffor, they act nothing, nor admit of a Lover that he fhall
not approve; at leaft, this Method ought
to be taken, and is by almoft all of 'em;
tho' *Miranda* thought her Wit above it,
as her Spirit was.

But as thefe Women are, as I faid, of
the beft Quality, and live with the Reputation of being retir'd from the World
a little more than ordinary, and becaufe
there is a fort of Difficulty to approach
'em, they are the People the moft courted,
and liable to the greateft Temptations;
for as difficult as it feems to be, they receive Vifits from all the Men of the beft
Quality, efpecially Strangers. All the
Men of Wit and Converfation meet at
the Apartments of thefe fair *Filles Devotes*,
where all Manner of Gallantries are perform'd, while all the Study of thefe Maids
is to accomplifh themfelves for thefe noble Converfations. They receive Prefents,
Balls, Serenades, and Billets: All the
News, Wit, Verfes, Songs, Novels, Mufick, Gaming, and all fine Diverfion, is in
their Apartments, they themfelves being
of the beft Quality and Fortune. So that
to manage thefe Gallantries, there is
no fort of Female Arts they are not

K 2

practis'd

practis'd in, no Intrigue they are ignorant of, and no Management of which they are not capable.

Of this happy Number was the fair *Miranda*, whose Parents being dead, and a vast Estate divided between her self and a young Sister, (who liv'd with an unmarry'd old Uncle, whose Estate afterwards was all divided between 'em) she put her self into this uninclos'd religious House; but her Beauty, which had all the Charms that ever Nature gave, became the Envy of the whole *Sisterhood*. She was tall, and admirably shaped; she had a bright Hair, and Hazle-Eyes, all full of Love and Sweetness: No Art could make a Face so fair as hers by Nature, which every Feature adorn'd with a Grace that Imagination cannot reach: Every Look, every Motion charm'd, and her black Dress shew'd the Lustre of her Face and Neck. She had an Air, though gay as so much Youth could inspire, yet so modest, so nobly reserv'd, without Formality, or Stiffness, that one who look'd on her would have imagin'd her Soul the Twin-Angel of her Body; and both together made her appear something divine. To this she had a great deal of Wit, read much, and retain'd all that serv'd her Purpose. She sung delicately, and danc'd well, and play'd on the Lute to a Miracle.

cle. She fpoke feveral Languages naturally ; for being Co-heirefs to fo great a
Fortune. She was bred with the niceft
Care, in all the fineft Manners of Education ; and was now arriv'd to her Eigh-
teenth Year.

'Twere needlefs to tell you how great
a Noife the Fame of this young Beauty,
with fo confiderable a Fortune, made in
the World : I may fay, the World, rather than confine her Fame to the fcanty
Limits of a Town ; it reach'd to many
others : And there was not a Man of any
Quality that came to *Antwerp*, or pafs'd
thro' the City, but made it his Bufinefs
to fee the lovely *Miranda*, who was uni-
verfally ador'd : Her Youth and Beauty,
her Shape, and Majefty of Mein, and Air
of Greatnefs, charm'd all her Beholders ;
and thoufands of People were dying by
her Eyes, while fhe was vain enough to
glory in her Conquefts, and make it her
Bufinefs to wound. She lov'd nothing fo
much as to behold fighing Slaves at her
Feet, of the greateft Quality ; and treated them all with an Affability that gave
them Hope. Continual Mufick, as foon
as it was dark, and Songs of dying Lovers, were fung under her Windows ;
and fhe might well have made herfelf a
great Fortune (if fhe had not been fo already) by the rich Prefents that were

                hourly

hourly made her; and every body daily expected when she would make some one happy, by suffering her self to be conquer'd by Love and Honour, by the Assiduities and Vows of some one of her Adorers. But *Miranda* accepted their Presents, heard their Vows with Pleasure, and willingly admitted all their soft Addresses; but would not yield her Heart, or give away that lovely Person to the Possession of one, who could please itself with so many. She was naturally amorous, but extremely inconstant: She lov'd one for his Wit, another for his Face, and a third for his Mein; but above all, she admir'd Quality: Quality alone had the Power to attach her entirely; yet not to one Man, but that Virtue was still admir'd by her in all: Where-ever she found that, she lov'd, or at least acted the Lover with such Art, that (deceiving well) she fail'd not to compleat her Conquest; and yet she never durst trust her fickle Humour with Marriage. She knew the Strength of her own Heart, and that it could not suffer itself to be confin'd to one Man, and wisely avoided those Inquietudes, and that Uneasiness of Life she was sure to find in that married State, which would, against her Nature, oblige her to the Embraces of one, whose Humour was, to love all the Young and
the

the Gay. But Love, who had hitherto only play'd with her Heart, and given it nought but pleasing wanton Wounds, such as afforded only soft Joys, and not Pains, resolv'd, either out of Revenge to those Numbers she had abandon'd, and who had sigh'd so long in vain, or to try what Power he had upon so fickle a Heart, to send an Arrow dipp'd in the most tormenting Flames that rage in Hearts most sensible. He struck it home and deep, with all the Malice of an angry God.

There was a Church belonging to the *Cordeliers*, whither *Miranda* often repair'd to her Devotion; and being there one Day, accompany'd with a young Sister of the Order, after the Mass was ended, as 'tis the Custom, some one of the Fathers goes about the Church with a Box for Contribution, or Charity-money : It happen'd that Day, that a young Father, newly initiated, carried the Box about, which, in his Turn, he brought to *Miranda*. She had no sooner cast her Eyes on this young Friar, but her Face was overspread with Blushes of Surprize : She beheld him stedfastly, and saw in his Face all the Charms of Youth, Wit, and Beauty; he wanted no one Grace that could form him for Love, he appear'd all that is adorable to the Fair Sex, nor could the mis-shapen Habit hide from her the

K 4

lovely

lovely Shape it endeavour'd to cover, nor thofe delicate Hands that approach'd her too near with the Box. Befides the Beauty of his Face and Shape, he had an Air altogether great, in fpite of his profefs'd Poverty, it betray'd the Man of Quality; and that Thought weigh'd greatly with *Miranda.* But Love, who did not defign fhe fhould now feel any fort of thofe eafy Flames, with which fhe had heretofore burnt, made her foon lay all thofe Confiderations afide, which us'd to invite her to love, and now lov'd fhe knew not why.

She gaz'd upon him, while he bow'd before her, and waited for ·her Charity, till fhe perceiv'd the lovely Friar to blufh, and caft his Eyes to the Ground. This awaken'd her Shame, and fhe put her Hand into her Pocket, and was a good while in fearching for her Purfe, as if fhe thought of nothing lefs than what fhe was about; at laft fhe drew it out, and gave him a Piftole; but with fo much Deliberation and Leifure, as eafily betray'd the Satisfaction fhe took in looking on him; while the good Man, having receiv'd her Bounty, after a very low Obeyfance, proceeded to the reft; and *Miranda* cafting after him a Look all languifhing, as long as he remain'd in the Church, departed with a Sigh as foon as
fhe

she saw him go out, and returned to her Apartment without speaking one Word all the Way to the young *Fille Devote,* who attended her; so absolutely was her Soul employ'd with this young Holy Man. *Cornelia* (so was this Maid call'd who was with her) perceiving she was so silent, who us'd to be all Wit and good Humour, and observing her little Disorder at the Sight of the young Father, tho' she was far from imagining it to be Love, took an Occasion, when she was come home, to speak of him. 'Madam, *said she,* did you ' not observe that fine young *Cordelier,* ' who brought the Box?' At a Question that nam'd that Object of her Thoughts, *Miranda* blush'd; and she finding she did so, redoubled her Confusion, and she had scarce Courage enough to say,——*Yes, I did observe him:* And then, forcing herself to smile a little, continu'd, 'And I wonder'd ' to see so jolly a young Friar of an Or- ' der so severe and mortify'd.—Madam, ' *(reply'd* Cornelia) when you know his ' *Story,* you will not wonder.' *Miranda,* who was impatient to know all that con- cern'd her new Conqueror, obliged her to tell his Story; and *Cornelia* obey'd, and .proceeded.

K 5   *The*

The Story of Prince Henrick.

'YOU muſt know, Madam, that
' this young Holy Man is a Prince
' of *Germany*, of the Houſe of ——, whoſe
' Fate it was, to fall moſt paſſionately in
' Love with a fair young Lady, who lov'd
' him with an Ardour equal to what he
' vow'd her. Sure of her Heart, and
' wanting only the Approbation of her
' Parents, and his own, which her Quali-
' ty did not ſuffer him to deſpair of, he
' boaſted of his Happineſs to a young
' Prince, his elder Brother, a Youth amo-
' rous and fierce, impatient of Joys, and
' ſenſible of Beauty, taking Fire with all
' fair Eyes : He was his Father's Darling,
' and Delight of his fond Mother ; and, by
' an Aſcendant over both their Hearts,
' rul'd their Wills.

' This young Prince no ſooner ſaw, but
' lov'd the fair Miſtreſs of his Brother;
' and with an Authority of a Sovereign,
' rather than the Advice of a Friend,
' warn'd his Brother *Henrick* (this now
' young Friar) to approach no more this
' Lady, whom he had ſeen ; and ſeeing,
' lov'd.

' In vain the poor ſurpriz'd Prince
' pleads his Right of Love, his Exchange
' of

‘ of Vows, and Affurance of a Heart that
‘ could never be but for himfelf.   In vain
‘ he urges his Nearnefs of Blood, his
‘ Friendfhip, his Paffion, or his Life, which
‘ fo entirely depended on the Poffeffion
‘ of the charming Maid. All his Plead-
‘ ing ferv’d but to blow his Brother’s
‘ Flame ; and the more he implores, the
‘ more the other burns ; and while *Hen-*
‘ *rick* follows him, on his Knees, with
‘ humble Submiffions, the other flies from
‘ him in Rages of tranfported Love ; nor
‘ could his Tears, that purfu’d his Bro-
‘ ther’s Steps, move him to Pity : Hot-
‘ headed, vain-conceited of his Beauty,
‘ and greater Quality, as elder Brother,
‘ he doubts not of Succefs, and refolv’d to
‘ facrifice all to the Violence of his new-
‘ born Paffion.

‘ In fhort, he fpeaks of his Defign to his
‘ Mother, who promis’d him her Affif-
‘ tance ; and accordingly propofing it firft
‘ to the Prince her Hufband, urging the Lan-
‘ guifhment of her Son, fhe foon wrought
‘ fo on him, that a Match being concluded
‘ between the Parents of this young Beau-
‘ ty and *Henrick*’s Brother, the Hour was
‘ appointed before fhe knew of the Sacri-
‘ fice fhe was to be made. And while this
‘ was in Agitation, *Henrick* was fent on
‘ fome great Affairs, up into *Germany*, far
‘ out of the Way ; not but his boding

K 6

Heart

‘ Heart, with perpetual Sighs and Throbs,
‘ eternally foretold him his Fate.

‘ All the Letters he wrote were inter-
‘ cepted, as well as thofe fhe wrote to him.
‘ She finds herfelf every Day perplex’d
‘ with the Addreffes of the Prince fhe ha-
‘ ted ; he was ever fighing at her Feet. In
‘ vain were all her Reproaches, and all her
‘ Coldnefs, he was on the furer Side; for
‘ what he found Love would not do, Force
‘ of Parents would.

‘ She complains, in her Heart, of young
‘ *Henrick*, from whom fhe could never re-
‘ ceive one Letter ; and at laft could not
‘ forbear burfting into Tears, in fpite of
‘ all her Force, and feign’d Courage,
‘ when, on a Day, the Prince told her,
‘ that *Henrick* was withdrawn to give him
‘ Time to court her; to whom he faid,
‘ he confefs’d he had made fome Vows,
‘ but did repent of ’em, knowing himfelf
‘ too young to make ’em good : That it
‘ was for that Reafon he brought him firft
‘ to fee her ; and for that Reafon, that af-
‘ ter that, he never faw her more, nor fo
‘ much as took Leave of her ; when, in-
‘ deed, his Death lay upon the next Vifit,
‘ his Brother having fworn to murder him ;
‘ and to that End, put a Guard upon him,
‘ till he was fent into *Germany*.

‘ All this he utter’d with fo many paf-
‘ fionate Afleverations, Vows, and feem-

‘ ing

‘ ing Pity for her being fo inhumanly
‘ abandon’d, that fhe almoft gave Credit to
‘ all he had faid, and had much ado to
‘ keep herfelf within the Bounds of Mo-
‘ deration, and filent Grief. Her Heart
‘ was breaking, her Eyes languifh’d, and
‘ her Cheeks grew pale, and fhe had like
‘ to have fallen dead into the treacherous
‘ Arms of him that had reduc’d her to this
‘ Difcovery ; but fhe did what fhe could
‘ to affume her Courage, and to fhew as
‘ little Refentment as poffible for a Heart,
‘ like hers, opprefs’d with Love, and now
‘ abandon’d by the dear Subject of its Joys
‘ and Pains.

‘ But, Madam, not to tire you with this
‘ Adventure, the Day arriv’d wherein our
‘ ftill weeping Fair Unfortunate was to be
‘ facrific’d to the Capricioufnefs of Love ;
‘ and fhe was carry’d to Court by her Pa-
‘ rents, without knowing to what End,
‘ where fhe was even compell’d to marry
‘ the Prince.

‘ *Henrick*, who all this While knew no
‘ more of his Unhappinefs, than what his
‘ Fears fuggefted, returns, and paffes even
‘ to the Prefence of his Father, before he
‘ knew any Thing of his Fortune ; where
‘ he beheld his Miftrefs and his Brother,
‘ with his Father, in fuch a Familiarity,
‘ as he no longer doubted his Deftiny.
‘ ’Tis hard to judge, whether the Lady,

‘ or

‘ or himfelf, was moft furpriz’d ; fhe was
‘ all pale and unmoveable in her Chair,
‘ and *Henrick* fix’d like a Statue ; at laft
‘ Grief and Rage took Place of Amaze-
‘ ment, and he could not forbear crying
‘ out, *Ah, Traytor ! Is it thus you have*
‘ *treated a Friend and Brother? And you, O*
‘ *perjur’d Charmer! Is it thus you have re-*
‘ *warded all my Vows?* He could fay no
‘ more ; but reeling againft the Door, had
‘ fallen in a Swoon upon the Floor, had
‘ not his Page caught him in his Arms,
‘ who was entring with him. The good
‘ old Prince, the Father, who knew not
‘ what all this meant, was foon inform’d
‘ by the young weeping Princefs ; who, in
‘ relating the Story of her Amour with
‘ *Henrick*, told her Tale in fo moving a
‘ Manner, as brought Tears to the Old
‘ Man’s Eyes, and Rage to thofe of her
‘ Hufband ; he immediately grew jealous
‘ to the laft Degree : He finds himfelf in
‘ Poffeffion (’tis true) of the Beauty he
‘ ador’d, but the Beauty adoring another ;
‘ a Prince young and charming as the
‘ Light, foft, witty, and raging with an
‘ equal Paffion. He finds this dreaded Ri-
‘ val in the fame Houfe with him, with an
‘ Authority equal to his own ; and fan-
‘ cies, where two Hearts are fo entirely
‘ agreed, and have fo good an Underftand-
‘ ing, it would not be impoffible to find
‘ Op-

' Opportunities to satisfy and ease that
' mutual Flame, that burnt so equally in
' both ; he therefore resolved to send him
' out of the World, and to establish his
' own Repose by a Deed, wicked, cruel,
' and unnatural, to have him assassinated
' the first Opportunity he could find. This
' Resolution set him a little at Ease, and
' he strove to dissemble Kindness to *Hen-*
' *rick*, with all the Art he was capable of,
' suffering him to come often to the Apart-
' ment of the Princess, and to entertain
' her oftentimes with Discourse, when he
' was not near enough to hear what he
' spoke ; but still watching their Eyes, he
' found those of *Henrick* full of Tears,
' ready to flow, but restrain'd, looking all
' dying, and yet reproaching, while those
' of the Princess were ever bent to the
' Earth, and she as much as possible, shun-
' ning his Conversation. Yet this did not
' satisfy the jealous Husband ; 'twas not
' her Complaisance that could appease him ;
' he found her Heart was panting within,
' whenever *Henrick* approach'd her, and
' every Visit more and more confirmed his
' Death.

  ' The Father often found the Disorders
' of the Sons ; the Softness and Address
' of the one gave him as much Fear, as the
' angry Blushings, the fierce Looks, and
' broken Replies of the other, whenever
' he

‘ he beheld *Henrick* approach his Wife;
‘ fo that the Father, fearing fome ill Con-
‘ fequence of this, befought *Henrick* to
‘ withdraw to fome other Country, or
‘ travel into *Italy*, he being now of an
‘ Age that required a View of the World.
‘ He told his Father, That he would obey
‘ his Commands, tho’ he was certain, that
‘ Moment he was to be feparated from the
‘ Sight of the fair Princefs, his Sifter,
‘ would be the laft of his Life ; and, in
‘ fine, made fo pitiful a Story of his fuffer-
‘ ing Love, as almoft moved the old
‘ Prince to compaffionate him fo far, as to
‘ permit him to ftay ; but he faw inevi-
‘ vitable Danger in that, and therefore bid
‘ him prepare for his Journey.

‘ That which pafs’d between the Fa-
‘ ther and *Henrick*, being a Secret, none
‘ talked of his departing from Court ; fo
‘ that the Defign the Brother had went
‘ on ; and making a Hunting-Match one
‘ Day, where moft young People of Qua-
‘ lity were, he order’d fome whom he had
‘ hired to follow his Brother, fo as if he
‘ chanced to go out of the Way, to dif-
‘ patch him ; and accordingly, Fortune
‘ gave ’em an Opportunity ; for he lagg’d
‘ behind the Company, and turn’d afide
‘ into a pleafant Thicket of Hazles, where
‘ alighting, he walk’d on Foot in the moft
‘ pleafant Part of it, full of Thought,
‘ how

' how to divide his Soul between Love
' and Obedience. He was fenfible that he
' ought not to ftay; that he was but an
' Affliction to the young Princefs, whofe
' Honour could never permit her to eafe
' any Part of his Flame; nor was he fo
' vicious to entertain a Thought that fhould
' ftain her Virtue. He beheld her now as
' his Brother's Wife, and that fecured his
' Flame from all loofe Defires, if her na-
' tive Modefty had not been fufficient of
' itfelf to have done it, as well as that
' profound Refpect he paid her; and he
' confider'd, in obeying his Father, he left
' her at Eafe, and his Brother freed of a
' thoufand Fears; he went to feek a Cure,
' which if he could not find, at laft he
' could but die; and fo he muft, even at
' her Feet: However, that it was more
' noble to feek a Remedy for his Difeafe,
' than expect a certain Death by ftaying.
' After a thoufand Reflections on his hard
' Fate, and bemoaning himfelf, and bla-
' ming his cruel Stars, that had doom'd
' him to die fo young, after an Infinity of
' Sighs and Tears, Refolvings and Unre-
' folvings, he, on the fudden, was inter-
' rupted by the trampling of fome Horfes
' he heard, and their rufhing through the
' Boughs, and faw four Men make to-
' wards him: He had not time to mount,
' being walk'd fome Paces from his Horfe.
' One

‘ One of the Men advanced, and cry’d,
‘ *Prince, you muſt die——I do believe thee,*
‘ *(reply’d Henrick) but not by a Hand ſo*
‘ *baſe as thine:* And at the ſame Time
‘ drawing his Sword, run him into the
‘ Groin. When the Fellow found himſelf
‘ ſo wounded, he wheel’d off and cry’d,
‘ *Thou art a Prophet, and haſt rewarded my*
‘ *Treachery with Death.* The reſt came up,
‘ and one ſhot at the Prince, and ſhot him
‘ in the Shoulder; the other two haſtily
‘ laying hold (but too late) on the Hand
‘ of the Murderer, cry’d, *Hold, Traytor;*
‘ *we relent, and he ſhall not die.* He re-
‘ ply’d, *’Tis too late, he is ſhot; and ſee,*
‘ *he lies dead. Let us provide for ourſelves,*
‘ *and tell the Prince, we have done the*
‘ *Work; for you are as guilty as I am.*
‘ At that they all fled, and left the Prince
‘ lying under a Tree, weltering in his
‘ Blood.

‘ About the Evening, the Foreſter go-
‘ ing his Walks, ſaw the Horſe richly ca-
‘ pariſon’d, without a Rider, at the En-
‘ trance of the Wood; and going farther,
‘ to ſee if he could find its Owner, found
‘ there the Prince almoſt dead; he imme-
‘ diately mounts him on the Horſe, and
‘ himſelf behind, bore him up, and car-
‘ ry’d him to the Lodge; where he had
‘ only one old Man, his Father, well ſkil-
‘ led in Surgery, and a Boy. They put
‘ him

' him to Bed ; and the old Forester, with
' what Art he had, dress'd his Wound,
' and in the Morning sent for an abler
' Surgeon, to whom the Prince enjoin'd
' Secrecy, because he knew him.. The
' Man was faithful, and the Prince in
' Time was recover'd of his Wound ; and
' as soon as he was well, he come for *Flan-*
' *ders*, in the Habit of a Pilgrim, and after
' some Time took the Order of St. *Francis*,
' none knowing what became of him,
' till he was profess'd ; and then he wrote
' his own Story to the Prince his Father,
' to his Mistress, and his ungrateful Bro-
' ther. The young Princess did not long
' survive his Loss, she languished from the
' Moment of his Departure ; and he had
' this to confirm his devout Life, to know
' she dy'd for him.

' My Brother, Madam, was an Officer
' under the Prince his Father, and knew
' his Story perfectly well ; from whose
' Mouth I had it.'

What ! (reply'd *Miranda* then) *is Father*
Henrick *a Man of Quality? Yes, Madam,*
(said *Cornelia*) *and has changed his Name to*
Francisco. But *Miranda*, fearing to betray the Sentiments of her Heart, by asking any more Questions about him, turned
the Discourse ; and some Persons of Quality came in to visit her (for her Apartment was about six o'Clock, like the Pre-
sence-

fence-Chamber of a Queen, always filled
with the greateft People) : There meet all
the *Beaux Efprits*, and all the Beauties.
But it was vifible *Miranda* was not fo gay
as fhe ufed to be; but penfive, and an-
fwering *mal a propos* to all that was faid
to her. She was a thoufand times going
to fpeak, againft her Will, fomething of
the charming Friar, who was never from
her Thoughts; and fhe imagined, if he
could infpire Love in a coarfe, grey, ill-
made Habit, a fhorn Crown, a Hair-cord
about his Waift, bare-legg'd, in Sandals
inftead of Shoes; what muft he do, when
looking back on Time, fhe beholds him in
a Profpect of Glory, with all that Youth,
and illuftrious Beauty, fet off by the Advantage of Drefs and Equipage ? She
frames an Idea of him all gay and fplendid,
and looks on his prefent Habit as fome
Difguife proper for the Stealths of Love ;
fome feigned put-on Shape, with the more
Security to approach a Miftrefs, and make
himfelf happy ; and that the Robe laid by,
fhe has the Lover in his proper Beauty,
the fame he would have been, if any other
Habit (though ever fo rich) were put off:
In the Bed, the filent gloomy Night, and
the foft Embraces of her Arms, he lofes
all the Friar, and affumes all the Prince ;
and that aweful Reverence, due alone to his
Holy Habit, he exchanges for a thoufand
Dalliances,

Dalliances, for which his Youth was made ;
for Love, for tender Embraces, and all the
Happiness of Life. Some Moments she
fancies him a Lover, and that the fair Object that takes up all his Heart, has left no
Room for her there ; but that was a
Thought that did not long perplex her,
and which, almost as soon as born, she
turned to her Advantage. She beholds him
a Lover, and therefore finds he has a Heart
sensible and tender ; he had Youth to be
fir'd, as well as to inspire ; he was far from
the loved Object, and totally without
Hope ; and she reasonably consider'd,
that Flame would of itself soon die, that
had only Despair to feed on. She beheld
her own Charms ; and Experience, as well
as her Glass, told her, they never failed of
Conquest, especially where they designed
it : And she believed *Henrick* would be
glad, at least, to quench that Flame in
himself, by an Amour with her, which
was kindled by the young Princess of ——
his Sister.

These, and a thousand other Self-flat-
teries, all vain and indiscreet, took up her
waking Nights, and now more retired
Days ; while Love, to make her truly
wretched, suffered her to sooth herself
with fond Imaginations ; not so much as
permitting her Reason to plead one Moment to save her from undoing : She

would

would not suffer it to tell her, he had
taken Holy Orders, made sacred and
solemn Vows of everlasting Chastity, that
it was impossible he could marry her, or
lay before her any Argument that might
prevent her Ruin ; but Love, mad malicious Love, was always called to Counsel,
and, like easy Monarchs, she had no Ears,
but for Flatterers.

Well then, she is resolv'd to love, without considering to what End, and what
must be the Consequence of such an Amour.
She now miss'd no Day of being at that
little Church, where she had the Happinefs, or rather the Misfortune (so Love ordained) to see this Ravisher of her Heart
and Soul ; and every Day she took new
Fire from his lovely Eyes. Unawares,
unknown, and unwillingly, he gave her
Wounds, and the Difficulty of her Cure
made her rage the more : She burnt, she
languish'd, and died for the young Innocent, who knew not he was the Author of
so much Mischief.

Now she resolves a thousand Ways in
her tortur'd Mind, to let him know her
Anguish, and at last pitch'd upon that of
writing to him soft Billets, which she had
learn'd the Art of doing ; or if she had not,
she had now Fire enough to inspire her
with all that could charm and move.
These she deliver'd to a young Wench,
who

who waited on her, and whom she had entirely subdu'd to her Interest, to give to a certain Lay-Brother of the Order, who was a very simple harmless Wretch, and who served in the Kitchen, in the Nature of a Cook, in the Monastery of *Cordeliers.* She gave him Gold to secure his Faith and Service; and not knowing from whence they came (with so good Credentials) he undertook to deliver the Letters to Father *Francisco;* which Letters were all afterwards, as you shall hear, produced in open Court. These Letters failed not to come every Day; and the Sense of the first was, to tell him, that a very beautiful young Lady, of a great Fortune, was in love with him, without naming her; but it came as from a third Person, to let him know the Secret, that she desir'd he would let her know whether she might hope any Return from him; assuring him, he needed but only see the fair Languisher, to confess himself her Slave.

This Letter being deliver'd him, he read by himself, and was surpriz'd to receive Words of this Nature, being so great a Stranger in that Place; and could not imagine, or would not give himself the Trouble of guessing who this should be, because he never designed to make Returns.

The

The next Day, *Miranda*, finding no
Advantage from her Meſſenger of Love, in
the Evening ſends another (impatient of
Delay) confeſſing that ſhe who ſuffer'd the
Shame of writing and imploring, was the
Perſon herſelf who ador'd him. 'Twas
there her raging Love made her ſay all
Things that diſcover'd the Nature of its
Flame, and propoſe to flee with him to
any Part of the World, if he would quit
the Convent ; that ſhe had a Fortune conſiderable enough to make him happy ; and
that his Youth and Quality were not given him to ſo unprofitable an End as to
loſe themſelves in a Convent, where Poverty and Eaſe was all the Buſineſs. In
fine, ſhe leaves nothing unurg'd that might
debauch and invite him ; not forgetting to
ſend him her own Character of Beauty,
and left him to judge of her Wit and Spirit by her Writing, and her Love by the
Extremity of Paſſion ſhe profeſs'd. To all
which the lovely Friar made no Return, as
believing a gentle Capitulation or Exhor-
tation to her would but inflame her the
more, and give new Occaſions for her con-
tinuing to write. All her Reaſonings,
falſe and vicious, he deſpis'd, pity'd the
Error of her Love, and was Proof againſt
all ſhe could plead. Yet notwithſtanding
his Silence, which left her in Doubt, and
more tormented her, ſhe ceas'd not to
purſue

purſue him with her Letters, varying her Style ; ſometimes all wanton, looſe and raving ; ſometimes feigning a Virgin-Modeſty all over, accuſing her ſelf, blaming her Conduct, and ſighing her Deſtiny, as one compell'd to the ſhameful Diſcovery by the Auſterity of his Vow and Habit, aſking his Pity and Forgiveneſs; urging him in Charity to uſe his Fatherly Care to perſuade and reaſon with her wild Deſires, and by his Counſel drive the God from her Heart, whoſe Tyranny was worſe than that of a Fiend ; and he did not know what his pious Advice might do. But ſtill ſhe writes in vain, in vain ſhe varies her Style, by a Cunning, peculiar to a Maid poſſeſs'd with ſuch a ſort of Paſſion.

This cold Neglect was ſtill Oil to the burning Lamp, and ſhe tries yet more Arts, which for want of right Thinking were as fruitleſs. She has Recourſe to Preſents ; her Letters came loaded with Rings of great Price, and Jewels, which Fops of Quality had given her. Many of this Sort he receiv'd, before he knew where to return 'em, or how ; and on this Occaſion alone he ſent her a Letter, and reſtor'd her Trifles, as he call'd them : But his Habit having not made him forget his Quality and Education, he wrote to her with all the profound Reſpect imaginable ; believing by her Prefents, and the Liberality with which fhe parted with 'em, that fhe was of Quality. But the whole Letter, as he told me afterwards, was to perfuade her from the Honour fhe did him, by loving him; urging a thoufand Reafons, folid and pious, and affuring her, he had wholly devoted the reft of his Days to Heaven, and had no Need of thofe gay Trifles fhe had fent him, which were only fit to adorn Ladies fo fair as herfelf, and who had Bufinefs with this glittering World, which he difdain'd, and had for ever abandon'd. He fent her a thoufand Bleffings, and told her, fhe fhould be ever in his Prayers, tho' not in his Heart, as fhe defir'd : And abundance of Goodnefs more he exprefs'd, and Counfel he gave her, which had the fame Effect with his Silence; it made her love but the more, and the more impatient fhe grew. She now had a new Occafion to write, fhe now is charm'd with his Wit; this was the new Subject. She rallies his . Refolution, and endeavours to re-call him to the World, by all the Arguments that human Invention is capable of.

But when fhe had above four Months languifh'd thus in vain, not miffing one Day, wherein fhe went not to fee him, without difcovering herfelf to him ; fhe refolv'd, as her laft Effort, to fhew her Perfon, and fee what that, affifted by her

Tears,

Tears, and soft Words from her Mouth, could do, to prevail upon him.

It happen'd to be on the Eve of that Day when she was to receive the Sacrament, that she, covering herself with her Veil, came to *Vespers,* purposing to make Choice of the conquering Friar for her Confessor.

She approach'd him; and as she did so, she trembled with Love. At last she cry'd, *Father, my Confessor is gone for some Time from the Town, and I am oblig'd To-morrow to receive, and beg you will be pleas'd to take my Confession.*

He could not refuse her; and let her into the *Sacrifty,* where there is a Confession-Chair, in which he seated himself; and on one Side of him she kneel'd down, over-against a little Altar, where the Priests Robes lye, on which were plac'd some lighted Wax-Candles, that made the little Place very light and splendid, which shone full upon *Miranda.*

After the little Preparation usual in Confession, she turn'd up her Veil, and discover'd to his View the most wondrous Object of Beauty he had ever seen, dress'd in all the Glory of a young Bride; her Hair and Stomacher full of Diamonds, that gave a Lustre all dazling to her brighter Face and Eyes. He was surpriz'd at her amazing Beauty, and question'd

whe-

whether he faw a Woman, or an Angel at
his Feet. Her Hands, which were elevated,
as if in Prayer, feem'd to be form'd of po-
lifh'd Alabafter ; and he confefs'd, he had
never feen any Thing in Nature fo perfect,
and fo admirable.

He had fome Pain to compofe himfelf
to hear her Confeffion, and was oblig'd to
turn away his Eyes, that his Mind might
not be perplex'd with an Object fo diverting ; when *Miranda*, opening the fineft
Mouth in the World, and difcovering new
Charms, began her Confeffion.

' Holy Father *(faid fhe)* amongft the
' Number of my vile Offences, that which
' afflicts me to the greateft Degree, is, that
' I am in love : Not *(continued fhe)* that I
' believe fimple and virtuous Love a Sin,
' when 'tis plac'd on an Object proper and
' fuitable ; but, my dear Father, *(faid fhe,*
' *and wept)* I love with a Violence which
' cannot be contain'd within the Bounds
' of Reafon, Moderation, or Virtue. I
' love a Man whom I cannot poffefs with-
' out a Crime, and a Man who cannot
' make me happy without being perjur'd.
' Is he marry'd ? *(reply'd the Father.)* No ;
' *(anfwer'd* Miranda.) Are you fo ? *(con-*
' *tinued he.)* Neither, *(faid fhe.)* Is he
' too near ally'd to you ? *(faid* Francifco :)
' a Brother, or Relation ? Neither of
' thefe, *(faid fhe.)* He is unenjoy'd, un-
                              ' promis'd ;

' promis'd ; and fo am I : Nothing oppo-
' fes our Happinefs, or makes my Love a
' Vice, but you——'Tis you deny me
' Life : 'Tis you that forbid my Flame :
' 'Tis you will have me die, and feek my
' Remedy in my Grave; when I complain
' of Tortures, Wounds, and Flames. O
' cruel Charmer ! 'tis for you I languifh ;
' and here, at your Feet, implore that Pity,
' which all my Addreffes have fail'd of pro-
' curing me.——

With that, perceiving he was about to
rife from his Seat, fhe held him by his Habit, and vow'd fhe would in that Pofture
follow him, where-ever he flew from her.
She elevated her Voice fo loud, he was
afraid fhe might be heard, and therefore
fuffer'd her to force him into his Chair
again ; where being feated, he began, in
the moft paffionate Terms imaginable, to
diffuade her ; but finding fhe the more
perfifted in Eagernefs of Paffion, he us'd
all the tender Affurance that he could
force from himfelf, that he would have
for her all the Refpect, Efteem and Friendfhip that he was capable of paying ; that
he had a real Compaffion for her : and at
laft fhe prevail'd fo far with him, by her
Sighs and Tears, as to own he had a Ten-
dernefs for her, and that he could not behold fo many Charms, without being fenfibly touch'd by 'em, and finding all thofe

L 3

Effects,

Effects, that a Maid fo fair and young caufes in the Souls of Men of Youth and Senfe: But that, as he was affured, he could never be fo happy to marry her, and as certain he could not grant any Thing but honourable Paffion, he humbly befought her not to expect more from him than fuch. And then began to tell her how fhort Life was, and tranfitory its Joys; how foon fhe would grow weary of Vice, and how often change to find real Repofe in it, but never arrive to it. He made an End, by new Affurance of his eternal Friendfhip, but utterly forbad her to hope.

Behold her now deny'd, refus'd and defeated, with all her pleading Youth, Beauty, Tears, and Knees, imploring, as fhe lay, holding faft his *Scapular*, and embracing his Feet. What fhall fhe do? She fwells with Pride, Love, Indignation and Defire; her burning Heart is burfting with Defpair, her Eyes grow fierce, and from Grief fhe rifes to a Storm; and in her Agony of Paffion, with Looks all difdainful, haughty, and full of Rage, fhe began to revile him, as the pooreft of Animals; tells him his Soul was dwindled to the Meannefs of his Habit, and his Vows of Poverty were fuited to his degenerate Mind. ' And ' *(faid fhe)* fince all my nobler Ways have ' fail'd me; and that, for a little Hypo-
' critical

‘ critical Devotion, you refolve to lofe the
‘ greateft Bleffings of Life, and to facri-
‘ fice me to your Religious Pride and Va-
‘ nity, I will either force you to abandon
‘ that dull Diffimulation, or you fhall die,
‘ to prove your Sanctity real.   Therefore
‘ anfwer me immediately, anfwer my
‘ Flame, my raging Fire, which your Eyes
‘ have kindled ; or here, in this very Mo-
‘ ment, I will ruin thee ; and make no
‘ Scruple of revenging the Pains I fuffer,
‘ by that which fhall take away your Life
‘ and Honour.’

The trembling young Man, who, all
this While, with extreme Anguifh of Mind,
and Fear of the dire Refult, had liften'd to
her Ravings, full of Dread, demanded
what fhe would have him do ?   When fhe
reply'd——“ Do that which thy Youth
‘ and Beauty were ordain'd to do :——
‘ this Place is private, a facred Silence
‘ reigns here, and no one dares to pry in-
‘ to the Secrets of this Holy Place : We
‘ are as fecure from Fears of Interruption,
‘ as in Defarts uninhabited, or Caves for-
‘ faken by wild Beafts.   The Tapers too
‘ fhall veil their Lights, and only that
‘ glimmering Lamp fhall be Witnefs of our
‘ dear Stealths of Love——Come to my
‘ Arms, my trembling, longing Arms ;
‘ and curfe the Folly of thy Bigotry, that
L 4   ‘ has

' has made thee fo long lofe a Bleffing, for
' which fo many Princes figh in vain.'

At thefe Words fhe rofe from his Feet,
and fnatching him in her Arms, he could
not defend himfelf from receiving a thoufand Kiffes from the lovely Mouth of the
charming Wanton ; after which, fhe ran
herfelf, and in an Inftant put out the Candles.   But he cry'd to her, ' In vain, O too
' indifcreet Fair One, in vain you put out
' the Light ; for Heaven ftill has Eyes,
' and will look down upon my broken
' Vows.   I own your Power, I own I
' have all the Senfe in the World of your
' charming Touches ; I am frail Flefh and
' Blood, but —— yet —— yet I can re-
' fift ; and I prefer my Vows to all your
' powerful Temptations. —— I will be
' deaf and blind, and guard my Heart
' with Walls of Ice, and make you know,
' that when the Flames of true Devotion
' are kindled in a Heart, it puts out all
' other Fires ; which are as ineffectual,
' as Candles lighted in the Face of the
' Sun. —— Go, vain Wanton, and re-
' pent, and mortify that Blood which has
' fo fhamefully betray'd thee, and which
' will one Day ruin both thy Soul and
' Body.——

At thefe Words *Miranda*, more enrag'd,
the nearer fhe imagin'd her felf to Happinefs, made no Reply ; but throwing her
felf,

felf, in that Inftant, into the Confefling-
Chair, and violently pulling the young
Friar into her Lap, fhe elevated her Voice
to fuch a Degree, in crying out, *Help,
Help! A Rape! Help, Help!* that fhe was
heard all over the Church, which was full
of People at the Evening's Devotion;
who flock'd about the Door of the *Sacrifty,*
which was fhut with a Spring-Lock on
the Infide, but they durft not open the
Door.

'Tis eafily to be imagin'd, in what Condition our young Friar was, at this laft
devilifh Stratagem of his wicked Miftrefs.
He ftrove to break from thofe Arms that
held him fo faft; and his Buftling to get
away, and her's to retain him, diforder'd
her Hair and Habit to fuch a Degree, as
gave the more Credit to her falfe Accu-
fation.

The Fathers had a Door on the other
Side, by which they ufually enter'd, to
drefs in this little Room; and at the
Report that was in an Inftant made 'em,
they hafted thither, and found *Miranda*
and the good Father very indecently
ftruggling; which they mif-interpreted,
as *Miranda* defir'd; who, all in Tears,
immediately threw her felf at the Feet
of the Provincial, who was one of thofe
that enter'd; and cry'd, ' O holy Fa-
L 5 ' ther

‘ ther! revenge an innocent Maid, un-
‘ done and loft to Fame and Honour,
‘ by that vile Monfter, born of Goats,
‘ nurs’d by Tygers, and bred up on fa-
‘ vage Mountains, where Humanity and
‘ Religion are Strangers.   For, O holy
‘ Father, could it have enter’d into the
‘ Heart of Man, to have done fo barba-
‘ rous and horrid a Deed, as to attempt
‘ the   Virgin-Honour of an unfpotted
‘ Maid, and one of my Degree, even in
‘ the Moment of my Confeffion, in that
‘ holy Time, when I was proftrate be-
‘ fore him and Heaven, confeffing thofe
‘ Sins that prefs’d my tender Confcience ;
‘ even then to load my Soul with the
‘ blackeft of Infamies, to add to my
‘ Number a Weight that muft fink me
‘ to Hell?   Alas! under the Security of
‘ his innocent Looks, his holy Habit,
‘ and his aweful Function, I was led into
‘ this Room to make my Confeffion ;
‘ where, he locking the Door, I had no
‘ fooner began, but he gazing on me,
‘ took Fire at my fatal Beauty ; and
‘ ftarting up, put out the Candles and
‘ caught me in his Arms ; and raifing me
‘ from the Pavement, fet me in the Con-
‘ feffion Chair ; and then —— Oh, fpare
‘ me the reft.’

With

With that a Shower of Tears burſt from her fair diſſembling Eyes, and Sobs ſo naturally acted, and ſo well manag'd, as left no Doubt upon the good Men, but all ſhe had ſpoken was Truth.

'——— At firſt, *(proceeded ſhe)* I was
' unwilling to bring ſo great a Scandal
' on his Order, as to cry out; but ſtrug-
' gled as long as I had Breath; pleaded
' the Heinouſneſs of the Crime, urging
' my Quality, and the Danger of the At-
' tempt. But he, deaf as the Winds,
' and ruffling as a Storm, purſu'd his
' wild Deſign with ſo much Force and
' Inſolence, as I at laſt, unable to reſiſt,
' was wholly vanquiſh'd, robb'd of my
' native Purity. With what Life and
' Breath I had, I call'd for Aſſiſtance, both
' from Men and Heaven; but oh, alas!
' your Succours came too late:——You
' find me here a wretched, undone, and
' raviſh'd Maid. Revenge me, Fathers;
' revenge me on the perfidious Hypo-
' crite, or elſe give me a Death that may
' ſecure your Cruelty and Injuſtice from
' ever being proclaim'd over the World;
' or my Tongue will be eternally re-
' proaching you, and curſing the wicked
' Author of my Infamy.'

She ended as ſhe began, with a thouſand Sighs and Tears; and received

L 6

from

from the Provincial all Assurances of Revenge.

The innocent betray'd Victim, all the while she was speaking, heard her with an Astonishment that may easily be imagined; yet shew'd no extravagant Signs of it, as those would do, who feign it, to be thought innocent; but being really so, he bore with an humble, modest, and blushing Countenance, all her Accusations; which silent Shame they mistook for evident Signs of his Guilt.

When the Provincial demanded, with an unwonted Severity in his Eyes and Voice, what he could answer for himself? calling him Profaner of his Sacred Vows, and Infamy to the Holy Order; the injur'd, but innocently accus'd, only reply'd: ‘ May Heaven forgive that bad ‘ Woman, and bring her to Repentance! ‘ For his Part, he was not so much in Love ‘ with Life, as to use many Arguments ‘ to justify his Innocence; unless it were ‘ to free that Order from a Scandal, of ‘ which he had the Honour to be profess'd. ‘ But as for himself, Life or Death were ‘ Things indifferent to him, who heartily ‘ despis'd the World.’

He said no more, and suffer'd himself to be led before the Magistrate; who committed him to Prison, upon the Accusation

cusation

cufation of this implacable Beauty; who, with fo much feign'd Sorrow, profecuted the Matter, even to his Tryal and Condemnation; where he refus'd to make any great Defence for himfelf. But being daily vifited by all the Religious, both of his own and other Orders, they oblig'd him (fome of 'em knowing the Aufterity of his Life, others his Caufe of Griefs that firft brought him into Orders, and others pretending a nearer Knowledge, even of his Soul it felf) to ftand upon his Juftification, and difcover what he knew of that wicked Woman; whofe Life had not been fo exemplary for Virtue, not to have given the World a thoufand Sufpicions of her Lewdnefs and Proftitutions.

The daily Importunities of thefe Fathers made him produce her Letters: But as he had all the Gown-men on his Side, fhe had all the Hats and Feathers on her's; all the Men of Quality taking her Part, and all the Church-men his. They heard his daily Proteftations and Vows, but not a Word of what paffed at Confeffion was yet difcover'd: He held that as a Secret facred on his Part; and what was faid in Nature of a Confeffion, was not to be revealed, though his Life depended on the Difcovery. But as to the

the Letters, they were forc'd from him, and expos'd; however, Matters were carry'd with so high a Hand against him, that they serv'd for no Proof at all of his Innocence, and he was at last condemn'd to be burn'd at the Market-Place.

After his Sentence was pass'd, the whole Body of Priests made their Ad-dresses to the Marquis *Castel Roderigo,* the then Governor of *Flanders,* for a Reprieve; which, after much ado, was granted him for some Weeks, but with an absolute Denial of Pardon: So pre-vailing were the young Cavaliers of his Court, who were all Adorers of this Fair Jilt.

About this time, while the poor inno-cent young *Henrick* was thus languishing in Prison, in a dark and dismal Dungeon, and *Miranda,* cured of her Love, was triumphing in her Revenge, expecting and daily giving new Conquests; and who, by this time, had re-assum'd all her wonted Gaiety; there was a great Noise about the Town, that a Prince of mighty Name, and fam'd for all the Excellencies of his Sex, was arriv'd; a Prince young, and gloriously attended, call'd Prince *Tarquin.*

We

We had often heard of this great
Man, and that he was making his Travels in *France* and *Germany:* And we
had alſo heard, that ſome Years before,
he being about Eighteen Years of Age,
in the Time when our King *Charles,* of
bleſſed Memory, was in *Bruſſels,* in the
laſt Year of his Baniſhment, that all on
a ſudden, this young Man roſe up upon
'em like the Sun, all glorious and dazling,
demanding Place of all the Princes in
that Court. And when his Pretence was
demanded, he own'd himſelf Prince *Tarquin,* of the Race of the laſt Kings of
Rome, made good his Title, and took his
Place accordingly. After that he travell'd for about ſix Years up and down the
World, and then arriv'd at *Antwerp,*
about the Time of my being ſent thither
by King *Charles.*

Perhaps there could be nothing ſeen ſo
magnificent as this Prince: He was, as
I ſaid, extremely handſome, from Head
to Foot exactly form'd, and he wanted
nothing that might adorn that native
Beauty to the beſt Advantage. His Parts
were ſuitable to the reſt: He had an Accompliſhment fit for a Prince, an Air
haughty, but a Carriage affable, eaſy in
Converſation, and very entertaining, liberal and good-natur'd, brave and inoffenſive.

five. I have feen him pafs the Streets with twelve Footmen, and four Pages; the Pages all in green Velvet Coats lac'd with Gold, and white Velvet Tunicks; the Men in Cloth, richly lac'd with Gold; his Coaches, and all other Officers, fuitable to a great Man.

He was all the Difcourfe ·of the Town; fome laughing at his Title, others reverencing it: Some cry'd, that he was an Impoftor; others, that he had made his Title as plain, as if *Tarquin* had reign'd but a Year ago. Some made Friendfhips with him, others would have nothing to fay to him: But all wonder'd where his Revenue was, that fupported this Grandeur; and believ'd, tho' he could make his Defcent from the *Roman* Kings very well out, that he could not lay fo good a Claim to the *Roman* Land. Thus every body meddled with what they had nothing to do; and, as in other Places, thought themfelves on the furer Side, if, in thefe doubtful Cafes, they imagin'd the worft.

But the Men might be of what Opinion they pleas'd concerning him; the Ladies were all agreed that he was a Prince, and a young handfome Prince, and a Prince not to be refifted: He had all their Wifhes, all their Eyes, and all
their

their Hearts. They now dreſs'd only for him ; and what Church he grac'd, was ſure, that Day, to have the Beauties, and all that thought themſelves ſo.

You may believe, our amorous *Miranda* was not the leaſt Conqueſt he made. She no ſooner heard of him, which was as ſoon as he arriv'd, but ſhe fell in Love with his very Name. *Jeſu!* —— A young King of *Rome!* Oh, it was ſo novel, that ſhe doated on the Title ; and had not car'd whether the reſt had been Man or Monkey almoſt : She was reſolved to be the *Lucretia* that this young *Tarquin* ſhould raviſh.

To this End, ſhe was no ſooner up the next Day, but ſhe ſent him a *Billet Doux*, aſſuring him how much ſhe admired his Fame ; and that being a Stranger in the Town, ſhe begged the Honour of introducing him to all the *Belle* Converſations, *&c.* which he took for the Invitation of ſome Coquet, who had Intereſt in fair Ladies ; and civilly return'd her an Anſwer, that he would wait on her. She had him that Day watched to Church ; and impatient to ſee what ſhe heard ſo many People flock to ſee, ſhe went alſo to the ſame Church ; thoſe ſanctified Abodes being too often profaned by ſuch Devotees, whoſe Buſineſs is to ogle and enſnare.

But

But what a Noife and Humming was heard all over the Church, when *Tarquin* enter'd ! His Grace, his Mein, his Fafhion, his Beauty, his Drefs, and his Equipage, furpriz'd all that were prefent: And by the good Management and Care of *Miranda*, fhe got to kneel at the Side of the Altar, juft over againft the Prince, fo that, if he would, he could not avoid looking full upon her. She had turned up her Veil, and all her Face and Shape appear'd fuch, and fo inchanting, as I have defcribed; and her Beauty heighten'd with Blufhes, and her Eyes full of Spirit and Fire, with Joy, to find the young *Roman* Monarch fo charming, fhe appear'd like fomething more than mortal, and compelled his Eyes to a fixed gazing on her Face; She never glanc'd that Way, but fhe met them ; and then would feign fo modeft a Shame, and caft her Eyes downwards with fuch inviting Art, that he was wholly ravifh'd and charmed, and fhe over-joy'd to find he was fo.

The Ceremony being ended, he fent a Page to follow that Lady Home, himfelf purfuing her to the Door of the Church, where he took fome holy Water, and threw upon her, and made her a profound Reverence. She forc'd an innocent

nocent Look, and a modeft Gratitude in her Face, and bow'd, and pafs'd forward, half affured of her Conqueft ; leaving her, to go home to his Lodging, and impatiently wait the Return of his Page. And all the Ladies who faw this firft Beginning between the Prince and *Miranda*, began to curfe and envy her Charms, who had deprived them of half their Hopes.

After this, I need not tell you, he made *Miranda* a Vifit ; and from that Day never left her Apartment, but when he went home at Nights, or unlefs he had Bufinefs ; fo entirely was he conquer'd by this Fair One. But the Bifhop, and feveral Men of Quality, in Orders, that profefs'd Friendfhip to him, advifed him from her Company ; and fpoke feveral Things to him, that might (if Love had not made him blind) have reclaimed him from the Purfuit of his Ruin. But whatever they trufted him with, fhe had the Art to wind her felf about his Heart, and make him unravel all his Secrets ; and then knew as well, by feign'd Sighs and Tears, to make him difbelieve all ; fo that he had no Faith but for her ; and was wholly inchanted and bewitch'd by her. At laft, in fpite of all that would have oppofed it, he marry'd this
famous

famous Woman, poffefs'd by fo many great Men and Strangers before, while all the World was pitying his Shame and Misfortunes.

Being marry'd, they took a great Houfe; and as fhe was indeed a great Fortune, and now a great Princefs, there was nothing wanting that was agreeable to their Quality; all was fplendid and magnificent. But all this would not acquire them the World's Efteem; they had an Abhorrence for her former Life, and defpifed her; and for his efpoufing a Woman fo infamous, they defpifed him. So that though they admir'd, and gazed upon their Equipage, and glorious Drefs, they forefaw the Ruin that attended it, and paid her Quality little Refpect.

She was no fooner married, but her Uncle died; and dividing his Fortune between *Miranda* and her Sifter, leaves the young Heirefs, and all her Fortune, entirely in the Hands of the Princefs.

We will call this Sifter *Alcidiana*; fhe was about fourteen Years of Age, and now had chofen her Brother, the Prince, for her Guardian. If *Alcidiana* were not altogether fo great a Beauty as her Sifter, fhe had Charms fufficient to procure her a great many Lovers, though her Fortune had not been fo confiderable as it was;

but

but with that Addition, you may believe, she wanted no Courtships from those of the best Quality; tho' every body deplor'd her being under the Tutorage of a Lady so expert in all the Vices of her Sex, and so cunning a Manager of Sin, as was the Princess; who, on her Part, failed not, by all the Caresses, and obliging Endearments, to engage the Mind of this young Maid, and to subdue her wholly to her Government. All her Senses were eternally regaled with the most bewitching Pleasures they were capable of: She saw nothing but Glory and Magnificence, heard nothing but Musick of the sweetest Sounds; the richest Perfumes employ'd her Smelling; and all she eat and touch'd was delicate and inviting; and being too young to consider how this State and Grandeur was to be continu'd, little imagined her vast Fortune was every Day diminishing, towards its needless Support.

When the Princess went to Church, she had her Gentleman bare before her, carrying a great Velvet Cushion, with great Golden Taffels, for her to kneel on, and her Train borne up a most prodigious Length, led by a Gentleman Usher, bare; follow'd by innumerable Footmen, Pages, and Women. And in this State she

fhe would walk in the Streets, as in thofe
Countries it is the Fafhion for the great
Ladies to do, who are well ; and in her
Train two or three Coaches, and perhaps
a rich Velvet Chair embroider'd, would
follow in State.

It was thus for fome time they liv'd, and
the Princefs was daily prefs'd by young
fighing Lovers, for her Confent to marry
Alcidiana ; but fhe had ftill one Art or
other to put them off, and fo continually
broke all the great Matches that were propofed to her, notwithftanding their Kindred
and other Friends had induftrioufly endeavour'd to make feveral great Matches for
her ; but the Princefs was ftill pofitive
in her Denial, and one Way or other
broke all. At laft it happened, there was
one propofed, yet more advantageous, a
young Count, with whom the young Maid
grew paffionately in Love, and befought
her Sifter to confent that fhe might have
him, and got the Prince to fpeak in her
Behalf ; but he had no fooner heard the
fecret Reafons *Miranda* gave him, but
(entirely her Slave) he chang'd his Mind,
and fuited it to hers, and fhe, as before, broke off that Amour : Which fo
extremely incenfed *Alcidiana*, that fhe,
taking an Opportunity, got from her
Guard, and ran away, putting her felf
into

into the Hands of a wealthy Merchant, her Kinfman, and one who bore the greateft Authority in the City; him fhe chufes for her Guardian, refolving to be no longer a Slave to the Tyranny of her Sifter. And fo well fhe ordered Matters, that fhe writ to this young Cavalier, her laft Lover, and retrieved him; who came back to *Antwerp* again, to renew his Courtfhip.

Both Parties being agreed, it was no hard Matter to perfuade all but the Princefs. But though fhe oppofed it, it was refolved on, and the Day appointed for Marriage, and the Portion demanded; demanded only, but never to be paid, the beft Part of it being fpent. However, fhe put them off from Day to Day, by a thoufand frivolous Delays; and when fhe faw they would have Recourfe to Force, and that all her Magnificence would be at an End, if the Law fhould prevail againft her; and that without this Sifter's Fortune, fhe could not long fupport her Grandeur; fhe bethought her felf of a Means to make it all her own, by getting her Sifter made away; but fhe being out of her Tuition, fhe was not able to accomplifh fo great a Deed of Darknefs. But fince it was refolved it muft be done, fhe contrives a thoufand Stratagems;

tagems; and at laſt pitches upon an effectual one.

She had a Page call'd *Van Brune,* a
Youth of great Addreſs and Wit, and one
ſhe had long managed for her Purpoſe.
This Youth was about ſeventeen Years of
Age, and extremely beautiful; and in
the Time when *Alcidiana* lived with the
Princeſs, ſhe was a little in Love with this
handſome Boy; but it was checked in
its Infancy, and never grew up to a
Flame: Nevertheleſs, *Alcidiana* retained
ſtill a ſort of Tenderneſs for him, while
he burn'd in good Earneſt with Love for
the Princeſs.

The Princeſs one Day ordering this
Page to wait on her in her Cloſet, ſhe
ſhut the Door; and after a thouſand
Queſtions of what he would undertake to
ſerve her, the amorous Boy finding himſelf alone, and careſs'd by the fair Perſon he ador'd, with joyful Bluſhes that
beautify'd his Face, told her, ' There
' was nothing upon Earth, he would not
' do, to obey her leaſt Commands.' She
grew more familiar with him, to oblige
him; and ſeeing Love dance in his Eyes,
of which ſhe was ſo good a Judge, ſhe
treated him more like a Lover, than a
Servant; till at laſt the raviſhed Youth,
wholly tranſported out of himſelf, fell

at

at her Feet, and impatiently implor'd to receive her Commands quickly, that he might fly to execute them ; for he was not able to bear her charming Words, Looks, and Touches, and retain his Duty. At this she smil'd, and told him, the Work was of such a Nature, as would mortify all Flames about him ; and he would have more Need of Rage, Envy, and Malice, than the Aids of a Passion so soft as what she now found him capable of. He assur'd her, he would stick at nothing, tho' even against his Nature, to recompense for the Boldness he now, through his Indiscretion, had discover'd. She smiling, told him, he had committed no Fault ; and that possibly, the Pay he should receive for the Service she required at his Hands, should be——what he most wish'd for in the World. At this he bow'd to the Earth ; and kissing her Feet, bad her command : And then she boldly told him, *'Twas to kill her Sister* Alcidiana. The Youth, without so much as starting or pausing upon the Matter, told her, *It should be done* ; and bowing low, immediately went out of the Closet. She call'd him back, and would have given him some Instruction ; but he refused it, and said, ' The Action and ' the Contrivance should be all his own.'

And offering to go again, she ———— again recalled him; putting into his Hand a Purse of a hundred Pistoles, which he took, and with a low Bow departed.

He no sooner left her Presence, but he goes directly, and buys a Dose of Poison, and went immediately to the House where *Alcidiana* lived; where desiring to be brought to her Presence, he fell a weeping; and told her, his Lady had fallen out with him, and dismissed him her Service; and since from a Child he had been brought up in the Family, he humbly besought *Alcidiana* to receive him into her's, she being in a few Days to be marry'd. There needed not much Intreaty to a Thing that pleased her so well, and she immediately received him to Pension : And he waited some Days on her, before he could get an Opportunity to administer his devilish Potion. But one Night, when she drank Wine with roasted Apples, which was usual with her; instead of Sugar, or with the Sugar, the baneful Drug was mixed, and she drank it down.

About this Time, there was a great Talk of this Page's coming from one Sister, to go to the other. And Prince *Tarquin*, who was ignorant of the De-

sign

fign from the Beginning to the End,
hearing fome Men of Quality at his Table
fpeaking of *Van Brune*'s Change of
Place (the Princefs then keeping her
Chamber upon fome trifling Indifpofi-
tion) he anfwer'd, ' That furely they
' were miftaken, that he was not dif-
' miffed from the Princefs's Service : '
And calling fome of his Servants, he
asked for *Van Brune* ; and whether any
Thing had happen'd between her High-
nefs and him, that had occafion'd his
being turned off. They all feem'd ignorant of this Matter ; and thofe who had
fpoken of it, began to fancy there was
fome Juggle in the Cafe, which Time
would bring to Light.

The enfuing Day 'twas all about the
Town, that *Alcidiana* was poifon'd ; and
though not dead, yet very near it ; and
that the Doctors faid, fhe had taken
Mercury. So that there was never fo
formidable a Sight as this fair young
Creature ; her Head and Body fwoln,
her Eyes ftarting out, her Face black,
and all deformed : So that diligent Search
was made, who it fhould be that did
this ; who gave her Drink and Meat.
The Cook and Butler were examined, the
Footmen called to an Account ; but all
concluded, fhe received nothing but from

the Hand of her new Page, fince he came
into her Service. He was examined, and
fhew'd a thoufand guilty Looks : And
the Apothecary, then attending among
the Doctors, proved he had bought
Mercury of him three or four Days before ; which he could not deny ; and
making many Excufes for his buying it,
betray'd him the more ; fo ill he chanced
to diffemble. He was immediately fent
to be examined by the Margrave or Juftice, who made his *Mittimus,* and fent him
to Prifon.

'Tis eafy to imagine, in what Fears and
Confufion the Princefs was at this News :
She took her Chamber upon it, more to
hide her guilty Face, than for any Indifpo-
fition. And the Doctors apply'd fuch
Remedies to *Alcidiana,* fuch Antidotes
againft the Poifon, that in a fhort Time
fhe recover'd ; but loft the fineft Hair in
the World, and the Complexion of her Face
ever after.

It was not long before the Trials for
Criminals came on ; and the Day being
arrived, *Van Brune* was try'd the firft of
all ; every Body having already read
his Deftiny, according as they wifhed
it ; and none would believe, but juft indeed as it was : So that for the Revenge
they hoped to fee fall upon the Princefs,

every

every one wifhed he might find no Mercy, that fhe might fhare of his Shame and Mifery.

The Seffions-Houfe was filled that Day with all the Ladies, and chief of the Town, to hear the Refult of his Trial; and the fad Youth was brought, loaded with Chains, and pale as Death; where every Circumftance being fufficiently proved againft him, and he making but a weak Defence for himfelf, he was convicted, and fent back to Prifon, to receive his Sentence of Death on the Morrow; where he owned all, and who fet him on to do it. He own'd 'twas not Reward of Gain he did it for, but Hope he fhould command at his Pleafure the Poffeffion of his Miftrefs, the Princefs, who fhould deny him nothing, after having entrufted him with fo great a Secret; and that befides, fhe had elevated him with the Promife of that glorious Reward, and had dazzled his young Heart with fo charming a Profpect, that blind and mad with Joy, he rufhed forward to gain the defired Prize, and thought on nothing but his coming Happinefs: That he faw too late the Follies of his prefumptuous Flame, and curfed the deluding Flatteries of the fair Hypocrite, who had foothed him to his Undoing:

M 3

That

That he was a miferable Victim to her
Wickednefs ; and hoped he fhould warn
all young Men, by his Fall, to avoid
the Diffimulation of the deceiving Fair :
That he hoped they would have Pity on
his Youth, and attribute his Crime to
the fubtle Perfuafions alone of his Miftrefs the Princefs : And that fince *Alcidiana* was not dead, they would grant him
Mercy, and permit him to live to repent
of his grievous Crime, in fome Part of
the World, whither they might banifh
him.

He ended with Tears, that fell in abundance from his Eyes ; and immediately
the Princefs was apprehended, and brought
to Prifon, to the fame Prifon where
yet the poor young Father *Francifco*
was languifhing, he having been from
Week to Week reprieved, by the In-
terceffion of the Fathers ; and poffibly
fhe there had Time to make fome Reflections.

You may imagine *Tarquin* left no
Means uneffay'd, to prevent the Imprifonment of the Princefs, and the publick
Shame and Infamy fhe was likely to un-
dergo in this Affair : But the whole
City being over-joy'd that fhe fhould be
punifhed, as an Author of all this Mifchief, were generally bent againft her,
both

both Priests, Magistrates and People; the whole Force of the Stream running that Way, she found no more Favour than the meanest Criminal. The Prince therefore, when he saw 'twas impossible to rescue her from the Hands of Justice, suffer'd with Grief unspeakable, what he could not prevent, and led her himself to the Prison, follow'd by all his People, in as much State as if he had been going to his Marriage; where, when she came, she was as well attended and served as before, he never stirring one Moment from her.

The next Day she was tried in open and common Court; where she appeared in Glory, led by *Tarquin,* and attended according to her Quality: And she could not deny all the Page had alledged against her, who was brought thither also in Chains; and after a great many Circumstances, she was found Guilty, and both received Sentence; the Page to be hanged till he was dead, on a Gibbet in the Market-Place; and the Princess to stand under the Gibbet, with a Rope about her Neck, the other End of which was to be faſtned to the Gibbet where the Page was hanging; and to have an Inscription, in large Characters, upon her Back and Breast, of the Cause why; where ſhe was to ſtand from ten in the Morning to twelve.

This Sentence, the People with one Accord, believed too favourable for ſo ill a Woman, whoſe Crimes deſerved Death, equal to that of *Van Brune*. Nevertheleſs, there were ſome who ſaid, it was infinitely more ſevere than Death it ſelf.

The following *Friday* was the Day of Execution, and one need not tell of the Abundance of People, who were flocked together in the Market-Place : And all the Windows were taken down, and filled with Spectators, and the Tops of Houſes ; when at the Hour appointed, the fatal Beauty appear'd. She was dreſs'd in a black Velvet Gown, with a rich Row of Diamonds all down the fore Part of her Breaſt, and a great Knot of Diamonds at the Peak behind; and a Petticoat of flower'd Gold, very rich, and laced; with all Things elſe ſuitable. A Gentleman carry'd her great Velvet Cuſhion before her, on which her Prayer-Book, embroider'd, was laid ; her Train was borne up by a Page, and the Prince led her, bare ; followed by his Footmen, Pages, and other Officers of his Houſe.

When they arrived at the Place of Execution, the Cuſhion was laid on the Ground,

Ground, upon a *Portugal* Mat, spread there for that Purpose ; and the Princess stood on the Cushion, with her Prayer-Book in her Hand, and a Priest by her Side ; and was accordingly tied up to the Gibbet.

She had not stood there ten Minutes, but she had the Mortification (at least one would think it so to her) to see her sad Page, *Van Brune*, approach, fair as an Angel, but languishing and pale. That Sight moved all the Beholders with as much Pity, as that of the Princess did with Disdain and Pleasure.

He was dressed all in Mourning, and very fine Linen, bare-headed, with his own Hair, the fairest that could be seen, hanging all in Curls on his Back and Shoulders, very long. He had a Prayer-Book of black Velvet in his Hand, and behaved himself with much Penitence and Devotion.

When he came under the Gibbet, he seeing his Mistress in that Condition, shew'd an infinite Concern, and his fair Face was cover'd over with Blushes ; and falling at her Feet, he humbly ask'd her Pardon for having been the Occasion of so great an Infamy to her, by a weak Confession, which the Fears of Youth, and Hopes of Life, had obliged him to make, fo greatly to her Difhonour ; for indeed he wanted that manly Strength, to bear the Efforts of dying, as he ought, in Silence, rather than of committing fo great a Crime againft his Duty, and Honour itfelf ; and that he could not die in Peace, unlefs fhe would forgive him. The Princefs only nodded her Head, and cried, *I do*——

And after having fpoken a little to his Father-Confeffor, who was with him, he chearfully mounted the Ladder, and in Sight of the Princefs he was turned off, while a loud Cry was heard thro' all the Market-Place, efpecially from the Fair Sex ; he hanged there till the Time the Princefs was to depart ; and then fhe was put into a rich embroider'd Chair, and carry'd away, *Tarquin* going into his, for he had all that Time ftood fupporting the Princefs under the Gallows, and was very weary. She was fent back, till her Releafement came, which was that Night about feven o'Clock ; and then fhe was conducted to her own Houfe in great State, with a Dozen White Wax Flambeaux about her Chair.

If the Guardian of *Alcidiana*, and her Friends, before were impatient of having the Portion out of the Hands of thefe Extravagants, it is not to be imagined,
but

but they were now much more fo ; and the next Day they fent an Officer, according to Law, to demand it, or to fummon the Prince to give Reafons why he would not pay it. The Officer received for Anfwer, That the Money fhould be call'd in, and paid in fuch a Time, fetting a certain Time, which I have not been fo curious as to retain, or put in my Journal-Obfervations ; but I am fure it was not long, as may be eafily imagined, for they every Moment fufpected the Prince would pack up, and be gone, fome time or other, on the fudden ; and for that Reafon they would not truft him without Bail, or two Officers to remain in his Houfe, to watch that nothing fhould be remov'd or touch'd. As for Bail, or Security, he could give none ; every one flunk their Heads out of the Collar, when it came to that : So that he was oblig'd, at his own Expence, to maintain Officers in his Houfe.

The Princefs finding her felf reduced to the laft Extremity, and that fhe muft either produce the Value of a hundred thoufand Crowns, or fee the Prince her Husband lodged for ever in a Prifon, and all their Glory vanifh ; and that it was impoffible to fly, fince guarded ; fhe had Recourfe to an Extremity, worfe than

 the

the Affair of *Van Brune.* And in order
to this, she first puts on a world of Sorrow and Concern, for what she feared
might arrive to the Prince : And indeed,
if ever she shed Tears which she did not
dissemble, it was upon this Occasion. But
here she almost over-acted : She stirred not
from her Bed, and refused to eat, or sleep,
or see the Light ; so that the Day being
shut out of her Chamber, she lived by
Wax-lights, and refus'd all Comfort and
Consolation.

The Prince, all raving with Love, tender Compassion and Grief, never stirred
from her Bed-side, nor ceased to implore, that she would suffer her self to
live. But she, who was not now so passionately in Love with *Tarquin,* as she was
with the Prince ; nor so fond of the Man
as his Titles, and of Glory ; foresaw the
total Ruin of the last, if not prevented
by avoiding the Payment of this great
Sum ; which could not otherwise be, than
by the Death of *Alcidiana :* And therefore, without ceasing, she wept, and
cry'd out, ' She could not live, unless
' *Alcidiana* died. This *Alcidiana (conti-*
' *nued she)* who has been the Author of
' my Shame ; who has expos'd me un-
' der a Gibbet, in the Publick Market-
' Place ——— Oh ! ——— I am deaf to
' all

' all Reason, blind to natural Affection. I
' renounce her, I hate her as my mortal
' Foe, my Stop to Glory, and the Finisher
' of my Days, e'er half my Race of Life
' be run.'

Then throwing her false, but snowy, charming Arms about the Neck of her Heart-breaking Lord, and Lover, who lay sighing, and listening by her Side, he was charmed and bewitch'd into saying all Things that appeased her; and lastly, told her, ' *Alcidiana* should be no longer any
' Obstacle to her Repose; but that, if
' she would look up, and cast her Eyes of
' Sweetness and Love upon him, as here-
' tofore; forget her Sorrow, and redeem
' her lost Health; he would take what
' Measures she should propose to dispatch
' this fatal Stop to her Happiness, out of
' the Way.'

These Words failed not to make her caress him in the most endearing Manner that Love and Flattery could invent; and she kiss'd him to an Oath, a solemn Oath, to perform what he had promised; and he vow'd liberally. And she assumed in an Instant her Good-Humour, and suffer'd a Supper to be prepared, and did eat; which in many Days before she had not done: So obstinate and powerful was she in dissembling well.

The

The next Thing to be confider'd was, which Way this Deed was to be done; for they doubted not, but when it was done, all the World would lay it upon the Princefs, as done by her Command: But fhe urged, Sufpicion was no Proof; and that they never put to Death any one, but when they had great and certain Evidence who were the Offenders. She was fure of her own Conftancy, that Racks and Tortures fhould never get the Secret from her Breaft; and if he were as confident on his Part, there was no Danger. Yet this Preparation fhe made towards laying the Fact on others, that fhe caufed feveral Letters to be wrote from *Germany*, as from the Relations of *Van Brune*, who threaten'd *Alcidiana* with Death, for depriving their Kinfman (who was a Gentleman) of his Life, though he had not taken away hers. And it was the Report of the Town, how this young Maid was threaten'd. And indeed, the Death of the Page had fo afflicted a great many, that *Alcidiana* had procured her felf abundance of Enemies upon that Account, becaufe fhe might have faved him if fhe had pleafed; but, on the contrary, fhe was a Spectator, and in full Health and Vigour, at his Execution: And People were not fo much concerned

for

for her at this Report, as they would have been.

The Prince, who now had, by reafoning the Matter foberly with *Miranda*, found it abfolutely neceffary to difpatch *Alcidiana*, refolved himfelf, and with his own Hand, to execute it; not daring to truft to any of his moft favourite Servants, though he had many, who poffibly would have obey'd him; for they loved him as he deferved, and fo would all the World, had he not been fo purely deluded by this fair Enchantrefs. He therefore, as I faid, refolved to keep this great Secret to himfelf; and taking a Piftol, charged well with two Bullets, he watch'd an Opportunity to fhoot her as fhe fhould go out or into her Houfe, or Coach, fome Evening.

To this End he waited feveral Nights near her Lodgings, but ftill, either fhe went not out, or when fhe return'd, fhe was fo guarded with Friends, her Lover, and Flambeaux, that he could not aim at her without endangering the Life of fome other. But one Night above the reft, upon a *Sunday*, when he knew fhe would be at the Theatre, for fhe never miffed that Day feeing the Play, he waited at the Corner of the Stadt-Houfe, near the Theatre, with his Cloak caft

over

over his Face, and a black Periwig, all
alone, with his Piftol ready cock'd ; and
remain'd not very long but he faw her
Kinfman's Coach come along ; 'twas almoft dark, Day was juft fhutting up her
Beauties, and left fuch a Light to govern
the World, as ferved only juft to diftin-
guifh one Object from another, and
a convenient Help to Mifchief. He faw
alight out of the Coach only one young
Lady, the Lover, and then the deftin'd
Victim ; which he (drawing near) knew
rather by her Tongue than Shape. The
Lady ran into the Play-Houfe, and left
Alcidiana to be conducted by her Lover
into it : Who led her to the Door, and
went to give fome Order to the Coach-
man ; fo that the Lover was about twenty
yards from *Alcidiana* ; when fhe ftood
the faireft Mark in the World, on the
Threfhold of the Entrance of the Theatre, there being many Coaches about the
Door, fo that hers could not come fo
near. *Tarquin* was refolved not to lofe
fo fair an Opportunity, and advanc'd,
but went behind the Coaches ; and when
he came over-againft the Door, through
a great booted Velvet Coach, that ftood
between him and her, he fhot ; and fhe
having the Train of her Gown and Petticoat on her Arm, in great Quantity, he
miffed

'miffed her Body, and fhot through her Clothes, between her Arm and her Body. She, frighten'd to find fomething hit her, and to fee the Smoke, and hear the Report of the Piftol; running in, cried, *I am fhot, I am dead.*

This Noife quickly alarm'd her Lover; and all the Coachmen and Footmen immediately ran, fome one Way, and fome another. One of 'em feeing a Man hafte away in a Cloak; he being a lufty, bold *German*, ftopped him; and drawing upon him, bad him ftand, and deliver his Piftol, or he would run him through.

Tarquin being furprifed at the Boldnefs of this Fellow to demand his Piftol, as if he pofitively knew him to be the Murderer (for fo he thought himfelf, fince he believed *Alcidiana* dead) had fo much Prefence of Mind as to confider, if he fuffered himfelf to be taken, he fhould poorly die a publick Death; and therefore refolv'd upon one Mifchief more, to fecure himfelf from the firft: And in the Moment that the *German* bad him deliver his Piftol, he cry'd, *Though I have no Piftol to deliver, I have a Sword to chaftife thy Infolence.* And throwing off his Cloak, and flinging his Piftol from him, he drew, and wounded, and difarmed the Fellow.

This

This Noife of Swords brought every body to the Place; and immediately the Bruit ran, *The Murderer was taken, the Murderer was taken:* Tho' none knew which was he, nor as yet fo much as the Caufe of the Quarrel between the two fighting Men; for it was now darker than before. But at the Noife of the Murderer being taken, the Lover of *Alcidiana,* who by this Time found his Lady unhurt, all but the Trains of her Gown and Petticoat, came running to the Place, juft as *Tarquin* had difarm'd the *German,* and was ready to kill him; when laying hold of his Arm, they arrefted the Stroke, and redeemed the Footman.

They then demanded who this Stranger was, at whofe Mercy the Fellow lay; but the Prince, who now found himfelf venturing for his laft Stake, made no Reply; but with two Swords in his Hands went to fight his Way through the Rabble: And tho' there were above a hundred Perfons, fome with Swords, others with long Whips, (as Coachmen) fo invincible was the Courage of this poor unfortunate Gentleman at that Time, that all thefe were not able to feize him; but he made his Way through the Ring that encompaffed him, and ran away; but was, however, fo clofely purfued,

the

the Company ftill gathering as they ran, that toiled with fighting, oppreffed with Guilt, and Fear of being taken, he grew fainter and fainter, and fuffered himfelf, at laft, to yield to his Purfuers, who foon found him to be Prince *Tarquin* in Dif- guife : And they carry'd him directly to Prifon, being *Sunday*, to wait the coming Day, to go before a Magiftrate.

In an Hour's Time the whole fatal Ad- venture was carried all over the City, and every one knew that *Tarquin* was the intended Murderer of *Alcidiana* ; and not one but had a real Sorrow and Com- paffion for him. They heard how brave- ly he had defended himfelf, how many he had wounded before he could be ta- ken, and what Numbers he had fought through : And even thofe that faw his Valour and Bravery, and who had affift- ed at his being feiz'd, now repented from the Bottom of their Hearts their having any Hand in the Ruin of fo gallant a Man ; efpecially fince they knew the La- dy was not hurt. A thoufand Addreffes were made to her, not to profecute him ; but her Lover, a hot-headed Fellow, more fierce than brave, would by no Means be pacified, but vowed to purfue him to the Scaffold.

The

The *Monday* came, and the Prince being examined, confeſſed the Matter of Fact, ſince there was no Harm done; believing a generous Confeſſion the beſt of his Game: But he was ſent back to cloſer Impriſonment, loaded with Irons, to expect the next Seſſions. All his Houſhold-Goods were ſeiz'd, and all they could find, for the Uſe of *Alcidiana*. And the Princeſs, all in Rage, tearing her Hair, was carried to the ſame Priſon, to behold the cruel Effects of her helliſh Deſigns.

One need not tell here how ſad and horrid this Meeting appear'd between her Lord and her: Let it ſuffice, it was the moſt melancholy and mortifying Object that ever Eyes beheld. On *Miranda's* Part, 'twas ſometimes all Rage and Fire, and ſometimes all Tears and Groans; but ſtill 'twas ſad Love, and mournful Tenderneſs on his. Nor could all his Sufferings, and the Proſpect of Death itſelf, drive from his Soul one Spark of that Fire the obſtinate God had fatally kindled there: And in the midſt of all his Sighs, he would re-call himſelf, and cry, —— *I have* Miranda *ſtill.*

He was eternally viſited by his Friends and Acquaintance; and this laſt Action of Bravery had got him more than all his

former

former Conduct had lost. The Fathers were perpetually with him ; and all join'd with one common Voice in this, That he ought to abandon a Woman so wicked as the Princess ; and that however Fate dealt with him, he could not shew himself a true Penitent, while he laid the Author of so much Evil in his Bosom : That Heaven would never bless him, till he had renounced her : And on such Conditions he would find those that would employ their utmost Interest to save his Life, who else would not stir in this Affair. But he was so deaf to all, that he could not so much as dissemble a Repentance for having married her.

He lay a long Time in Prison, and all that Time the poor Father *Francisco* remained there also : And the good Fathers who daily visited these two amorous Prisoners, the Prince and Princess ; and who found, by the Management of Matters, it would go very hard with *Tarquin*, entertained 'em often with holy Matters relating to the Life to come ; from which, before his Trial, he gathered what his Stars had appointed, and that he was destin'd to die.

This gave an unspeakable Torment to the now repenting Beauty, who had reduced

duced him to it; and she began to appear with a more solid Grief: Which being perceived by the good Fathers, they resolved to attack her on the yielding Side; and after some Discourse upon the Judgment for Sin, they came to reflect on the Business of Father *Francisco;* and told her, she had never thriven since her accusing of that Father, and laid it very home to her Conscience; assuring her that they would do their utmost in her Service, if she would confess that secret Sin to all the World, so that she might atone for the Crime, by the saving that good Man. At first she seemed inclined to yield; but Shame of being her own Detector, in so vile a Matter, recalled her Goodness, and she faintly persisted in it.

At the End of six Months, Prince *Tarquin* was called to his Tryal; where I will pass over the Circumstances, which are only what is usual in such criminal Cases, and tell you, that he being found guilty of the Intent of killing *Alcidiana*, was condemned to lose his Head in the Market-Place, and the Princess to be banished her Country.

After Sentence pronounced, to the real Grief of all the Spectators, he was carry'd back to Prison. And now the Fathers
attack

attack her anew; and fhe, whofe Griefs daily encreafed, with a Languifhment that brought her very near her Grave, at laft confefs'd all her Life, all the Lewdnefs of her Practices with feveral Princes and great Men, befides her Lufts with People that ferved her, and others in mean Capacity: And laftly, the whole Truth of the young Friar; and how fhe had drawn the Page, and the Prince her Hufband, to this defign'd Murder of her Sifter. This fhe figned with her Hand, in the Prefence of the Prince, her Hufband, and feveral Holy Men who were prefent. Which being fignify'd to the Magiftrates, the Friar was immediately deliver'd from his Irons (where he had languifhed more than two whole Years) in great Triumph, with much Honour, and lives a moft exemplary pious Life, as he did before; for he is now living in *Antwerp*.

After the Condemnation of thefe two unfortunate Perfons, who begot fuch different Sentiments in the Minds of the People (the Prince, all the Compaffion and Pity imaginable; and the Princefs, all the Contempt and Defpite;) they languifhed almoft fix Months longer in Prifon: fo great an Intereft there was made, in order to the faving his Life,

by

by all the Men of the Robe. On the other ſide, the Princes, and great Men of all Nations, who were at the Court of *Bruſſels*, who bore a ſecret Revenge in their Hearts againſt a Man who had, as they pretended, ſet up a falſe Title, only to take Place of them ; who indeed was but a Merchant's Son of *Holland*, as they ſaid ; ſo incens'd them againſt him, that they were too hard at Court for the Church-men. However, this Diſpute gave the Prince his Life ſome Months longer than was expected ; which gave him alſo ſome Hope, that a Reprieve for ninety Years would have been granted, as was deſired. Nay, Father *Franciſco* ſo intereſted himſelf in this Concern, that he writ to his Father, and ſeveral Princes of *Germany*, with whom the Marquis *Caſtel Roderigo* was well acquainted, to intercede with him for the ſaving of *Tarquin ;* ſince 'twas more by his Perſuaſions, than thoſe of all who attacked her, that made *Miranda* confeſs the Truth of her Affair with him. But at the End of ſix Months, when all Applications were found fruitleſs and vain, the Prince receiv'd News, that in two Days he was to die, as his Sentence had been before pronounced, and for which he prepared himſelf with all Chearfulneſs.

On

On the following *Friday*, as soon as it was light, all People of any Condition came to take their Leaves of him; and none departed with dry Eyes, or Hearts unconcern'd to the last Degree: For *Tarquin*, when he found his Fate inevitable bore it with a Fortitude that shewed no Signs of Regret; but addres'd himself to all about him with the same chearful, modest, and great Air, he was wont to do in his most flourishing Fortune. His Valet was dressing him all the Morning, so many Interruptions they had by Visitors; and he was all in Mourning, and so were all his Followers; for even to the last he kept up his Grandeur, to the Amazement of all People. And indeed, he was so passionately belov'd by them, that those he had dismis'd, serv'd him voluntarily, and would not be persuaded to abandon him while he liv'd.

The Princess was also dress'd in Mourning, and her two Women; and notwith-standing the unheard-of Lewdness and Villanies she had confess'd of her self, the Prince still ador'd her; for she had still those Charms that made him first do so; nor, to his last Moment, could he be brought to wish, that he had never seen her; but on the contrary, as a Man yet vainly proud of his Fetters, he said, ' All

‘ the Satisfaction this fhort Moment of
‘ Life could afford him, was, that he
‘ died in endeavouring to ferve *Miranda,*
‘ his adorable Princefs.’

After he had taken Leave of all, who
thought it neceffary to leave him to himfelf
for fome Time, he retir’d with his Confeffor; where they were about an Hour in
Prayer, all the Ceremonies of Devotion
that were fit to be done, being already paft.
At laft the Bell toll’d, and he was to take
Leave of the Princefs, as his laft Work
of Life, and the moft hard he had to accomplifh. He threw himfelf at her Feet,'
and gazing on her as fhe fat more dead
than alive, overwhelm’d with filent Grief,
they both remain’d fome Moments fpeech-
lefs ; and then, as if one rifing Tide of
Tears had fupply’d both their Eyes, it
burft out in Streams at the fame Inftant:
and when his Sighs gave Way, he utter’d
a thoufand Farewels, fo foft, fo paffionate, and moving, that all who were by
were extremely touch’d with it, and faid,
That nothing could be feen more deplorable
and melancholy. A thoufand Times they
bad Farewel, and ftill fome tender Look,
or Word, would prevent his going ; then
embrace, and bid Farewel again. A thoufand Times fhe ask’d his Pardon for being
the Occafion of that fatal Separation ; a
thou-

thousand Times assuring him, she would follow him, for she could not live without him. And Heaven knows when their soft and sad Caresses would have ended, had not the Officers assur'd him 'twas Time to mount the Scaffold. At which Words the Princess fell fainting in the Arms of her Woman, and they led *Tarquin* out of Prison.

When he came to the Market-Place, whither he walked on Foot, follow'd by his own Domesticks, and some bearing a black Velvet Coffin with Silver Hinges ; the Head's-man before him with his fatal Scimiter drawn, his Confessor by his Side, and many Gentlemen and Church-men, with Father *Francisco* attending him, the People showring Millions of Blessings on him, and beholding him with weeping Eyes, he mounted the Scaffold ; which was strewed with some Saw dust, about the Place where he was to kneel, to receive the Blood : For they behead People kneeling, and with the Back-Stroak of a Scimiter ; and not lying on a Block, and with an Axe, as we in *England.* The Scaffold had a low Rail about it, that every body might more conveniently see. This was hung with black, and all that State that such a Death could have, was here in most decent Order.

N 2   He

He did not fay much upon the Scaffold: The Sum of what he faid to his Friends was, to be kind, and take Care of the poor Penitent his Wife: To others, recommending his honeft and generous Servants, whofe Fidelity was fo well known and commended, that they were foon promifed Preferment. He was fome time in Prayer, and a very fhort time in fpeaking to his Confeffor; then he turned to the Head's-man, and defired him to do his Office well, and gave him twenty *Louis d'Ors;* and undreffing himfelf with the Help of his Valet and Page, he pull'd off his Coat, and had underneath a white Sattin Waiftcoat: He took off his Periwig, and put on a white Sattin Cap, with a Holland one done with Point under it, which he pulled over his Eyes; then took a chearful Leave of all, and kneel'd down, and faid, ' When he ' lifted up his Hands the third Time, ' the Head's-man fhould do his Office.' Which accordingly was done, and the Head's man gave him his laft Stroke, and the Prince fell on the Scaffold. The People with one common Voice, as if it had been but one entire one, pray'd for his Soul; and Murmurs of Sighs were heard from the whole Multitude,

titude, who ſcrambled for ſome of the blood Saw-duſt, to keep for his Memory.

The Head's-man going to take up the Head, as the Manner is, to ſhew it to the People, he found he had not ſtruck it off, and that the Body ſtirr'd ; with that he ſtepped to an Engine, which they always carry with 'em, to force thoſe who may be refractory ; thinking, as he ſaid, to have twiſted the Head from the Shoulders, conceiving it to hang but by a ſmall Matter of Fleſh. Tho' 'twas an odd Shift of the Fellow's, yet 'twas done, and the beſt Shift he could ſuddenly propoſe. The Margrave, and another Officer, old Men, were on the Scaffold, with ſome of the Prince's Friends, and Servants ; who ſeeing the Head's-man put the Engine about the Neck of the Prince, began to call out, and the People made a great Noiſe. The Prince, who found himſelf yet alive ; or rather, who was paſt thinking but had ſome Senſe of Feeling left, when the Head's-man took him up, and ſet his Back againſt the Rail, and clapp'd the Engine about his Neck, got his two Thumbs between the Rope and his Neck, feeling himſelf preſs'd there ; and ſtruggling between Life and Death, and

N 3　　　bending

bending himſelf over the Rail backward, while the Head's-man pulled forward, he threw himſelf quite over the Rail, by Chance, and not Deſign, and fell upon the Heads and Shoulders of the People, who were crying out with amazing Shouts of Joy. The Head's-man leap'd after him, but the Rabble had lik'd to have pulled him to Pieces ; All the City was in an Uproar, but none knew what the Matter was, but thoſe who bore the Body of the Prince, whom they found yet living ; but how, or by what ſtrange Miracle preſerv'd, they knew not, nor did examine ; but with one Accord, as if the whole Crowd had been one Body, and had had but one Motion, they bore the Prince on their Heads about a hundred Yards from the Scaffold, where there is a Monaſtery of Jeſuits ; and there they ſecur'd him. All this was done, ·his beheading, his falling, and his being ſecur'd, almoſt in a Moment's Time ; the People rejoiceing, as at ſome extraordinary Victory won. One of the Officers being, as I ſaid, an old timorous Man, was ſo frighten'd at the Accident, the Buſtle, the Noiſe, and the Confuſion, of which he was wholly ignorant, that he dy'd with Amazement and Fear ; and the other was fain to be let blood.

The

The Officers of Juftice went to demand the Prifoner, but they demanded in vain ; the Jefuits had now a Right to protect him, and would do fo. All his overjoy'd Friends went to fee in what Condition he was, and all of Quality found Admittance : They faw him in Bed, going to be drefs'd by the moft fkilful Surgeons, who yet could not affure him of Life. They defired no body fhould fpeak to him, or afk him any Queftions. They found that the Head's-man had ftruck him too low, and had cut him into the Shoulder-bone. A very great Wound, you may be fure ; for the Sword, in fuch Executions, carries an extreme Force: However, fo great Care was taken on all Sides, and fo greatly the Fathers were concern'd for him, that they found an Amendment, and Hopes of a good Effect of their incomparable Charity and Goodnefs.

At laft, when he was permitted to fpeak, the firft News he afk'd was after the Princefs. And his Friends were very much afflicted to find, that all his Lofs of Blood had not quenched that Flame, not let out that which made him ftill love that bad Woman. He was follicited daily to think no more of her: And all her Crimes are laid fo open

N 4

to

to him, and fo fhamefully reprefented ; and on the other Side, his Virtues fo admir'd ; and which, they faid, would have been eternally celebrated, but for his Folly with this infamous Creature ; that at laft, by affuring him of all their Affiftance if he abandon'd her ; and to renounce him, and deliver him up, if he did not ; they wrought fo far upon him, as to promife, he would fuffer her to go alone into Banifhment, and would not follow her, or live with her any more. But alas ! this was but his Gratitude that compell'd this Complaifance, for in his Heart he refolv'd never to abandon her ; nor was he able to live, and think of doing it: However, his Reafon affur'd him, he could not do a Deed more juftifiable, and one that would regain his Fame fooner.

His Friends ask'd him fome Queftions concerning his Efcape; and fince he was not beheaded, but only wounded, why he did not immediately rife up ? But he replied, he was fo abfolutely prepoffeffed, that at the third lifting up his Hands he fhould receive the Stroke of Death, that at the fame Inftant the Sword touch'd him, he had no Senfe ; nay, not even of Pain, fo abfolutely dead he was with Imagination ; and knew not
that

that he 'ſtirr'd, as the Head's-man found he did ; nor did he remember any Thing, from the lifting up of his Hands, to his fall ; and then awaken'd, as out of a Dream, or rather a Moment's Sleep without Dream, he found he liv'd, and wonder'd what was arriv'd to him, or how he came to live ; having not, as yet, any Senſe of his Wound, tho' ſo terrible an one.

After this, *Alcidiana*, who was extremely afflicted for having been the Proſecutor of this great Man ; who, bating this laſt Deſign againſt her, which ſhe knew was at the Inſtigation of her Siſter, had oblig'd her with all the Civility imaginable ; now ſought all Means poſſible of getting his Pardon, and that of her Siſter ; tho' of an hundred thouſand Crowns, which ſhe ſhould have paid her, ſhe could get but ten thouſand ; which was from the Sale of her rich Beds, and ſome other Furniture. So that the young Count, who before ſhould have marry'd her, now went off for want of Fortune ; and a young Merchant (perhaps the beſt of the two) was the Man to whom ſhe was deſtin'd.

At laſt, by great Interceſſion, both their Pardons were obtain'd ; and the Prince, who would be no more ſeen in

a Place that had prov'd every way fo
fatal to him, left *Flanders*, promifing never to live with the Fair Hypocrite more;
but e'er he departed, he wrote her a Letter,
wherein he order'd her, in a little Time,
to follow him into *Holland;* and left a Bill
of Exchange with one of his trufty Servants,
whom he had left to wait upon her, for
Money for her Accommodation; fo that
fhe was now reduced to one Woman, one
Page, and this Gentleman. The Prince,
in this Time of his Imprifonment, had feveral Bills of great Sums from his Father,
who was exceeding rich, and this all the
Children he had in the World, and whom
he tenderly loved.

As foon as *Miranda* was come into *Holland*, fhe was welcom'd with all imaginable
Refpect and Endearment by the old Father; who was impos'd upon fo, as that he
knew not fhe was the fatal Occafion of all
thefe Difafters to his Son; but rather look'd
on her as a Woman, who had brought him
an hundred and fifty thoufand Crowns,
which his Misfortunes had confumed. But,
above all, fhe was receiv'd by *Tarquin* with
a Joy unfpeakable; who, after fome Time,
to redeem his Credit, and gain himfelf a
new Fame, put himfelf into the *French* Army, where he did Wonders; and after three
Campaigns, his Father dying, he return'd
home,

home, and retir'd to a Country-House :
where, with his Princess, he liv'd as a private Gentleman, in all the Tranquillity of
a Man of good Fortune. They say *Miranda* has been very penitent for her Life
past, and gives Heaven the Glory for have-
ing given her these Afflictions that have
reclaim'd her, and brought her to as perfect
a State of Happiness, as this troublesome
World, can afford.

Since I began this Relation, I heard that
Prince *Tarquin*, dy'd about three Quarters
of a Year ago.

 THE

THE

N U N :

OR, THE

Perjur'd Beauty.

A True NOVEL.

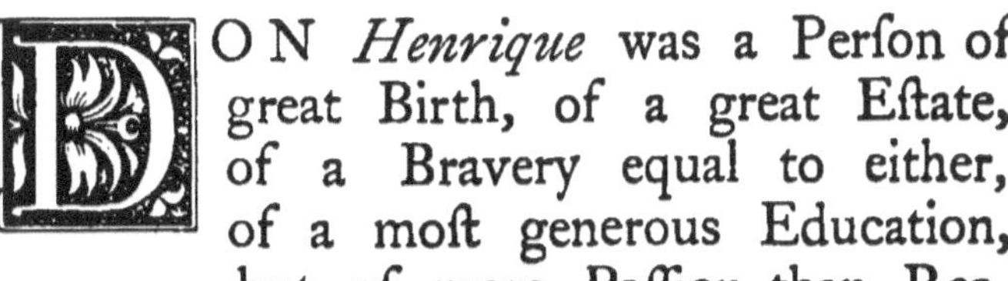

DON *Henrique* was a Perfon of great Birth, of a great Eftate, of a Bravery equal to either, of a moft generous Education, but of more Paffion than Reafon : He was befides of an opener and freer Temper than generally his Countrymen

V:I P.288
J. Pine inv. sculp. 1733

trymen are (I mean, the *Spaniards*) and always engag'd in some Love-Intrigue or other.

One Night as he was retreating from one of those Engagements, Don *Sebastian*, whose Sister he had abus'd with a Promise of Marriage, set upon him at the Corner of a Street, in *Madrid,* and by the Help of three of his Friends, design'd to have dispatch'd him on a doubtful Embassy to the Almighty Monarch : But he receiv'd their first Instructions with better Address than they expected, and dismiss'd his Envoy first, killing one of Don *Sebastian*'s Friends. Which so enrag'd the injur'd Brother, that his Strength and Resolution seem'd to be redoubled, and so animated his two surviving Companions, that (doubtless) they had gain'd a dishonourable Victory, had not Don *Antonio* accidentally come in to the Rescue; who after a short Dispute, kill'd one of the two who attack'd him only; whilst Don *Henrique*, with the greatest Difficulty, defended his Life, for some Moments, against *Sebastian,* whose Rage depriv'd him of Strength, and gave his Adversary the unwish'd Advantage of his seeming Death, tho' not without bequeathing some bloody Legacies to Don *Henrique. Antonio* had receiv'd but one

slight

flight Wound in the left Arm, and his furviving Antagonift none; who however thought it not advifeable to begin a frefh Difpute againft two, of whofe Courage he had but too fatal a Proof, tho' one of 'em was fufficiently difabled. The Conquerors, on the other Side, politickly retreated, and quitting the Field to the Conquer'd, left the Living to bury the Dead, if he could, or thought convenient.

As they were marching off, Don *Antonio*, who all this while knew not whofe Life he had fo happily preferv'd, told his Companion in Arms, that he thought it indifpenfibly neceffary that he fhould quarter with him that Night, for his further Prefervation. To which he prudently confented, and went, with no little Uneafinefs, to his Lodgings; where he furpriz'd *Antonio* with the Sight of his deareft Friend. For they had certainly the neareft Sympathy in all their Thoughts, that ever made two brave Men unhappy: And, undoubtedly, nothing but Death, or more fatal Love, could have divided them. However, at prefent, they were united and fecure.

In the mean time, Don *Sebaftian's* Friend was juft going to call Help to carry off the Bodies, as the —— came
by;

by ; who feeing three Men lie dead,
feiz'd the fourth : who as he was about
to juftify himfelf, by difcovering one of
the Authors of fo much Blood-fhed, was
interrupted by a Groan from his fuppofed
dead Friend Don *Sebaftian* ; whom, after
a brief Account of fome Part of the Matter, and the Knowledge of his Quality,
they took up, and carried to his Houfe ;
where, within a few Days he was recovered paft the Fear of Death.   All this
While *Henrique* and *Antonio* durft not appear, fo much as by Night ; nor could
be found, tho' diligent and daily Search
was made after the firft ; but upon Don
Sebaftian's Recovery, the Search ceafing,
they took the Advantage of the Night,
and, in Difgnife, retreated to *Seville.*
'Twas there they thought themfelves
moft fecure, where indeed they were in
the greateft Danger ; for tho' (haply)
they might there have efcap'd the murderous Attempt of Don *Sebaftian*, and
his Friends, yet they could not there a-
void the malicious Influence of their
Stars.

This City gave Birth to *Antonio*, and
to the Caufe of his greateft Misfortunes,
as well as of his Death.   Dona *Ardelia*
was born there, a Miracle of Beauty and
Falfhood.   'Twas more than a Year fince
Don

Don *Antonio* had firft feen and loved her.
For 'twas impoffible any Man fhould
do one without the other. He had had
the unkind Opportunity of fpeaking and
conveying a Billet to her at Church ; and
to his greater Misfortune, the next Time
he found her there, he met with too Kind
a Return both from her Eyes and from her
Hand, which privately flipt a Paper into
his ; in which he found abundantly more
than he expected, directing him in that,
how he fhould proceed, in order to carry
her off from her Father with the leaft Danger he could look for in fuch an Attempt ;
fince it would have been vain and fruitlefs
to have afked her of her Father, becaufe
their Families had been at Enmity for feveral Years ; tho' *Antonio* was as well defcended as fhe, and had as ample a Fortune ;
nor was his Perfon, according to his Sex,
any way inferior to her's ; and certainly,
the Beauties of his Mind were more excellent, efpecially if it be an Excellence to be
conftant.

He had made feveral Attempts to
take Poffeffion of her, but all prov'd ineffectual ; however, he had the good
Fortune not to be known, tho' once or
twice he narrowly efcap'd with Life,
bearing off his Wounds with Difficulty.
—(Alas

—— (Alas, that the Wounds of Love fhould caufe thofe of Hate!) Upon which fhe was ftrictly confin'd to one Room, whofe only Window was towards the Garden, and that too was grated with Iron ; and, once a Month, when fhe went to Church, fhe was conftantly and carefully attended by her Father, and a Mother-in-Law, worfe than a *Duegna.* Under this miferable Confinement *Antonio* underftood fhe ftill continued, at his Return to *Seville,* with Don *Henrique,* whom he acquainted with his invincible Paffion for her ; lamenting the Severity of her prefent Circumftances, that admitted of no Profpect of Relief ; which caus'd a generous Concern in Don *Henrique,* both for the Sufferings of his Friend, and of the Lady. He propofed feveral Ways to Don *Antonio,* for the Releafe of the fair Prifoner ; but none of them was thought practicable, or at leaft likely to fucceed. But *Antonio,* who (you may believe) was then more nearly engag'd, bethought himfelf of an Expedient that would undoubtedly reward their Endeavours. 'Twas, that Don *Henrique,* who was very well acquainted with *Ardelia*'s Father, fhould make him a Vifit, with Pretence of begging his Confent and Admiffion to make his Addreffes to his

' Daughter ;

Daughter ; which, in all Probability, he could not refuse to Don *Henrique's* Quality and Estate ; and then this Freedom of Access to her would give him the Opportunity of delivering the Lady to his Friend. This was thought so reasonable, that the very next Day it was put in Practice ; and with so good Success, that Don *Henrique* was received by the Father of *Ardelia* with the greatest and most respectful Ceremony imaginable : And when he made the Proposal to him of marrying his Daughter, it was embraced with a visible Satisfaction and Joy in the Air of his Face. This their first Conversation ended with all imaginable Content on both Sides ; Don *Henrique* being invited by the Father to Dinner the next Day, when Dona *Ardelia* was to be present ; who, at that Time, was said to be indispos'd, (as 'tis very probable she was, with so close an Imprisonment.) *Henrique* returned to *Antonio*, and made him happy with the Account of his Reception ; which could not but have terminated in the perfect Felicity of *Antonio*, had his Fate been just to the Merits of his Love. The Day and Hour came which brought *Henrique*, with a private Commission from his Friend, to *Ardelia*. He saw her ;———

(ah !

(ah ! would he had only feen her veil'd !)
and, with the firſt Opportunity, gave her
the Letter, which held ſo much Love,
and ſo much Truth, as ought to have
preſerved him in the Empire of her
Heart. It contained, beſides, a Diſcovery
of his whole Deſign upon her Father,
for the compleating of their Happineſs ; which nothing then could ob-
ſtruct but her ſelf. But *Henrique* had
feen her ; he had gaz'd, and ſwallowed
all her Beauties at his Eyes. How gree-
dily his Soul drank the ſtrong Poiſon
in ! But yet his Honour and his Friendſhip were ſtrong as ever, and bravely
fought againſt the Uſurper Love, and
got a noble Victory ; at leaſt he thought
and wiſh'd ſo. With this, and a ſhort
Anſwer to his Letter, *Henrique* return'd
to the longing *Antonio* ; who, receiving
the Paper with the greateſt Devotion,
and kiſſing it with the greateſt Zeal,
open'd and read theſe Words to himſelf :

Don Antonio,

YO U have, at laſt, made Uſe of the
beſt and only Expedient for my Enlargement ; for which I thank you, ſince I
know it is purely the Effect of your Love.
Your

Your Agent has a mighty Influence on my Father : And you may affure yourfelf, that as you have advis'd and defir'd me, he fhall have no lefs on me, who am

Your's entirely,

And only your's,

A R D E L I A.

Having refpectfully and tenderly kifs'd the Name, he could not chufe but fhew the *Billet* to his Friend ; who reading that Part of it which concern'd himfelf, ftarted and blufh'd : Which *Antonio* obferving, was curious to know the Caufe of it. *Henrique* told him, That he was furpriz'd to find her exprefs fo little Love, after fo long an Abfence. To which his Friend reply'd for her, That, doubtlefs, fhe had not Time enough to attempt fo great a Matter as a perfect Account of her Love ; and added, that it was Confirmation enough to him of its Continuance, fince fhe fubfcrib'd her felf his entirely, and only his. —— How blind is Love ! Don *Henrique* knew how to make it bear another Meaning ; which, however, he had the Difcretion to conceal. *Antonio,* who was as real in his
Friend-

Friendſhip, as conſtant in his Love, aſk'd him what he thought of her Beauty ? To which the other anſwer'd, that he thought it irreſiſtable to any, but to a Soul prepoſſeſs'd, and nobly fortify'd with a perfect Friendſhip : —— Such as is thine, my *Henrique* (added *Antonio* ;) yet as ſincere and perfect as that is, I know you muſt, nay, I know you do love her.   As I ought to do, (reply'd *Henrique.*) Yes, yes, (return'd his Friend) it muſt be ſo ; otherwiſe the Sympathy which unites our Souls would be want-ing, and conſequently our Friendſhip were in a State of Imperfection. How induſ-triouſly you would argue me into a Crime, that would tear and deſtroy the Foundation of the ſtrongeſt Ties of Truth and Honour ! (ſaid *Henrique.*) But (he continu'd) I hope within a few Days, to put it out of my Power to be guilty of ſo great a Sacrilege.   I can't determine (ſaid *Antonio*) if I knew that you lov'd one another, whether I could eaſier part with my Friend, or my Miſtreſs. Tho' what you ſay, is highly generous, (reply'd *Henrique*) yet give me Leave to urge, that it looks like a Trial of Friend-ſhip, and argues you inclinable to Jea-louſy : But, pardon me, I know it to be ſincerely meant by you ; and muſt
therefore

therefore own, that 'tis the beſt, becauſe 'tis the nobleſt Way of ſecuring both your Friend and Miſtreſs.   I need not make uſe of any Arts to ſecure me of either, (reply'd *Antonio*) but expeᴄt to enjoy 'em both in a little Time.

Henrique, who was a little uneaſy with a Diſcourſe of this Nature, diverted it, by reflecting on what had paſs'd at *Madrid*, between them two and Don *Sebaſtian* and his Friends ; which caus'd *Antonio* to bethink himſelf of the Danger to which he expos'd his Friend, by appearing daily, tho' in Diſguiſe : For, doubtleſs, Don *Sebaſtian* would purſue his Revenge to the utmoſt Extremity.   Theſe Thoughts put him upon deſiring his Friend, for his own Sake, to haſten the Performance of his Attempt ; and accordingly, each Day Don *Henrique* brought *Antonio* nearer the Hopes of Happineſs, while he himſelf was hourly ſinking into the loweſt State of Miſery.   The laſt Night before the Day in which *Antonio* expeᴄted to be bleſs'd in her Love, Don *Henrique* had a long and fatal Conference with her about her Liberty.   Being then with her alone in an Arbour of the Garden, which Privilege he had had for ſome Days ; after a long Silence, and obſerving Don *Henrique* in much Diſorder, by the
Motion

Motion of his Eyes, which were fometimes ftedfaftly fix'd on the Ground, then
lifted up to her or Heaven, (for he could
fee nothing more beautiful on Earth) fhe
made ufe of the Privilege of her Sex, and
began the Difcourfe firft, to this Effect :
—— Has any Thing happened, Sir, fince
our Retreat hither, to occafion that Diforder which is but too vifible in your
Face, and too dreadful in your continued
Silence ? Speak, I befeech you, Sir, and
let me know if I have any Way unhappily contributed to it ! No, Madam, (re-
plyed he) my Friendfhip is now likely
to be the only Caufe of my greateft Mifery ; for To-morrow I muft be guilty of
an unpardonable Crime, in betraying the
generous Confidence which your noble Father has plac'd in me : To-morrow (added he, with a piteous Sigh) I muft deliver you into the Hands of one whom
your Father hates even to Death, inftead
of doing myfelf the Honour of becoming
his Son-in-Law within a few Days more.
—— But —— I will confider and remind
myfelf, that I give you into the Hands
of my Friend ; of my Friend, that loves
you better than his Life, which he has
often expos'd for your Sake ; and what
is more than all, to my Friend, whom
you love more than any Confideration on
Earth.

Earth.——And muſt this be done ? (ſhe ask'd.) Is it inevitable as Fate ?—— Fix'd as the Laws of Nature, Madam, (reply'd he) don't you find the Neceſſity of it, *Ardelia ?* (continued he, by Way of Queſtion :) Does not your Love require it ? Think, you are going to your dear *Antonio,* who alone can merit you, and whom only you can love. Were your laſt Words true (returned ſhe) I ſhould yet be unhappy in the Diſpleaſure of a dear and tender Father, and infinitely more, in being the Cauſe of your Infidelity to him : No, Don *Henrique* (continued ſhe) I could with greater Satisfaction return to my miſerable Confinement, than by any Means diſturb the Peace of your Mind, or occaſion one Moment's Interruption of your Quiet. —— Would to Heaven you did not, (ſigh'd he to himſelf.) Then addreſſing his Words more diſtinctly to her, cry'd he, Ah, cruel ! ah, unjuſt *Ardelia !* theſe Words belong to none but *Antonio* ; why then would you endeavour to perſuade me, that I do, or ever can merit the Tenderneſs of ſuch an Expreſſion ? —— Have a Care ! (purſued he) have a Care *Ardelia !* your outward Beauties are too powerful to be reſiſted ; even your Frowns have ſuch a Sweetneſs that they attract the very Soul that is

not

not ftrongly prepoffeffed with the nobleft
Friendfhip, and the higheft Principles of
Honour : Why then, alas! did you add
fuch fweet and charming Accents ? Why
——ah, Don *Henrique !* (fhe interrupted)
why did you appear to me fo charming
in your Perfon, fo great in your Friendfhip, and fo illuftrious in your Reputation ? Why did my Father, ever fince
your firft Vifit, continually fill my Ears
and Thoughts with noble Characters and
glorious Ideas, which yet but imperfect-
ly and faintly reprefent the inimitable
Original ! —— But —— (what is moft fevere and cruel) why, Don *Henrique,* why
will you defeat my Father in his Ambition of your Alliance, and ₁me of thofe
glorious Hopes with which you had blefs'd
my Soul, by cafting me away from you
to *Antonio !* —— Ha ! (cry'd he, ftarting)
what faid you, Madam ! What did *Ardelia* fay ? That I had blefs'd your Soul
with Hopes ! That I would caft you
away to *Antonio !* —— Can they who
fafely arrive in their wifh'd-for Port, be
faid to be fhipwreck'd ? Or, can an abject
indigent Wretch make a King ? ———
Thefe are more than Riddles, Madam ;
and I muft not think to expound 'em.
No, (faid fhe) let it alone, Don *Henrique* ; I'll eafe you of that Trouble, and

tell you plainly that I love you. Ah!
(cry'd he) now all my Fears are come
upon me!———— How! (afk'd fhe)
were you afraid I fhould love you? Is
my Love fo dreadful then? Yes, when
mifplac'd (reply'd he ;) but 'twas your
Falfhood that I fear'd: Your Love was
what I would have fought with the ut-
moft Hazard of my Life, nay, even of
my future Happinefs, I fear, had you
not been engag'd; ftrongly oblig'd to
love elfewhere, both by your own Choice
and Vows, as well as by his dangerous
Services, and matchlefs Conftancy. For
which (faid fhe) I do not hate him, tho'
his Father kill'd my Uncle: Nay, perhaps
(continu'd fhe) I have a Friendfhip for
him, but no more. No more, faid you,
Madam? (cry'd he ;) ———— but tell me,
did you never love him? Indeed, I did,
(reply'd fhe ;) but the Sight of you has
better inftructed me, both in my Duty to
my Father, and in caufing my Paffion for
you, without whom I fhall be eternally
miferable. Ah, then purfue your honourable Propofal, and make my Father happy in my Marriage! It muft not be (return'd Don *Henrique)* my Honour, my
Friendfhip forbids it. No (fhe return'd)
your Honour requires it; and if your
Friendfhip oppofes your Honour, it can
have

have no sure and solid Foundation. Female Sophiftry ! (cried *Henrique :)* but you need no Art nor Artifice, *Ardelia*, to make me love you : Love you ! (purfu'd he :) By that bright Sun, the Light and Heat of all the World, you are my only Light and Heat —— Oh, Friendfhip ! Sacred Friendfhip, now affift me ! ——— [Here for a Time he paus'd, and then afrefh proceeded thus,] ——You told me, or my Ears deceiv'd me, that you lov'd me, *Ardelia.* I did, fhe reply'd ; and that I do love you, is as true as that I told you fo. 'Tis well ;——But would it were not fo ! Did ever Man receive a Blefling thus ?—— Why, I could wifh I did not love you, *Ardelia !* But that were impoffible —— At leaft unjuft, (interrupted fhe.) Well then (he went on) to fhew you that I do fincerely confult your particular Happinefs, without any Regard to my own, To-morrow I will give you to Don *Antonio* ; and as a Proof of your Love to me, I expect your ready Confent to it. To let you fee, Don *Henrique*, how perfectly and tenderly I love you, I will be facrificed To-morrow to Don *Antonio*, and to your Quiet. Oh, ftrongeft, deareft Obligation ! —— cry'd *Henrique :* To-morrow then, as I have told your Father, I am to bring you to

O 2

fee

fee the deareft Friend I have on Earth, who dares not appear with this City for fome unhappy Reafons, and therefore cannot be prefent at our Nuptials ; for which Caufe, I could not but think it my Duty to one fo nearly related to my Soul, to make him happy in the Sight of my beautiful Choice, e'er yet fhe be my Bride. I hope (faid fhe) my loving Obedience may merit your Compaffion ; and that at laft, e'er the Fire is lighted that muft confume the Offering, I mean the Marriage-Tapers (alluding to the old *Roman* Ceremony) that you or fome other pitying Angel, will fnatch me from the Altar. Ah, no more, *Ardelia !* fay no more, (cry'd he) we muft be cruel, to be juft to our felves. [Here their Difcourfe ended, and they walked into the Houfe, where they found the good old Gentleman and his Lady, with whom he ftay'd till about an Hour after Supper, when he returned to his Friend with joyful News, but a forrowful Heart.]

Antonio was all Rapture with the Thoughts of the approaching Day ; which tho' it brought Don *Henrique* and his dear *Ardelia* to him, about five o'Clock in the Evening, yet at the fame Time brought his laft and greateft Misfortune. He faw her then at a She Relation's of his,

above

above three Miles from *Seville*, which was the Place affigned for their fatal Interview. He faw her, I fay; but ah! how ftrange! how altered from the dear, kind *Ardelia* fhe was when laft he left her! 'Tis true, he flew to her with Arms expanded, and with fo fwift and eager a Motion, that fhe could not avoid, nor get loofe from his Embrace, till he had kiffed, and fighed, and dropt fome Tears, which all the Strength of his Mind could not reftrain; whether they were the Effects of Joy, or whether (which rather may be feared) they were the Heat-drops which preceded and threaten'd the Thunder and Tempeft that fhould fall on his Head, I cannot pofitively fay; yet all this fhe was then forced to endure, e'er fhe had Liberty to fpeak, or indeed to breathe. But as foon as fhe had freed herfelf from the loving Circle that fhould have been the dear and lov'd Confinement or Centre of a faithful Heart, fhe began to dart whole Showers of Tortures on him from her Eyes; which that Mouth that he had juft before fo tenderly and facredly kifs'd, feconded with whole Volleys of Deaths crammed in every Sentence, pointed with the keeneft Affliction that ever pierc'd a Soul. *Antonio*, (fhe began) you have treated me

O 3

now

now as if you were never like to fee me
more : and would to Heaven you were
not!———Ha! (cry'd he, ftarting and
ftaring wildly on her ;) What faid you
Madam ? What faid you, my *Ardelia ?*
If you like the Repetition, take it ! (reply'd fhe, unmoved) *Would to Heaven you
were never like to fee me more !* Good !
very Good ! (cry'd he, with a Sigh that
threw him trembling into a Chair behind him, and gave her the Opportunity of proceeding thus :)———Yet, *Antonio,* I muft not have my Wifh ; I muft
continue with you, not out of Choice,
but by Command, by the ftricteft and
fevereft Obligation that ever bound Humanity ; Don *Henrique,* your Friend, commands it ; Don *Henrique,* the deareft
Object of my Soul, enjoins it ; Don *Henrique,* whofe only Averfion I am, will
have it fo. Oh, do not wrong me, Madam ! (cry'd Don *Henrique.*) Lead me,
lead me a little more by the Light of
your Difcourfe, I befeech you (faid Don
Antonio) that I may fee your Meaning !
for hitherto 'tis Darknefs all to me. Attend therefore with your beft Faculties
(purfu'd *Ardelia*) and know, That I do
moft fincerely and moft paffionately love
Don *Henrique;* and as a Proof of my
Love to him, I have this Day confented

to

to be delivered up to you by him; not for your Sake in the leaft, *Antonio*, but purely to facrifice all the Quiet of my Life to his Satisfaction. And now, Sir, (continued fhe, addreffing her felf to Don *Henrique*) now, Sir, if you can be fo cruel, execute your own moft dreadful Decree, and join our Hands, though our Hearts never can meet.   All this to try me! It's too much, *Ardelia* —— (faid *Antonio:*) And then turning to Don *Henrique*, he went on, Speak thou! if yet thou art not Apoftate to our Friendfhip! Yet fpeak, however! Speak, though the Devil has been tampering with thee too! Thou art a Man, a Man of Honour once.   And when I forfeit my juft Title to that (interrupted Don *Henrique)* may I be made moft miferable! —— May I lofe the Bleffings of thy Friendfhip!—— May I lofe thee!———— Say on then, *Henrique* (cry'd *Antonio:*) And I charge thee, by all the facred Ties of Friendfhip, fay, Is this a Trial of me? Is't Illufion, Sport, or fhameful murderous Truth? —— Oh, my Soul burns within me, and I can bear no longer! —— Tell! Speak! Say on!——[Here, with folded Arms, and Eyes fixed ftedfaftly on *Henrique*, he ftood like a Statue, without Motion; unlefs fometimes, when his

fwelling Heart raifed his over-charged Breaft.] After a little Paufe, and a hearty Sigh or two, *Henrique* began ; —— Oh, *Antonio !* Oh my Friend ! prepare thy felf to hear yet more dreadful Accents !——I am (purfu'd he) unhappily the greateft and moft innocent Criminal that e'er till now offended :——I love her, *Antonio,*—— I love *Ardelia* with a Paffion ftrong and violent as thine !—— Oh ! fummon all that us'd to be more than Man about thee, to fuffer to the End of my Difcourfe, which nothing but a Refolution like thine can bear ! I know it by myfelf. ———— Tho' there be Wounds, Horror, and Death in each Syllable (interrupted *Antonio*) yet prithee now go on, but with all Hafte. I will, (returned Don *Henrique)* tho' I feel my own Words have the fame cruel Effects on me. I fay again, my Soul loves *Ardelia :* And how can it be otherwife ? Have we not both the felf-fame Appetites, the fame Difgufts ? How then could I avoid my Deftiny, that has decreed that I fhould love and hate juft as you do ? Oh, hard Neceffity ! that obliged you to ufe me in the Recovery of this Lady ! Alas, can you think that any Man of Senfe or Paffion could have feen, and not have lov'd her ! Then how fhould I, whofe Thoughts are Unifons to
yours,

yours, evade thofe Charms that had prevail'd on you ?———And now, to let you
know, 'tis no Illufion, no Sport, but ferious and amazing woeful Truth, *Ardelia*,
beft can tell you whom fhe loves. What
I have already faid, is true, by Heaven
(cry'd fhe) 'tis you, Don *Henrique*, whom
I only love, and who alone can give me
Happinefs : Ah, would you would !——
With you, *Antonio*, I muft remain unhappy, wretched, curfed : Thou art my Hell;
Don *Henrique* is my Heaven. And thou
art mine, (returned he) which here I
part with to my deareft Friend. Then
taking her Hand, Pardon me, *Antonio*,
(purfued he) that I thus take my laft
Farewel of all the Taftes of Blifs from
your *Ardelia*, at this Moment. [At which
Words he kifs'd her Hand, and gave it
to Don *Antonio ;* who received it, and
gently preffed it clofe to his Heart, as
if he would have her feel the Diforders
fhe had caus'd there.] Be happy, *Antonio*, (cry'd *Henrique :)* Be very tender of
her ; To-morrow early I fhall hope to
fee thee. ——————— *Ardelia*, (purfued he)
All Happinefs and Joy furround thee !
May'ft thou ne'er want thofe Bleffings
thou can'ft give *Antonio !* —— Farewel
to both ! (added he, going out.) Ah
(cry'd fhe) Farewel to all Joys, Bleffings,

Happinefs, if you forfake me. —— Yet
do not go! —— Ah, cruel! (continu'd
fhe, feeing him quit the Room) but you
fhall take my Soul with you. Here fhe
fwooned away in Don *Antonio's* Arms ;
who, though he was happy that he had
her faft there, yet was obliged to call in
his Coufin, and *Ardelia's* Attendants, e'er
fhe could be perfectly recovered. In the
mean while Don *Henrique* had not the
Power to go out of Sight of the Houfe,
but wandred to and fro about it, dif-
tracted in his Soul ; and not being able
longer to refrain her Sight, her laft Words
ftill refounding in his Ears, he came
again into the Room where he left her
with Don *Antonio*, juft as fhe revived,
and called him, exclaiming on his Cruelty, in leaving her fo foon. But when,
turning her Eyes towards the Door, fhe
faw him ; Oh! with what eager Hafte
fhe flew to him! then clafped him round
the Waift, obliging him, with all the
tender Expreffions that the Soul of a
Lover, and a Woman's too, is capable
of uttering, not to leave her in the
Poffeffion of Don *Antonio*. This fo amaz'd
her flighted Lover, that he knew not,
at firft, how to proceed in this tormenting Scene ; but at laft, fummoning all
his wonted Refolution, and Strength of
Mind,

Mind, he told her, He would put her out of his Power, if she would consent to retreat for some few Hours to a Nunnery that was not above half a Mile distant from thence, till he had discoursed his Friend, Don *Henrique* something more particularly than hitherto, about this Matter : To which she readily agreed, upon the Promise that Don *Henrique* made her, of seeing her with the first Opportunity. They waited on her then to the Convent, where she was kindly and respectfully received by the Lady Abbess ; but it was not long before her Grief renewing with greater Violence, and more afflicting Circumstances, had obliged them to stay with her till it was almost dark, when they once more begged the Liberty of an Hour's Absence ; and the better to palliate their Design, *Henrique* told her, that he would make use of her Father Don *Richardo*'s Coach, in which they came to Don *Antonio*'s, for so small a Time : which they did, leaving only *Eleonora* her Attendant with her, without whom she had been at a Loss, among so many fair Strangers ; Strangers, I mean, to her unhappy Circumstances : Whilst they were carry'd near a Mile farther, where, just as 'twas dark, they lighted from the Coach, Don *Hen-*
rique

rique, ordering the Servants not to ftir thence till their Return from their private Walk, which was about a Furlong, in a Field that belong'd to the Convent. Here Don *Antonio* told Don *Henrique,* That he had not acted honourably ; That he had betray'd him, and robb'd him at once both of a Friend and Miftrefs. To which t'other returned, That he underftood his Meaning, when he propofed a particular Difcourfe about this Affair, which he now perceived muft end in Blood : But you may remind your felf (continued he) that I have kept my Promife in delivering her to you. Yes, (cry'd *Antonio*) after you had practis'd foully and bafely on her. Not at all ! (returned *Henrique*) It was her Fate that brought this Mischief on her ; for I urged the Shame and Scandal of Inconftancy, but all in vain, to her. But don't you love her, *Henrique?* (the other ask'd.) Too well, and cannot live without her, though I fear I may feel the curfed Effects of the fame Inconftancy : However, I had quitted her all to you, but you fee how fhe refents it. And you fhall fee, Sir, (cry'd *Antonio*, drawing his Sword in a Rage) how I refent it. Here, without more Words, they fell to Action ; to bloody Action. (Ah ! how wretched are

our

our Sex, in being the unhappy Occafion
of fo many fatal Mifchiefs, even between
the deareft Friends!) They fought on
each Side with the greateft Animofity of
Rivals, forgetting all the facred Bonds
of their former Friendfhip; till Don *Antonio* fell, and faid, dying, ' Forgive me,
'. *Henrique!* I was to blame ; I could not
' live without her :———— I fear fhe will
' betray thy Life, which hafte and pre-
' ferve, for my fake——Let me not die
' all at once!——Heaven pardon both
' of us!——Farewel! Oh, hafte! Fare-
' wel! (*returned Don* Henrique) Farewel,
' thou braveft, trueft Friend! Farewel
' thou nobleft Part of me!——And Fare-
' wel all the Quiet of my Soul.' Then
ftooping, he kiffed his Cheek; but, rifing,
he found he muft retire in time, or elfe
muft perifh through Lofs of Blood, for
he had received two or three dangerous
Wounds, befides others of lefs Confequence: Wherefore he made all the convenient Hafte he could to the Coach, into
which, by the Help of the Footmen, he
got, and order'd 'em to drive him directly
to Don *Richardo*'s with all imaginable
Speed; where he arriv'd in little more
than half an Hour's Time, and was received by *Ardelia*'s Father with the greateft
Confufion and Amazement that is expref-
fible,

fible, feeing him return'd without his Daughter, and fo defperately wounded. Before he thought it convenient to afk him any Queftion more than to enquire of his Daughter's Safety, to which he receiv'd a fhort but fatisfactory Anfwer, Don *Richardo* fent for an eminent and able Surgeon, who probed and drefs'd Don *Henrique*'s Wounds, who was immediately put to Bed; not without fome Defpondency of his Recovery: but (thanks to his kind Stars, and kinder Conftitution!) he refted pretty well for fome Hours that Night, and early in the Morning, *Ardelia*'s Father, who had fcarce taken any Reft all that Night, came to vifit him, as foon as he underftood from the Servants who watched with him, that he was in a Condition to fuffer a fhort Difcourfe; which, you may be fure, was to learn the Circumftances of the paft Night's Adventure; of which Don *Henrique* gave him a perfect and pleafant Account, fince he heard that Don *Antonio*, his mortal Enemy, was killed; the Affurance of whofe Death was the more delightful to him, fince, by this Relation, he found that *Antonio* was the Man, whom his Care of his Daughter had fo often fruftrated. Don *Henrique* had hardly made an End of his Narration, e'er a Servant came haftily to give *Richardo*

chardo

chardo Notice, that the Officers were come to fearch for his Son-in-law that ·fhould have been ; whom the old Gentleman's wife Precaution had fecured in a Room fo unfufpected, that they might as reafonably have imagined the entire Walls of his Houfe had a Door made of Stones, as that there fhould have been one to that clofe Apartment : He went therefore boldly to the Officers, and gave them all the Keys of his Houfe, with free Liberty to examine every Room and Chamber ; which they did, but to no Purpofe ; and Don *Henrique* lay there undifcover'd, till his Cure was perfected.

In the mean time *Ardelia*, who that fatal Night but too rightly guefs'd that the Death of one or both her Lovers was the Caufe that they did not return to their Promife, the next Day fell into a high Fever, in which her Father found her foon after he had clear'd himfelf of thofe who come to fearch for a Lover. The Affurance which her Father gave her of *Henrique*'s Life, feemed a little to revive her ; but the Severity of *Antonio*'s Fate was no Way obliging to her, fince fhe could not but retain the Memory of his Love and Conftancy ; which added to her Afflictions, and heightned her Diftemper, infomuch that

that *Richardo* was conftrain'd to leave her under the Care of the good Lady Abbefs, and to the diligent Attendance of *Eleonora*, not daring to hazard her Life in a Removal to his own Houfe. All their Care and Diligence was however ineffectual; for fhe languifhed even to the leaft Hope of Recovery, till immediately after the firft Vifit of Don *Henrique*, which was the firft he made in a Month's Time, and that by Night *incognito*, with her Father, her Diftemper, vifibly retreated each Day: Yet when at laft fhe enjoy'd a perfect Health of Body, her Mind grew fick, and fhe plunged into a deep Melancholy; which made her entertain a pofitive Refolution of taking the Veil at the End of her Novitiate; which accordingly fhe did, notwithftanding all the Intreaties, Prayers, and Tears both of her Father and Lover. But fhe foon repented her Vow, and often wifh'd that fhe might by any means fee and fpeak to Don *Henrique*, by whofe Help fhe promis'd to her felf a Deliverance out of her voluntary Imprifonment: Nor were his Wifhes wanting to the fame Effect, tho' he was forc'd to fly into *Italy*, to avoid the Profecution of *Antonio*'s Friends. Thither fhe purfu'd him; nor could he any way fhun her, unlefs he

could

could have left his Heart at a Diftance
from his Body : Which made him take
a fatal Refolution of returning to *Seville*
in Difguife, where he wander'd about
the Convent every Night like a Ghoft
(for indeed his Soul was within, while
his inanimate Trunk was without) till
at laft he found Means to convey a Letter to her, which both furprized and delighted her. The Meffenger that brought
it her was one of her Mother-in-Law's
Maids, whom he had known before, and
met accidentally one Night as he was
going his Rounds, and fhe coming out
from *Ardelia* ; with her he prevail'd,
and with Gold obliged her to Secrecy
and Affiftance : Which proved fo fuccefsful, that he underftood from *Ardelia* her
ftrong Defire of Liberty, and the Continuance of her Paffion for him, together with the Means and Time moft
convenient and likely to fucceed for her
Enlargement. The Time was the fourteenth Night following, at twelve o'Clock,
which juft compleated a Month fince his
Return thither ; at which Time they both
promifed themfelves the greateft Happinefs on Earth. But you may obferve the
Juftice of Heaven, in their Difappointment.

Don

Don *Sebaſtian*, who ſtill purſu'd him
with a moſt implacable Hatred, had tra-
ced him even to *Italy*, and there narrowly miſſing him, poſted after him to
Toledo ; ſo ſure and ſecret was his Intelligence ! As ſoon as he arriv'd, he went
directly to the Convent where his Siſter
Elvira had been one of the Profeſs'd,
ever ſince Don *Henrique* had forſaken her,
and where *Ardelia* had taken her repented Vow. *Elvira* had all along conceal'd
the Occaſion of her coming thither from
Ardelia ; and tho' ſhe was her only Confident, and knew the whole Story of her
Misfortunes, and heard the Name of Don
Henrique repeated a hundred Times a Day,
whom ſtill ſhe lov'd moſt perfectly, yet
never gave her beautiful Rival any Cauſe of
Suſpicion that ſhe lov'd him, either by
Words or Looks : Nay more, when ſhe
underſtood that Don *Henrique* came to the
Convent with *Ardelia* and *Antonio*, and at
other Times with her Father ; yet ſhe had
ſo great a Command of her ſelf, as to refrain ſeeing him, or to be ſeen by him ;
nor ever intended to have ſpoken or writ
to him, had not her Brother Don *Sebaſtian*
put her upon the cruel Neceſſity of doing the laſt ; who coming to viſit his
Siſter (as I have ſaid before) found her
with

with Dona *Ardelia*, whom he never remembred to have feen, nor who ever had feen him but twice, and that was about fix Years before, when fhe was but ten Years of Age, when fhe fell paffionately in Love with him, and continu'd her Paffion till about the fourteenth Year of her Empire, when unfortunate *Antonio* firft began his Court to her. Don *Sebaftian* was really a very defirable Perfon, being at that time very beautiful, his Age not exceeding fix and twenty, of a fweet Converfation, very brave, but revengeful and irreconcilable (like moft of his Countrymen) and of an honourable Family. At the Sight of him *Ardelia* felt her former Paffion renew; which proceeded and continued with fuch Violence, that it utterly defac'd the Ideas of *Antonio* and *Henrique*. (No Wonder that fhe who could refolve to forfake her God for Man, fhould quit one Lover for another.) In fhort, fhe then only wifhed that he might love her equally, and then fhe doubted not of contriving the Means of their Happinefs betwixt 'em. She had her Wifh, and more, if poffible; for he lov'd her beyond the Thought of any other prefent or future Bleffing, and fail'd not to let her know it, at the fecond Interview;

when

when he receiv'd the greateſt Pleaſure
he could have wiſh'd, next to the Joys
of a Bridal Bed : For ſhe confeſſed her
Love to him, and preſently put him
upon thinking on the Means of her
Eſcape ; but not finding his Deſigns ſo
likely to ſucceed, as thoſe Meaſures ſhe
had ſent to Don *Henrique,* ſhe communi-
cates the very ſame to Don *Sebaſtian,*
and agreed with him to make uſe of
them on that very Night, wherein ſhe
had obliged Don *Henrique* to attempt
her Deliverance : The Hour indeed was
different, being determined to be at
Eleven. *Elvira,* who was preſent at the
Conference, took the Hint ; and not being willing to diſoblige a Brother who
had ſo hazarded his Life in Vindication
of her, either does not, or would not
ſeem to oppoſe his Inclinations at that
Time : However, when he retired with
her to talk more particularly of his intended Revenge on Don *Henrique,* who
he told her lay ſomewhere abſconded in
Toledo, and whom he had reſolved, as he
aſſured her, to ſacrifice to her injur'd
Honour, and his Reſentments ; ſhe op-
pos'd that his vindictive Reſolution with
all the forcible Arguments in a virtuous
and pious Lady's Capacity, but in vain :
ſo that immediately, upon his Retreat

from

from the Convent, fhe took the Opportunity of writing to Don *Henrique* as follows, the fatal Hour not being then feven Nights diftant.

Don *Henrique*,

MY Brother is now in Town, in Purfuit of your Life; nay more, of your Miftrefs, who has confented to make her Efcape from the Convent, at the fame Place of it, and by the fame Means on which fhe had agreed to give her felf entirely to you, but the Hour is eleven. I know, Henrique, *your* Ardelia *is dearer to you than your Life: But your Life, your dear Life, is more defired than any Thing in this World, by*

Your injur'd and forfaken

ELVIRA.

This fhe delivered to *Richardo*'s Servant, whom *Henrique* had gained that Night, as foon as fhe came to vifit *Ardelia*, at her ufual Hour, juft as fhe went out of the Cloifter.

Don *Henrique* was not a little furprized with this *Billet;* however, he could hardly refolve to forbear his accuftom'd
Vifits

Vifits to *Ardelia*, at firft: But upon more mature Confideration, he only chofe to converfe with her by Letters, which ftill prefs'd her to be mindful of her Promife, and of the Hour, not taking notice of any Caution that he had received of her Treachery. To which fhe ftill return'd in Words that might affure him of her Conftancy.

The dreadful Hour wanted not a Quarter of being perfect, when Don *Henrique* came; and having fixed his Rope-Ladder to that Part of the Garden-Wall, where he was expected, *Ardelia*, who had not ftirr'd from that very Place for a Quarter of an Hour before, prepar'd to afcend by it; which fhe did, as foon as his Servant had returned and fixed it on the inner-fide of the Wall: On the Top of which, at a little Diftance, fhe found another faften'd, for her to defcend on the out-fide, whilft Don *Henrique* eagerly waited to receive her. She came at laft, and flew into his Arms; which made *Henrique* cry out in a Rapture, *Am I at laft once more happy in having my* Ardelia *in my Poffeffion!* She, who knew his Voice, and now found fhe was betray'd, but knew not by whom, fhriek'd out, *I am ruin'd! help! help!* —— *Loofe me, I charge you,* Henrique! *Loofe me!* At that
very

very Moment, and at thofe very Words, came *Sebaftian*, attended by only one Servant ; and hearing *Henrique* reply, *Not all the Powers of Hell fhall fnatch you from me*, drawing his Sword, without one Word, made a furious Pafs at him : But his Rage and Hafte mifguided his Arm, for his Sword went quite through *Ardelia*'s Body, who only faid, *Ah, wretched Maid !* and drop'd from *Henrique*'s Arms, who then was obliged to quit her, to preferve his own Life, if poffible : however he had not had fo much Time as to draw, had not *Sebaftian* been amazed at this dreadful Miftake of his Sword ; but prefently recollecting himfelf, he flew with redoubled Rage to attack *Henrique* ; and his Servant had feconded him, had not *Henrique*'s, who was now defcended, otherwife diverted him. They fought with the greateft Animofity on both Sides, and with equal Advantage ; for they both fell together : *Ah, my* Ardelia, *I come to thee now ! (Sebaftian* groan'd out,)——*'Twas this unlucky Arm, which now embraces thee, that killed thee. Juft Heaven !* (fhe figh'd out,)——*Oh, yet have Mercy !* [Here they both dy'd.] *Amen,* cry'd *Henrique,* dying) *I want it moft* —— *Oh,* Antonio ! *Oh !* Elvira ! *Ah, there's the Weight that finks me down.* ——*And yet I wifh Forgivenefs.*——*Once more,*

more, sweet Heaven, have Mercy! He
could not out-live that last Word ; which
was echo'd by *Elvira*, who all this while
stood weeping, and calling out for Help,
as she stood close to the Wall in the Garden.

This alarmed the Rest of the Sisters,
who rising, caus'd the Bell to be rung out,
as upon dangerous Occasions it used to be ;
which rais'd the Neighbourhood, who came
time enough to remove the dead Bodies of
the two Rivals, and of the late fallen Angel *Ardelia*. The injur'd and neglected
Elvira, whose Piety designed quite contrary Effects, was immediately seiz'd with
a violent Fever ; which, as it was violent,
did not last long : for she dy'd within four
and twenty Hours, with all the happy
Symptoms of a departing Saint.

The End of the First Volume.